A Man
of My Own

Barbara Joe Williams

Amani Publishing, LLC
Barbara Joe Williams

Tallahassee, FL

This book is a work of fiction. and incidents are either th imagination or used fictitio actual persons, living or dead, or to actual events or locales is entirely coincidental.

Amani Publishing, LLC
P. O. Box 12045
Tallahassee, FL 32317
(850) 264-3341

A company based on faith, hope, and love

Visit our website at: **www.barbarajoewilliams.com**

Email us at: **amanipublishing@aol.com**

ISBN: 9780983366607
LCCN: 2011960515

Cover photo courtesy of: iStockphoto.com
Cover creation by: Diane Bass

PROLOGUE

"Dr. Hopson, I think I finally understand why I always fall in love with married men," Lisa began, using a low solemn voice. She was stretched out on the sofa in the doctor's high-rise office with her hands gently folded over her small chest. The back of her head was relaxed against a foam pillow with her long red wavy hair falling about her light freckled face. Lisa's beaming brown eyes were staring up at a fixed place in the ceiling as if she was in a hypnotic trance, visualizing scenes from her childhood that had probably haunted her subconsciousness for most of her forty-two years of life.

"After my father left my mother when I was four-years-old, he married another woman within three months of their divorce. My mother, Sadie, became a bitter and cold person while his second wife, Della, shined like an eternal ray of happiness." Lisa paused, swallowing hard. "I can remember being so angry at my father for leaving us. He turned my whole world upside down. Then when he stopped coming to visit us after he had other children, I felt like I wasn't good enough for anyone to love. So I've always imagined, doctor, that if I could get a married man to leave his wife and family for me, then it would prove that I was worthy of happiness, too. I thought maybe — just maybe, I would stop falling asleep every night with anger raging inside of me."

With a bewildered expression, Lisa turned to face the psychiatrist whom she'd come to trust over the past four months, "Do you think that's sick? Am I that crazy, Dr. Hopson?" Lisa asked, refusing to let a single tear fall from her batting eyes.

Taking note of her client's childlike voice, the salt and pepper-haired psychiatrist leaned in closer to Lisa's left ear. Softening her normally serious expression, she curved her rose-painted lips upward, and stated in an honest straightforward tone, "I've never thought you were crazy, Lisa. You just need to learn how to value yourself without basing your happiness and self-worth on a man, whether he's married or not."

"But, how can I do that? I'm forty something years old. You can't teach an old dog new tricks, can you?"

"Well now, I'm glad you asked that question. It just depends on how bad the old dog wants to learn," she replied, adding a light laugh after her statement. Leaning back in her cushioned armchair, Dr. Hopson pulled on the lapel of her off-white suit jacket. Relishing the progress her newest client had made in such a short period of time, she pressed her thin lips together. At that very second, one of her favorite sayings drifted through her mind. *God is good all the time and all the time, God is good. There might be some hope for Miss Lisa LaRaye Bradford after all.*

Dr. Hopson continued. "I've told you from the first day you entered my office, Lisa; you have to make recovery your number one priority. Anger will eat even the strongest person alive."

Suddenly, Lisa sat straight up on the sofa and blinked her teary eyes several times before speaking. "I understand that now, doctor, and all I want to have is a man of my own."

CHAPTER ONE
(LISA'S ARRIVAL)

"Hi, Uncle Johnny, thanks for picking me up at the airport." Lisa smiled, beaming her radiant brown eyes up at her distinguished-looking uncle. He was a tall, handsome, bald man even with the burn mark on the right side of his face he'd sustained in a house fire when Lisa was a teenager. Johnny Bradford was delighted to see the little freckled-face niece he used to bounce on his knees when he was a young man, was an amazing-looking ageless beauty. Lisa looked at least ten years younger than he calculated she had to be.

"No problem, Lisa. I'm glad you're going to be visiting with us for a while," he replied, removing her two brown leather suitcases from the Dallas-Fort Worth International Airport conveyor on a cool September morning. "Your Aunt Oretha is at home waiting on your arrival. She's fixing us a good Southern-style dinner, and from the looks of it, you could use a few decent meals."

"What are you implying?" she asked, standing on her tiptoes to give him a warm kiss on the cheek. Lisa was happy with her petite, size six frame, and didn't have any intentions of ever moving up to a larger size. Her forty-two-year-old body had served her well, so there wasn't any need trying to change it now. All of Lisa's designer clothing fit her narrow hips and barely-there breasts just the way she liked.

"I'm just teasing you about being so thin, girl. You know I love me some women with some juicy meat on their bones. You skinny women might be all right for one night, but when it comes to a lifetime, I need a woman who's big and fine," he said, laughing with his head thrown back. This was her favorite relative, the uncle who would come to visit her as a child, bringing gifts for her and her older sister, Jenna, even after her father, James Bradford, had abandoned his family and moved in with another woman. Uncle Johnny would show up on a monthly basis with a broad smile on his face giving them whatever treats they requested.

"Uncle Johnny, you are too crazy. How does Aunt Oretha trust you to work in your own bar and grill unsupervised?" Lisa asked, walking with her uncle out of the airport toward his parked silver Lincoln Town Car.

"Ah, my woman trusts me. She knows I love her," he replied, taking out his car keys to open the trunk of the car. "You know we've been married for twenty-five years, and I've never given her a reason not to believe in me. You see, those women working at the bar are nice, but they don't make me think about leaving my Oretha," he continued, lowering the two bags into the trunk. He opened the passenger side door for Lisa, slammed it shut, and then entered the car from the driver's side. "No, baby, Oretha and I have been through a lot together. Although we were never blessed to have any children, we still love each other. Nothing is worth giving up what we have."

Lisa simply smiled at her complacent uncle sitting behind the steering wheel, thankful he'd come to her official rescue. When Martin Carlisle, her former supervisor, dropped her off at the airport last night, she had to think about where she wanted to go since she had to leave Jacksonville, Florida, on such short notice. She didn't honestly believe Martin would actually carry out his threat of sending her to jail, but she wasn't foolish enough to hang around to find out either. After all, she was guilty of falsifying documents so she could work at M&M Software Developments with him and his partner, Michael Wayne. If they wanted to press charges, she could be incarcerated quite some time, and Lisa knew she was much too pretty to be some dyke's jailhouse bait. Since she didn't possess any fighting skills, Lisa knew she would more than likely be forced into a lesbian lifestyle just for her own personal survival. And she definitely wasn't about to take a chance on that occurring with a heterosexual sister like herself. So Lisa called up her best girlfriend and partner in crime, Ranetta Chadway, from the airport on her cellular telephone, politely requesting Ranetta pack up the remainder of her things and put them in a local storage unit until further notice. Since Ranetta's Chevrolet Impala had recently died on her in the middle of city traffic, Lisa sold her former college roommate the white convertible she'd proudly owned for over a year.

Then, considering the fact she had interfered with Michael Wayne's marriage to the point he was ready to outright strangle her, risking going to prison himself, Lisa rationalized it would be in her best interest to leave town peacefully as instructed for now. Even though she and Michael had been college sweethearts and recent lovers, he genuinely seemed committed to staying with his overweight dowdy wife, Alese. *Well, she can have him. He's not good enough for me, anyway. All of that money he has, and he don't even know how to spend it. No wonder I left him after college and moved to Washington, D. C. I don't know what possessed me to return to Jacksonville to try and get him back from his pitiful wife anyway. If he can turn down all this glory to be with a fat heifer, then so be it,* Lisa thought, looking down at her taupe, slim fitting pants and yellow, crisscross blouse. Pulling her hair back behind both ears, she continued in deep thought. *I'm sure there are plenty of rich men in Dallas who know how to treat a talented woman like me. It's going to be a pleasure getting to know some of them. I can't wait to see what the nightlife has to offer here.*

Uncle Johnny started the car, backed out, and headed home to the blue three bedroom wood-framed house located in Dallas. It was a gorgeous early September morning to arrive in one of the fastest growing cities in the South. Lisa was ready to reach their destination so she could take a quick shower and change out of the musty clothes she'd worn all night long. The long layover in Atlanta had gotten on her last nerve.

"What's on your mind, Lisa? Why are you being so quiet?" Uncle Johnny inquired. Lisa had her head turned away from him, looking out the side window. "You never did tell me why you were coming to visit us on such short notice. If I have to get up at the crack of dawn, I'd like to know why," he stated, glancing over in Lisa's direction.

Lisa snapped her head toward him. She'd already anticipated this question and had a prepared statement to fire back. "I was ready for a change, Uncle Johnny, and things didn't exactly work out for me in Jacksonville the way I wanted them to. So, I just decided to start fresh with my family in a different state. There was nothing for me to go back to in D.C. Of course, I could never live in Lake City with mama and Jenna, so I thought about you and Auntie O, and here I am," she said, sounding perky, lifting up both hands, flinging them away from her light-toned freckled face.

She'd skillfully left out the part about being threatened with prison out of her memorized equation. After carefully assessing her current predicament, Lisa had deduced that Uncle Johnny and Aunt Oretha didn't need to know all of her business. All they needed to know was that she had moved here to be with family, and a friend would be shipping the remainder of her clothes and furniture the following week.

"I see," he said, eyeing her suspiciously. He knew Lisa wasn't telling him the whole story, but this would suffice for now. Uncle Johnny would have plenty of time to drag the other details out of his niece later. "Well, you're welcome to stay with us for as long as you like. If you're looking for some work right away, I certainly need some assistance at the bar and grill. I tell you, good help is hard to find these days. My best bartender and the night manager both quit on me last week. I can do most of the bartending myself, but I need somebody who can step in and fill the management shoes. You have a college degree, don't you?"

"Yes, Uncle Johnny, you know I have a Computer Science degree with a minor in Business Administration."

"All right then, you're hired for the job, baby girl. Get you a good day's rest, and then you can hit the ground running tomorrow evening."

"I didn't apply for the job. I haven't decided where I want to work, but I don't have any intentions of working at a restaurant or a bar," Lisa stated, sounding just a little uppity.

"Oh, I get it. You think you're too good to work at my blue collar restaurant, huh? I'll have you know that a lot of famous people frequent my place of business. Most of those professional football players have been in my bar at some time or another. We're known for our quality drinks and the free hot wings we serve on a nightly basis."

A light bulb went off, flashing dollar signs in Lisa's head at the mere possibility of meeting a Dallas football player. Knowing that most of them were fine and had multimillion dollar contracts was enough to make Lisa reconsider her original negative comments. With a body like hers, she could easily get away with lying about her age. But that wouldn't be an issue, considering most young men enjoyed the company of an older woman, especially one who could teach them something. And even though she normally liked older men with money, a young, rich athlete would be just as good or twice as good in the bedroom, she rationalized.

"Now, you know I wasn't trying to imply that, Uncle Johnny. What I meant to say was that I would be happy to come in and help you keep things running smoothly while I figure out where I'm going to work permanently."

"Yeah, that's just what I thought. I'll swing you by there tomorrow morning so you can get a look at the set-up," he replied, pulling into the two-car garage at his modest home. Lisa could smell her Auntie O's home-cooking seeping through the open window screen the moment they pulled into the double-wide driveway. Exiting the vehicle, Lisa grabbed her brown, kidskin leather, saddle bag, and swung it across her right shoulder while closing the car door. Taking a quick glance around the neighborhood, Lisa quietly compared the other moderately priced homes to her uncle's. This wasn't one of the best neighborhoods in Dallas, but at least it would be a place where she could regroup in total peace and quiet while planning how to put the moves on another married man she hadn't even met.

Lisa didn't have any idea she would be meeting her unequivocal match in her future lover's wife. A diabolical madwoman who was so desperate to keep the rich husband that Lisa would later want, she would stop at nothing to drive her formidable enemy out of the picture. By the time his bitter spouse would be finished with Lisa Bradford, looking at another woman's husband would be the last thing on her pretty mind, forever.

CHAPTER TWO
(LISA'S JOB)

Lisa woke up around ten o'clock the next morning in a white, full-sized, poster bed with the warm Dallas sunlight shining on her smooth face. She could hear a few city workers in the street, and the sound of car horns honking in the distance. Stretching her arms upward, Lisa realized she'd fallen asleep in the nude last night and gently pulled the printed cotton sheet over her bare breasts. Carefully surveying the small bedroom that would be her new home for the next few months, she covered her mouth as she yawned. *Uncle Johnny and Auntie O may not have any children, but they must have been hoping and planning to have a little princess one day. The pink and white in this room is sickening. I definitely don't need to be trying to stay here in this little girl's fantasy room.*

Thinking she'd love to rent a car just to get out and see some of the great sites she'd heard about in the miraculous city, the rapid knock on the guest bedroom door interrupted her wavering thoughts. Lisa bolted up in bed clutching the sheet to her chest.

"Hey, it's Uncle Johnny!" he yelled through the closed door. "We need to be at the bar in one hour. We're open from noon to midnight, and I need to be there at least an hour early to make sure everything is in order. I really need you to start working today. I told you I'm in a bind right now."

"Good morning, Uncle Johnny!" Lisa yelled back. "I'll be out in a minute," she said, jumping up. Lisa scrambled around the room for her white terry cloth housecoat and threw it on. She cursed to herself. *I thought he was going to at least give me a whole day to rest before going to work in his dive bar. Well, so much for renting a car to go site-seeing today.*

Twenty minutes later, Lisa was showered and casually dressed in a FUBU short denim jacket with hip hugging jeans and a candy pink v-neck blouse. Wearing neutral colored make-up, she had her long wavy hair pulled up into a ponytail hanging down the back of her head. "I'm ready, Uncle Johnny," Lisa stated, entering the kitchen. Her uncle was seated at the round dining room table reading the daily newspaper. "How far is it to your restaurant?"

"Oh, it's only about fifteen minutes from here off the Central Expressway. We have a little time before we have to leave. Would you like a cup of hot coffee?"

"Yeah, sure. Where is Auntie O?"

"She left for work hours ago. She's working the day shift this week at Dallas Southwest Medical Center. You know, she's a registered nurse over there." Uncle Johnny got up to pour Lisa a steaming cup of black coffee, and placed it on the table in front of her.

"Yes, I remember. I'm sorry I missed her. I guess we won't be seeing each other today."

"No, you probably won't. I'll see her this evening when I come home for my dinner break. Most of the time I eat at the bar, but when she's working days, we try to have supper together."

"That's real sweet, Uncle Johnny. I'm happy to see that married life can be so grand," Lisa stated, taking a sip of her brew.

"Well, married life is whatever you make it. You just need to marry for the right reasons. That's all."

"I see. I'm hoping to get married one day, you know. I still haven't given up on my dream."

"And I don't see any reason why you should. I know quite a few women who have gotten married for the first time at fifty and sixty-years-old. So you still have plenty of time to find a mate."

"I'll certainly be looking while I'm in Dallas. It is listed as one of the largest growing cities for black professionals in America. I read that recently in one of the major magazines," Lisa stated with pride.

"I don't know about all of that, but it's a pretty decent place to live. I know the black on black crime rate seems to be going down for sure. Now finish up your coffee so we can get out of here."

Lisa didn't talk much on the way to her uncle's establishment. She was awed at the breathtaking view of the gorgeous city. Lisa had admired D.C. and Jacksonville because they had some beautiful sites, but Dallas was literally blowing away all of her senses. "I think I'm going to be happy here. This looks like a place where I could really get used to calling home. As soon as I save some money, I'll be looking for my own place."

"You don't have to rush away from us. We're glad to have you, and I really appreciate you being willing to help me out at the bar. Do you know how to mix drinks?"

"Yeah, I can do that," she replied. "I have a little bit of experience working inside a club. I worked at a bar awhile in D.C."

Less than twenty minutes later, Uncle Johnny pulled his silver Lincoln Town Car into a parking place with his name posted on the sign directly in front of the cream colored restaurant. Lisa looked up at the huge red and black sign displaying, "J's Bar & Grill."

"You can come on in and take a look around while I go work on a few things in my office," Uncle Johnny said, opening the front door for Lisa to enter his restaurant. He left her standing at the entrance as he headed to the main office located in the rear of the facility. To Lisa's left was a well-stocked bar area, and to her right was an open area with small tables, a few booths, and a stage area against the far wall.

It didn't look anything like the dive she had clearly imagined it to be. In fact, it was quite a classy-looking place, especially on the inside, with the red and purplish decor. Even though she could tell it was an older building, it had been recently updated and well-maintained. Walking through the dimly-lit facility, Lisa was reminded of the many days she had worked in a similar type bar in D.C. Placing those days behind her, she'd moved to Jacksonville, Florida, in search of a better life and hoping to rekindle a broken romance with her college sweetheart, Michael Wayne. When her plans to secure his hand in marriage failed, Lisa was forced to leave the city with barely the clothes on her back. Now, here she was in Dallas, one of the largest cities in the United States, about to embark on a new industrious life. She surveyed the building thinking, *I'll just have to make the best of it until I find another man to fill up some lonely nights or snag one of those pro football players.* Lisa's eyes finally landed on a cute brother about her height wearing a crisp white shirt with a black bowtie. He was standing behind the long bar sporting tiny dreadlocks and pearly white teeth. *Oh, no, what is up with his hair? I hate those dreadful looking things. No wonder they call them dreadlocks.*

"Hi, I'm Jason. Your uncle told me you'd be coming in today," he said, extending his hand to Lisa. His smile told Lisa he had been anticipating her visit.

Taking his firm, sable brown hand into hers, she introduced herself in return. "Hello, I'm Lisa Bradford, and I'm very pleased to meet you," she stated, noticing he was a medium-built young man, probably in his late twenties with a soft face, and a very proper speaking voice. Something about Jason's voice and mannerisms gave her an eerie feeling. Lisa couldn't quite put her finger on it, but her "gay-dar" was on full alert.

"So, Lisa, tell me what brings you to Dallas?" he asked, leaning on both elbows from behind the counter, stretching his eyes at her. Jason picked up a white towel and started wiping down the bar counter.

"I'm moving here to help out my uncle with his business for a while. I understand he's been having some problems keeping a manager around here."

"He sure has. Does that mean you're going to be working with me everyday?"

"I'll just be helping out until he can find a suitable replacement." *Or I can find a suitable man*, she thought, flashing him an eighteen-karat smile.

"Well, I'm looking forward to spending time with you. Let me take you around and introduce you to the rest of the crew before we officially open for business today."

Jason took his time showing Lisa the rest of the facility, introducing her to the other staff members, and telling her about some of the highlights of the city. He generously offered to be her escort for any day she chose to visit the Big Town Mall or Rodeo Center, as well as a few other places. He already had her pegged as a shopaholic. However, Lisa didn't want to waste any time with small fish, so she sweetly declined his invitation. Looking broken-hearted, Jason simply smiled, dropped her off at Uncle Johnny's office door, and then turned around. Lisa took another look at him as he swished away. Although he'd openly hit on her, Lisa's sixth sense was still telling her that he was either bi-sexual or gay. But something was definitely going on with that one.

"Hey, come on in here and let me show you how to handle the books for my business," Uncle Johnny stated, pulling Lisa through the door of his midsize office. "I can't be here every night so I'm putting you in charge of closing up the place for me at midnight. I can work with you every night for an entire week. That should be long enough for you to learn the ropes. Then I'll help you get a car, and you're on your own."

"All right. Now tell me how things are organized around here. Do you have a special night that the professional football players come in?"

Uncle Johnny let out a slight laugh. He knew Lisa was a hot number, but he had no idea she was so desperate for a man. "No, I don't, but I'm counting on you to change all that," He smiled, thinking about how Lisa was going to be real good for his place of business.

***

About a month later, Lisa was settled into a comfortable routine at her temporary dwelling in Dallas. She was enjoying the October climate and had her room fixed up nicely in bright floral colors which she loved. The curtains, comforter, and sheets were perfectly matched with a rose print on top of a green background. She was happy Auntie O had allowed her to remove all the pink and white girly stuff out of the room for a more sophisticated look.

Lisa would sleep until noon on most days, saunter into the bar around 4:00 p.m. and close around midnight. Since her arrival at the restaurant, she hadn't met any possible suitors. Of course, a few good prospects wandered into the bar every now and then, but overall the pickings were slim. Uncle Johnny needed to do something to create more interest in his bar, and she had the perfect idea for him. All Lisa needed now was the perfect approach to soften the blow she was about to throw.

Lisa knocked on her uncle's office door before entering. "It's open, come on in," he shouted. He looked up when Lisa entered the room and motioned with one hand for her to sit down.

Lisa eased into the cushioned armchair in front of Uncle Johnny's old wooden desk and crossed her bare legs. She tried to pull down the short peach-printed skirt that was well above her knees, but the fabric didn't budge. Then, she straightened up the twisted front of her cream-colored knit blouse. Smiling sweetly at her uncle, she began reciting her well-rehearsed presentation. "Uncle Johnny, you know, I've been thinking, and I have an idea that would draw a lot of business to your facility."

Uncle Johnny stopped counting receipts long enough to look up in her direction. "Yeah, I'm listening. What you got for me?"

"Just keep an open mind and listen to me before you react. This idea could make you a lot of money."

Uncle Johnny laughed. He knew something outrageous was coming. So he nodded for Lisa to keep talking.

"I've worked in several bars before. So I know what it takes to run a successful business like this. If you listen to me, we can increase your profits by a hundred percent in no time. Now I have looked around this neighborhood, and there are a lot of restaurants and businesses in this area. But there isn't one single strip joint within ten miles of us. How about changing the stage around, putting in a center pole, and hiring some girls to dance?"

"What are you talking about? I ain't trying to run no 'tittie bar.' My place is a respectable business. I'd never do anything like that. You must be out your mind."

"Look, it's just an idea. You asked me to be creative and help you bring in some business around here. I've spent a lot of time in the nightlife in D.C. and Jacksonville. Their biggest money makers were always places that served drinks, food, and women wrapped around a pole."

"Ha! I'm not surprised at that. It just won't be happening here," Uncle Johnny retorted. "Oretha is already riding my back about me serving alcoholic beverages in here with her being an usher at the church and all. If I bring strippers up in here, she'll have a stroke and throw me out the house for real. Are you trying to get me put out my house, woman?"

"No. I don't think Auntie O would go that far and put you out. She'll understand that it's strictly a business move," Lisa stated firmly. She wasn't ready to give up on her idea.

"Well, you don't know my wife as well as I do. I'm not doing that. Her friends at the church would never let her live it down. And I'd never be able to go to church with her again. No, no, forget that foolishness. I'm not that desperate to make a dollar," Uncle Johnny said, confirming his decision while shaking his head at Lisa. "But I do want you to look into one thing for me."

"What's that?" Lisa asked, letting out a frustrated sigh. *I'm fed up with these holy church folk thinking sex and money are evil. Either he wants to make money or not.*

"I've been thinking about maybe hiring a live band to come in here a couple of nights a week or at least on the weekends. Then we can charge a higher cover or something like that for those nights."

"All right, whatever you say. I'll see what I can come up with and get back with you," Lisa replied, dropping the subject for now. She sashayed out of his office in a huff thinking what a fool her uncle was. He could retire a millionaire if he only listened to her savvy advice. With the solid customer base he had, they would be making money hand over fist in no time flat.

"Hello, there. What's wrong with you, Miss Lisa? You look like you're about to blow a gasket." Jason was all in her face as she walked out of the office.

"Hey, Jason, what are you doing back here?" she asked, sounding like she didn't want to be bothered with him.

"I was just heading in to speak with Johnny. It seems we're running low on liquor tonight. I need to know what he wants to do about it."

"Come with me. I have the key to the storehouse," she said, leading the way. Jason closed his mouth for a second and followed Lisa.

"You know, you don't have to be the Ice Princess around here. It wouldn't hurt you to be a little friendly with some of us plain folk."

"What is that supposed to mean?" she asked, turning to look directly in his face as they neared the storage room.

"I'm just saying that you're not going to make many friends with that attitude of yours."

"Please, do I look like I need friends to you? I'm here on a temporary basis only," she replied, turning the key in the lock. They stepped in and took a quick survey of the liquor inventory. "Go ahead and take whatever you need. I'll do the paperwork and order the restocks later."

"Sure. Now, tell me something. When are you going to take me up on my dinner offer?"

"Well, if I thought you were serious, I'd give you an answer. But let me make myself clear: you cannot afford me. Remember, I know how much money you make."

"Oh, I see, you're one of those gold-digging wenches. I thought you were just a little stuck up, but now I can see your true colors."

Lisa didn't bother responding to any more of Jason's comments. She spun around on her sharp-heeled shoes, and walked out of the room. *He can think whatever he wants to think about me. I've got bigger fish to catch and fry. I haven't even gotten my feet wet in this city. Why would I waste my time with his gay-looking self? He's probably one of those DL brothers on the prowl anyway. So, no thank you.*

CHAPTER THREE
(LISA & HAMPTON)

The bar music was thumping Friday night. Uncle Johnny grabbed Lisa by the arm the second she entered the crowded room dressed in a hot pink low-cut sleeveless dress with a pair of matching leather platform sandals. The music was so loud he almost had to scream for her to understand what he was saying. "Hey, Lisa, I need you to work the bar for a little while tonight."

"Why? Where's the regular bartender?" she asked, frowning at him.

"He's running late. He had an emergency, but he'll be here later. He should be here before ten o'clock."

"You know how much I hate being behind the bar, Uncle Johnny. Where's Camille? Can't she run the bar tonight?"

"She's out there waiting tables right now. You know I'm short-handed, and the second happy hour is about to start. It's almost eight o'clock. Would you rather wait tables?"

"No, no. I don't want these stank men pawing on me. I'll tend the bar, but if he's not here by ten, I'm out," she said in a huff, stepping behind the counter.

"All right. If he's not here by then, I'll come back and take it over until closing. Right now, I need to run home and have dinner with my wife. I've been too busy to eat anything all day. If you need anything, Jason will be able to help you out," he said, turning away from Lisa. He was going to pass out from hunger if he didn't get home soon.

"That's right, I'm here to help you with anything you need," Jason chimed in, sliding his palm over the back of Lisa's hand resting on the counter.

"Thank you, but I'll be fine. I've worked every position in a bar before, so don't worry about me," she replied, snatching her hand down. Lisa didn't know what it was about Jason. For some reason, she just didn't like him. He seemed to have gay mannerisms, yet he constantly flirted with her. Anyway, whatever his problem was, she didn't want to be any part of the solution.

"Oh, if I didn't know any better, I could read something into that."

"Will you two stop yapping and get me these drinks," Camille butted in before Lisa could respond, handing her several slips with drink orders. She was sweating and fanning herself with a paper napkin as she leaned her thin waist against the counter to catch a quick breath. Her white top was sticking to her back, and she was trying to pull it off.

Jason snatched the orders from Lisa's hand. "I'll get these together while you take care of the customers at the bar."

"I'll be right back," Camille said, taking off again toward another section in the bar with waiting customers.

They were so busy that the next hour went very fast. Lisa had her back turned away from the bar counter when she heard a male voice say, "Good evening."

She swiftly turned around to see who owned the Billy Dee Williams baritone. "Am I too late to get at least one drink for happy hour?"

"No, you're not. What would you like?" Lisa asked, taking in the deep set gray eyes that went along with the deep sexy voice. He wasn't as light-skinned as she normally liked her men to be, but he smelled like new money. And judging from the length of his well-dressed upper body, he had to be a tall, thick muscled brother man. Lisa admired the slight gray areas around his temples and surmised that he was a distinguished-looking middle aged man. *Maybe he's a retired professional football player or a sports manager. He definitely has some money hidden somewhere, and I know just where to look. Let me see what he's about.*

"I'll take a Martini dry. Is that all right with you?" he asked, using a low seductive voice which had probably made many women squirm. If he had his way, Lisa would be one of them tonight.

"Sure, whatever you want is fine with me," she replied, using the sexy voice which she normally reserved for rich-looking customers. Lisa's eyes lingered on his one-carat diamond-studded earrings, then moved on to the Ralph Lauren Purple Label suit, shirt, and tie that draped his chiseled muscles like silk on chocolate. Just the thought of him caused Lisa to lick her lips as she turned to prepare his drink.

Minutes later, Lisa was serving the high powered gentleman a Martini dry with an extra twist of lime. She placed the drink on the counter in front of him while she stared into his penetrating gray eyes. "Here's your drink," she stated, leaning over the counter, making sure he got an eyeful of her pushed up breasts.

"If you don't mind me saying so, you sure are wearing that dress tonight. I love a woman in pink. It's my favorite color," he stated, grinning in Lisa's face.

"Thank you. I hope you like your drink as much as you like my dress." Lisa glanced at the drink on the counter and then looked back at him.

After taking one sip of his drink he asked, "What is your name, pretty lady?"

"Umh, I don't normally give out my name to the customers. But you can give me yours," she replied, giving him a devilish smile. Lisa was ready to have some fun in Dallas. Her ego hadn't been stroked since arriving in the fast city.

"Well, my name is Hampton Dupree," he said, extending his recently manicured right hand, showcasing a huge, diamond set gold ring. Lisa knew that manicured hands were a sign of a pampered, rich man.

"It's nice to meet you, Mr. Dupree. Do you have a business card?" she asked, lightly shaking his hand.

"Of course, I have one. Why do you need to see that?" he asked, raising an eyebrow.

"I just like to know something about the people I meet. That's all," she said sweetly, watching him pull a card out of his black leather wallet. He extended the card to Lisa, and she eased it out of his hand with a very charming smile.

"It says here that you're an attorney," she stated, eyeing the card. "Are you in private practice?"

"I'm a partner with three other attorneys over at Clark, Dupree, Knowles, and Tate. We all specialize in personal injury law. That's all we do. So, tell me. Why is a pretty lady like yourself serving drinks?"

"I'm the night manager. I'm helping out until the regular bartender gets here. He had a family emergency."

"Oh, I see. It's awful nice of you to help out. Otherwise, I might not have met you tonight. "

"Well, my uncle owns the place so I didn't have much choice."

"It's nice to know you can depend on family."

"Yes, I guess you're right. I have to get back to work, but I'll check back with you in a second, okay?"

"That sounds good to me. I'll be here," he replied, watching the curves beneath her dress as she turned away from him. Hampton licked his lips hoping that he'd struck gold tonight with the fine vixen he was observing who reminded him of Superhead, Karrine Steffins.

Minutes later, Lisa was back, giving Hampton her full attention. "I have two questions for you. What time do you get off from work, and what are you doing afterwards?" he asked, boldly staring her down.

"I might be getting off at midnight, and I might be going home, if it's any of your business," she replied, putting on her game face. She was beginning to enjoy their verbal exchange.

"Let's just say that I'm making it my business. We can go somewhere else and have a few drinks or we could go to my house if you'd like."

"Your house! Now why would I want to go to your house? Are you planning to have a threesome with your wife or something?" Lisa inquired, casting her eyes toward his gold and diamond-studded wedding band.

"Let's just say that my wife is not home tonight, and we have a very special understanding. However, I know another place we can go where you might feel more comfortable. It's a special club I visit when I want to relax."

"I see. Well, if you're still here at midnight Mr. Dupree, we'll see what happens."

"Oh, call me Hampton, and I'll still be around long after the midnight hour. I'll be waiting right here for you."

"Is that right?"

"Yeah, it's Friday night, and I never go to sleep on Fridays. I stay up all night long."

"Lisa, thanks for covering for me." Adam came strutting his tall, lanky figure behind the bar like he'd been relaxing all evening instead of tending to an emergency. He looked refreshed and smelled like he'd just stepped out of the shower stall.

"No problem. You can take over. I've got other things to do," she replied, looking directly into Hampton's deep-set gray eyes. The night was still young, and she had plenty of games she wanted to play before it was over. The handsome gentleman sitting in front of her looked like a prime candidate for Lisa's playmate of the year.

Winking at Hampton as she passed his seat, Lisa added an extra smooth sway in her hips. Knowing he was watching her backside, she took her time passing through the crowded room toward the main office. *I bet he'll be there whenever I decide to return. And that's the truth.*

***

It was almost one o'clock in the morning when Hampton and Lisa arrived at the dark club. Lisa left her car at the lounge and rode with her new friend in his charcoal Jaguar XKR 100 convertible sports coupe. The luxurious leather seats felt like warm butter on Lisa's thin back as they listened to the smooth jazz sounds of the latest Kem CD coming through Hampton's premium speakers. She became so immersed in the soft music and flattering conversation that she didn't really pay attention to the direction in which they headed. So, when they pulled up to park in front of a one-level brick house, Lisa thought they were at Hampton's home or maybe attending a private party since several other luxury cars lined the street. However, she couldn't have been more wrong.

Entering the dimly-lit club holding Hampton's hand, Lisa looked around to see what type of adult crowd was there. Immediately, she knew this wasn't a regular slow grind or booty shaking party. She'd seen these kinds of establishments all over the D. C. area, but she hadn't frequented one in years. This was similar to the strip clubs she'd visited in the Chocolate City, only it was a much higher level of adult entertainment going on up in there.

Carefully surveying the room, Lisa realized this was definitely a high class "sex club" or "mega sex party." The heavy smell of body fluids and alcohol tickled her sensitive nose as they continued walking through the crowd. One threesome, consisting of a tall, lanky man and two well-built women against the right partition, captured her attention for a few seconds. Lisa caught the man's pleasure-filled eyes and winked at him as she passed.

Making their way through the maze of naked bodies engaged in various levels of sexual activities across the sparsely furnished house, they strolled to an unoccupied room in the rear of the smoke-filled building. Leading the way into the candle-lit area, Hampton closed the door and locked it as soon as Lisa was inside. She could hear the soft music playing through the built-in speaker systems as she stepped across the doorway. The room had the distinctive musky smell of sex mixed with lavender candle wax, which only helped to heighten their senses even more. Lisa couldn't tell what type of furniture was in the room, but she was almost positive she could see the outline of a full-sized, made up bed underneath the open curtains in the moonlight.

"So, is this your type of scene?" Hampton asked, facing Lisa. His wide hands stroked her forearms.

"It used to be. I haven't been to one of these places in a long time. What made you bring me here?"

"I told you. This is where I come when I want to relax, and you looked like you needed to unwind," he stated, loosening his purple tie.

"I've been a good girl since I arrived in Dallas. I haven't seen any of the nightlife. I've been working at my uncle's club every night and..." Hampton's hot mouth covered hers as his deep tongue penetrated past her lips in one smooth player's move. He suckled her tongue without allowing her the opportunity to breathe for several seconds. When he released the grip he had on her succulent mouth, she gasped for air.

"Your mouth tastes good. I want to see how the rest of you tastes," he stated, placing her fingers into his mouth. Lisa moaned as he tasted each finger, using the same passion he'd kissed her lips with.

They enjoyed undressing each other, admiring the shape and tone of each other's well-defined bodies. They took turns kissing and licking one another's earlobes, cheeks, and necks. As they were standing face to face, Hampton squeezed her tender breasts, and then lowered his head so his face was nestled in her bosom. Lisa grabbed for his shirt, helping him undo the remaining buttons leading down to his silver belt buckle. Hampton stumbled backward onto the bed as she tried to undo his pants, and Lisa fell over on top of him.

They stayed there all night pleasing each other in various sexual positions. Like Hampton said, he didn't ever sleep on Friday nights. And this was one night that Lisa didn't have any intentions of sleeping either. She was all about pleasing a man.

***

Just before daylight the next day, he dropped Lisa off at J's Bar and Grill to pick up her vehicle. "Are you going to call me later?" she asked, smiling up at him, feeling like this would be the beginning of a mutually beneficial relationship.

"Ah, no, baby. I won't be calling you anytime soon," he replied, sounding serious as he looked Lisa directly in her bulging brown eyes.

"Why not?" she asked, trying to keep cool. "I thought we shared a special evening together."

"Yeah, we did, but that's all it was, one evening. Now, I would appreciate it if you would be adult about this and not call my place of business, all right?"

"What are you saying? You don't want to see me anymore?"

"Look, baby, we had our night of fun. So let's just leave it at that. I thought you were just looking for a good time like me?"

"Yeah, right, that's exactly what I was doing," Lisa replied, dropping her eyes, and realizing that she'd just been used as a jump-off.

Hampton reached across her chest, unlocked the car door, and pushed it open for Lisa. "Take care," he said, waiting for her to exit his vehicle.

Lisa scrambled out of the car seat with her last ounce of dignity. She grabbed the car door, gave him a death stare, and slammed it hard enough to shatter the glass. Hampton called her a "crazy whore" before he pressed the pedal to the metal and burned rubber toward the rising sun.

CHAPTER FOUR
(LISA'S DAY)

Lisa flipped through the classified section of the Dallas Morning News paper, faking like she was interested in finding a job for the sake of her aunt and uncle who were sitting at the breakfast table with her. Uncle Johnny was taking the last bite of his fried egg as Aunt Oretha stood up and started clearing the small wooden table. Still wearing her pink satin pajamas and house slippers, Lisa circled a couple of advertisements for the added effect. "Uncle Johnny, I have two job interviews this afternoon, so I'll probably be after four getting to the club."

"All right, no problem. As long as you make it in before dinner time and close up for me tonight, I'll be okay."

"It's been over a month. Have you interviewed anyone for the evening management position, yet?"

"Yeah, I talked with a few people last week, but none of them had the drive I'm looking for. I need someone I don't have to baby-sit everyday to get the job done, you know."

"Sure, I understand. I don't mind helping you out a little longer while I'm searching for employment." She wanted her uncle to feel like she was doing him a favor so he would be indebted to her for a long time. Lisa really wanted to tell Uncle Johnny she would continue helping him until she found a rich man who could take her to the other side of town. She had a strong gut feeling that was going to happen very soon.

After that fling with Hampton, she hadn't met anyone who was worth the time of day. Most of the men entering the bar looked decent, only they didn't look like the kind of money Lisa was seeking. Thinking it was time to move on to greener pastures, she decided to take some of her earnings and spend a luxury day shopping at one of the upscale centers in Dallas. Sure, she'd thought about harassing Hampton just for the thrill of it. Then, on second thought, he didn't seem like the type to take kindly to harassment. Besides, she'd had her fun with him anyway. *Someone has to be waiting for me in a city this size. I just need to get the right wardrobe and hit the right places.*

With that thought foremost in her mind, Lisa excused herself from the table, heading toward her bedroom to shower and change. In the back of her demented mind, she was hoping Uncle Johnny would change his decision and give her the green light for converting the bar into a strip club so they all could get rich real quick. Only she knew for a fact that would never happen. Uncle Johnny was a real cool guy and everything, but he wasn't interested in her grand ideas relating to that. He was too concerned about upsetting his Bible-toting wife to worry about making the real street money Lisa knew it was possible to make.

Taking the Tuesday afternoon off from her management duties at J's Bar & Grill, Lisa decided to visit the Highland Park Village on Mockingbird Lane at Preston Road for a day of leisurely browsing. Even for a weekday shopping excursion, she was fashionably dressed in a sharp-looking Escada orange pants suit with a pair of coordinating Stuart Weitzman, high-heeled pumps. Lisa wanted to look her best just in case she ran into someone important at the trendy location. She'd heard that this shopping center was as close as any shopper could get to Beverly Hill's Rodeo Drive in this city. Since it was built in the thirties, the ultrachic corner of high-end shopping nestled in Dallas' most exclusive neighborhood sported an eclectic mix of upscale boutiques and shops.

Smiling to herself, Lisa slid behind the wheel of her brand new silver convertible Chrysler PT Cruiser sports car. She didn't know what it was about her and drop top cars, but she loved having the wind blowing through her long wavy hair as she glided down the highway in the sunshine. One thing about it, Dallas had plenty of beautiful days like this where she could keep the top down all day long while driving through the ritzy sections of town. And since Uncle Johnny loaned her the money for a down payment and co-signed on the car loan last week, she was rolling down easy street.

Uncle Johnny had finally gotten tired of Lisa asking to borrow his car or Lisa begging him to take her on a fruitless job search every morning. So he relented to his niece's girlish whining and drove Lisa down to the nearest car lot, instructing her to pick out a new car before he lost his mind from fooling with her. "All right now, I don't have all day. You need to decide what car you want so we can get up out of here," he stated sternly, stashing both hands in his front pants pockets. When the neatly dressed young salesman came toward Uncle Johnny, he directed the man to Lisa.

Casting a sly smile across her devious face, Lisa drove away from the car dealership forty-five minutes later in the newest sporty edition of the PT Cruiser. Even though it was one of the most affordable convertibles available, it didn't look it. As a matter of fact, it cost less than the convertible she'd bought two years ago. Of course, she opted for the 220-horsepower, turbocharged four-cylinder engine.

Pressing her foot to the gas pedal a little bit harder, she checked the rearview mirror to make sure there weren't any cops behind her. She was anxious to get to the Highland Park Village to do some personal damage.

After visiting several shops, Lisa made one final stop at the International Perfumes counter to purchase a gift set including, a large-sized bottle of a newly released fragrance by one of the hottest female entertainers on the market. Although she already had nearly ten bottles of various perfumes on her dresser, Lisa wanted something new and fresh from the super diva. "This is a terrific fragrance, and it's really popular," the salesclerk bragged, spraying a tester card with the dark-colored liquid. "It's really the rage with the young people." That was all she needed to say to persuade Lisa to buy it.

Whipping out her VISA platinum card, Lisa charged the large-sized bottle as a present for herself. She left the shopping center humming the tune to Tweet's song featuring Missy Elliott, "Turn Da Lights Off," as she threw the bags in the back seat of her convertible.

Later that evening, Lisa stripped out of her clothes and headed to the bathroom. Slipping into the tub, she relaxed in the warm water, smelling the aromatic scent of the bubble fragrance. Lisa stayed there until she found herself becoming sleepy after almost an hour had passed. She wrapped herself in an ultra plush purple towel, and then headed to her room with thoughts running through her mind. *Now that I've had some time to get myself together, it's time for me to find another man to spend my evenings and bath time with. If I don't meet someone at the club real soon, I'll have to ease back into the nightlife on the other side of town. There's got to be some decent older married man around here somewhere looking for an experienced woman of the world.*

Lisa sprayed her neck with the heavy new scent prior to slipping into her red silk nightie and matching panties for the evening. *This scent reminds me of an updated version of Obsession, which I've always loved.* Admiring the shape of the uniquely designed bottle, she placed it on her dresser top. Hoping to have sweet dreams, Lisa hopped into her freshly made bed, and fell asleep in a few seconds.

An hour later, she was wide awake from a dream about her past lover, Michael Wayne, the man she thought had been her one true love since they began dating in college. Facing the fact that she'd lost him again after having a one night stand last year, he would always belong to Lisa in her dreams.

In the vision, she was making love to Michael the way they'd done when they were together over twenty years ago and truly in love with each other. Lisa recalled the sound of his distinctive masculine voice and the way he loved catering to her every desire. Michael had been the best lover she'd known and he would never be completely out of her system, whether he was married or not. If her scheming plan had worked, he'd be lying beside her right now instead of haunting her subconscious thoughts.

Vividly remembering the well-built man with the wavy hair and an ultra thin mustache from her dream, Lisa's left hand began roaming over her breasts while the other one crept downward. Moaning softly for herself the same way she'd moaned for Michael, Lisa visualized him pleasing her heated body all over again. Using the power of her imagination, she could actually feel the moisture from his lips roving over her smooth skin in place of her hands.

Just when she was ready to reach a roaring peak, Lisa buried her face in a fluffy bed pillow and let out a muffled scream. Before realizing it, Lisa was drifting off to sleep again visualizing Michael's gentle face staring down at her. *If only he hadn't married that...*

CHAPTER FIVE
(LISA & DESMOND)

Tossing and turning in her bed during the early morning hour while still deep-sleeping, Lisa began ferociously scratching her neck area. By the time she was awake enough to realize what was happening, her fair-colored skin was covered in a red rash from the top of her neck down to her chest. Turning on the pink bedside lamp, Lisa was so horrified at the sight of her skin that she rolled out of bed, hitting the floor like a sharp clap of thunder.

Seconds later, Aunt Oretha was knocking at Lisa's bedroom door. "Is everything okay in there?" she asked, clutching the front of a floral housecoat as she carried her tall, medium built frame through the door, She was almost as tall as her husband, Johnny, but much thinner, and a couple of shades darker.

"Auntie, please come on in. Look at me, Auntie O, my neck and chest are a mess," Lisa cried, holding her head back for her aunt to get a closer look.

"Child, what in the world happened to you? Why did you scratch yourself up like this?" her aunt asked, peering at Lisa through narrow eyes.

"I was asleep, but I scratched myself so hard I finally woke up from the pain. I believe it's from that new perfume I bought yesterday. What do you think?"

"I think you need to go see a dermatologist because you can't be sure if it's from the perfume or not. I could give you some over-the-counter cream, but from the look of your skin, I suggest you go see a specialist."

"Yeah, I do have very sensitive skin, and this itching is driving me crazy. Do you know a good dermatologist?"

"I know the best one in the city. He has his own practice right on this side of town. He also specializes in treating African-American skin. He's just the person you need to see. His name is Dr. Desmond Taylor. I'll go call him and make an appointment for you myself, all right?"

"Oh, thank you, auntie. I'll get dressed while you're doing that for me. Please try to get me in right away," Lisa begged, heading for the bathroom.

Five minutes later, Aunt Oretha had made an appointment for Lisa with Dr. Taylor at his private office. Since today was her day off from work and she knew the exact location of his business, Auntie O volunteered to drive her niece to the doctor's office in her cool vanilla Chrysler 300M. Lisa hurriedly pulled on a Phat Farm, light blue, zipper front spa suit trimmed in white and joined Aunt Oretha in the mid-sized vehicle.

"Auntie, I love your new car," Lisa cooed, surveying the interior. "This is really nice. It still has that new car smell."

"Thank you. I just figured it was time to buy a new car. When I saw the commercial for this vehicle, I immediately fell in love with it." She laughed.

"It's beautiful. What made you want this car?"

"Well, I drove a Honda Accord for twelve years, and it was running fine. We don't travel a lot so I never worried about getting a new car. But, then when I saw one of these in person, I knew it was the car for me. I went home and told Johnny I was buying me a brand new car."

"And what did he have to say about that?"

"He said it was about time. The next day we went to the dealership and came home with this baby."

They both laughed and talked the rest of the way to the doctor's office. *Auntie O can be fun when she's not talking all that religion stuff,* Lisa thought.

Almost thirty minutes later, they arrived at the elaborate office complex nestled in a cove of woods at the end of a busy west side street. They only had to wait a few minutes before the receptionist called Lisa back into one of the nicely decorated dressing rooms. One of the nurses came in, asked a few questions, wrote down Lisa's responses, kindly informed her that the doctor would be in shortly, and then left the room.

Sitting at the end of the white paper-covered examination table, Lisa was about to pick up a current issue of *People* magazine when she looked up at the sound of the door opening again. Walking toward her wearing a white laboratory jacket with a blue shirt and a silk printed necktie was the most magnificent male specimen she'd ever seen. Instantly, his height, strong build, and charismatic smile reminded her of the lost lover which had tormented her dreams last night. He was almost the spitting image of Michael Wayne except for the color of his skin and eyes. His mulatto coloring was much lighter than Michael's, of course, but he had the same shaped head, the wavy hair, the neatly trimmed mustache, and the thin sideburns leading down to a closely shaven beard. The only remarkable difference was that this man had the most beautiful, emerald green eyes humanly possible.

"Hi, I'm Dr. Desmond Taylor," he said, using his most professional voice as he walked over to the sink. After washing his hands for several seconds, he turned to face his new patient.

"Hello, I'm Lisa Bradford," she managed to get out of her mouth as she took in all of his overwhelming presence.

Dr. Taylor took a seat on a stool and pulled himself directly in front of Lisa. "What seems to be the problem today, young lady?" he asked, flashing a drop-your-panties smile.

"I — I used a new perfume last night, and I woke up this morning with this horrible rash all over my neck and chest." Lisa stumbled, unzipped her jacket, and carefully removed it because the rash was beginning to spread to her arms. Then, she slightly raised her head so he could have a closer look at her neck area, too.

"Did you spray the fragrance on any other parts of your body?" he asked, eyeing Lisa suspiciously.

"No, I didn't. I only spritzed the inside of my neck and chest."

"I see. That does look painful. You have almost scratched yourself raw."

"Yes, that happened while I was sleeping. By the time I woke up and realized what I'd done, it was too late. My aunt is a nurse, and she recommended I come see you."

"Really, well, I'm glad she did that," he stated, rising from his seat. "What's your aunt's name and where does she work?"

"Her name is Oretha Bradford, and she's employed at Dallas Southwest Medical Center as a registered nurse in the Emergency Room. Do you know her?"

"I don't recognize her name. Did she say whether or not she knew me?" he asked, maintaining eye contact with his patient.

"She only told me that you were the best dermatologist in the city and that you specialized in African-American skin. Is that true?" Lisa asked, giving him her signature vixen look.

"I would have to say yes on both counts, not that I'm trying to toot my own horn, you know," he replied, trying to sound modest.

Lisa let out a fake laugh. "Well, I'm sure you don't have to worry about doing that too often, tooting your own horn I mean," she stated, batting her long eyelashes.

"You're a very funny lady, Ms. Bradford," he said, chuckling at her response, watching the pink manicured hand she placed on his arm. "Please raise your head again so I can get a better look at your neck and see how far down the rash has spread." Lisa looked upward again and stuck out her chest as far as she could against the white sheer camisole top revealing her strapless push-up bra. Giving the doctor an ample look at her bosom, she tried to flash him a sexy smile.

Dr. Taylor took both of Lisa's hands and turned them over so he could inspect the inside of her arms. Thinking he held on to her soft hands a few seconds longer than necessary, Lisa's heart skipped a beat for Desmond as she absorbed the heat from his hands into her sweaty palms. Desmond smoothed his large hands up to her elbows and back down to her hands. Lisa held her breath, reveling in his exotic touch against her skin as she stared into his sparkling, emerald green eyes. For one second, Lisa thought she saw a speck of his soul behind those mesmerizing gems, a loving soul desiring to become intimately intertwined with hers.

"Okay, the rash is confined to the inside area of your upper arms and neck. I'm going to give you a prescription for a topical cream to use on this three times a day, all right," he said, releasing her hands. He pulled a pen out of his lab pocket, and began scribbling something on a notepad. "You know, you have wonderfully smooth skin on the parts that aren't irritated."

"Oh, thank you for noticing, Dr. Taylor. You have nice skin, too," Lisa cooed, reaching out and touching the back of the doctor's left hand.

"Thank you. If I didn't know any better, I'd think you were trying to flirt with an old man like me."

Lisa threw her head back, letting out a gentle laugh. "Come on now, you're not that old," she teased, batting her eyes again at the outrageously handsome creature standing before her. Lisa couldn't help noticing the solid gold, diamond-studded wedding band on his left hand, but that was only another part of the attraction.

"Forty-five may not be old, but it certainly feels like it to me. Let's just suffice it to say that I've had better days."

"Well, I'm sure some of your best days and nights are still ahead of you." Lisa gave him a beguiling smile, the one she'd used to capture many men's hearts.

"Wow, you do wonders for my ego, Ms. Bradford. I need you to make an appointment to come back and see me in a week or two."

"That sounds good to me, but I was hoping to make it sooner than that. How does lunch tomorrow sound to you?" she asked, lowering her head to one side, giving him a knowing eye.

"Ah, I'm afraid that I'm not available for lunch tomorrow. Thanks, anyway for the invitation just the same."

"You don't know what you're missing, but I understand," Lisa replied, eyeing his wedding band. She pulled up the zipper on her jacket, and smoothly slid down from the examining table.

Dr. Taylor gave a heavy sigh, handed Lisa the prescription, turned to leave the room, and then abruptly stopped with his right hand on the doorknob. Turning to face his stunning new client, he asked, "I don't suppose you'd be available for a late dinner tomorrow evening, would you?"

"How late did you have in mind?" Lisa replied, smiling inwardly. *Game. Set. Match. I can always get a married man.*

Lisa was already daydreaming about Desmond as she and her aunt pulled out of the parking lot. On their drive back home, she couldn't get the handsome, mulatto doctor out of her mind. Lisa was excited about how easily she'd met this distinguished gentleman without even setting out to do so, especially on a day when she wasn't feeling pretty at all. At least she'd managed to have her hair looking decent and a touch of make-up on her face, which probably helped to get his attention. Judging from the way he outright flirted with her today, he was ready for a diversion from his happy little married life. And Lisa was already planning how she was going to be his next wife.

As soon as she and Auntie O made it home with her prescription, Lisa rushed to her bedroom and turned on the Hewlett Packard laptop computer. While waiting for the machine to boot up, she smeared the cream over the infected areas of her arms and neck, and then scrubbed her hands with soap.

Signing on with the regular Internet service, she promptly went to Google.com and typed in the name of Dr. Desmond Taylor. In a few seconds, the screen flashed, revealing his work and home addresses. After printing out the information along with the directions from MapQuest, she carefully folded the paper and slid it into her purse. Picking up her car keys, Lisa headed out the door to go get a firsthand look at her future residence.

Pulling up to the gate with the convertible top and windows down, Lisa smiled to herself when she observed that a cute, young brother was providing the security for the prestigious gated community. He approached her car wearing a brown uniform and a childish grin, carrying a clipboard. She slowed down at his direction, threw her long hair back, and returned his curious stare.

"Hello. Could you pull up a little more so I can record your tag number?"

"Sure," she replied, easing the car up a little more. While he was diligently recording her license number on the clipboard, Lisa searched her mind for a plausible reason for being in the neighborhood this time of day.

"May I ask whom you're going to see?" he asked, returning to the side of her car.

"I'm not going to visit anyone, Rashid," Lisa replied, reading the name on his shirt. Extending her hand, she stated, "My name is Dr. Lisa Bradford. It's nice to meet you."

Taking her hand into his for a warm handshake, Rashid stated, "Hi, doctor, it's a pleasure to meet you."

"I'm new in town, and I just want to have a look around this area, if you don't mind. This is such a beautiful location and since I haven't found a permanent residence, I'd just like to drive through for a quick look at the homes out here."

"Well, we're really not supposed to let anyone in here unless they're going to a specific residence," the young man stated, leaning against the vehicle.

"I know what you mean," Lisa replied, placing her hand over the one he had resting on the car door. "But I'm looking for a place where I can have private parties without the prying eyes of nosy neighbors. I'm sure a good-looking man like yourself can understand what I mean."

"Yes, yes, I believe I do," he stated, standing straight up. Giving Lisa a knowing look, he tugged on his pants.

"That's good. I'll be out in fifteen minutes, I promise. I just want to drive around and see if there are any vacant homes available before I call my realtor. No one but you will ever know I've been here."

"Ahhh," he said, shaking his head at Lisa. "I just don't know about this. I could really get in trouble,"

"Look, let me give you this." Lisa reached in her purse, pulled out a sheet of note paper along with a pen and scribbled something down. Then, she handed it to the security guard, flashing every tooth in her mouth. "Give me a call later at this number, and I'll give you more details about the private parties I'm planning to have. Maybe you'll get a special invitation."

"Alright," he said, releasing a heavy sigh. He double-checked to make sure no one was in sight. Rashid took the paper from Lisa's hand and stashed it into his front pants pocket without looking at it first. "Listen, go on in and have a look around. There are a few homes available out here," he stated, returning to his station. He pressed the gate release button, and waved her on in.

It didn't take Lisa long to realize that Dr. Taylor had the largest house on his block. The three-story, red-brick mansion was a sight to behold. Lisa crept by three times, trying to take in the entire view of the gorgeous waterfront estate before leaving her dream world. Finally, she sped away with a vision of what she would someday own. As she slowed down for the exit gate, the young black man in the booth was still grinning from ear to ear, giving her an enthusiastic wave as she headed out.

Men are so stupid. They will risk their jobs, lives, and marriages for just a little bit of sex or even a promise of some stuff. And the married ones are always the easiest to persuade. If they have an opportunity to cheat with a beauty like me, the show is over, and the fat lady can sing for the rest of the night.

CHAPTER SIX
(DESMOND'S LIFE)

Dr. Desmond Taylor clicked the remote control button unlocking the doors to his brand new, red convertible Porsche Boxster in his reserved parking space right outside his brick office complex. This was his favorite time of day, when he could leave while the sun was still shining brightly. Feeling the warmth of the sun bearing down on the top of his head made Desmond appreciate being alive and in control of his destiny. Taking off the gray jacket to his thousand-dollar Kenneth Cole suit, he slid into the sharp vehicle humming a soulful tune. As he turned the key to start the automobile, listening to the unique engine sound invigorated his spirits. Looking through his music collection, he pulled out the latest Anthony Hamilton CD, and gently pushed it into the automatic player. He backed up, then pulled away as the masterful voice began to flow through the six speakers in his two-seater car.

Desmond loved riding in style, knowing that he was heading home to one of the most exclusive estates located in northern Dallas. It gave him a keen sense of pride. For the past twelve years, he and his wife, Belinda, had been the happy owners of a meticulously decorated, three-story, seven bedroom house situated on three acres of land. In Northwood Heights, north of I-635, the prestigious gated community where they resided had access to a private lake at the end of a cul-de-sac. He could almost smell the fish in the pond when he wasn't able to indulge in his favorite pastime of tossing out a fishing rod.

In addition, they had their own live-in housekeeper and cook, Ms. Rodriguez, an older Hispanic lady who had been with them for the past ten years. She lived in the third bedroom located on the first floor toward the rear end of the Taylors' seven thousand square foot home. She'd also been a nanny to the children when they were growing up and helped with the gardening as well as other outside chores around the house. Ms. Rodriguez was happy with her position and kindly indulged the doctor and his wife, along with both their kids, who were now teenagers. Justine, their daughter, had just turned into an innocent thirteen-year-old, while Jesse, their son, was sixteen-years-old with a fondness for the opposite sex, just like his father. Both kids were gorgeous with even-toned, blemish-free skin.

Coming from a long line of doctors, Desmond was an only child who had been spoiled rotten by his overprotective parents and grandparents. His father, David Taylor, was a noted African-American surgeon and chief of surgery at Dallas Memorial Hospital until he retired five years ago, while his mother, Eileen, a Caucasian woman, never worked a day in her pampered life. Therefore, Desmond was a product of his wealthy environment. He never had to want for food, money, or love during his childhood. So, once he became a fine-looking teenager with women from every economic level vying for his attention, Desmond decided to write his own rules for the player's handbook. The first rule was that Desmond Arnez Taylor would always be number one in any relationship he encountered. Ironically, most of the women he'd been involved with were fully aware of this rule, but they loved him anyway. Desmond was used to feeding women crumbs because he was only capable of giving his partners pieces of himself.

Desmond never really loved Belinda, but since she was one of the most devoted women in his league of lovers, he decided to marry her as a smart business investment. His parents had him set-up to receive a twenty million dollar trust fund at the age of thirty. The only catch was that he had to be married by that time or receive a much smaller fraction of the matured value. Belinda Hines wasn't the best looking girl he was boning, but she certainly was the most dependable. Desmond bet that the dark-skinned woman with the pretty almond-shaped eyes and very low self-esteem would always have his back no matter what. She wasn't bright enough to recognize her own value, but she held him in the highest regards.

Being that she was also from a prominent family, she was bred to become a rich man's wife. With that in mind, he believed Belinda wouldn't let anything or anyone compromise their multimillion dollar lifestyle. She would do whatever was necessary to keep him and their vast fortune away from enemy hands. And that was the only reason they'd managed to stay married for eighteen years. He trusted her devotion beyond a shadow of a doubt. She never even questioned him about the number of affairs he had during the course of their marriage. In all honesty, he would admit that a Harvard educated woman like Belinda probably had some ideas about his extracurricular activities, but since she was unable to prove anything, she just decided to go along with the program, which in his estimation, was a very intelligent move. She would never leave him, no matter what, so he could mistreat Belinda whenever he wanted to. As long as he threw some good loving her way every now and then, she'd be honored to be called his spouse.

Reliving every second he'd spent with Lisa today, Desmond knew the instant he entered the examining room that he'd met his future playmate. There was no denying the beauty of the woman who was an uninhibited flirter. Surely, she was accustomed to being a certified sex kitten for rich men. He recognized the traits of a fine woman used to being a well taken care of mistress. He didn't know exactly what it was, but the inner radar lodged somewhere in his brain started beeping whenever there was an attractive gold digger within fifty feet of him. Most of the time, it never went past the cat and mouse foreplay game unless he felt a special connection with the individual.

Today, what he was feeling could only be described as euphoria. It was a drugless high permeating through his entire system at the prospect of conquering a gorgeous new bed partner. One whiff of her natural aroma was comparable to snorting a line of the finest uncut cocaine powder available. Desmond never understood why women bathed themselves in perfume when the authentic essence of a female had always provided the greatest arousal for him.

He was floating on air from just touching Lisa's silky smooth skin. Imagining how fulfilling their first intimate encounter was going to be, Desmond had pulled into his long circular driveway before realizing how close he was to his fabulous home. Thinking how tomorrow night would be the start of an amazing romantic adventure, he exited his car. *I wonder how long this ride is going to last?*

Desmond entered his spacious bedroom, spoke to his wife, and gave her a quick peck on the cheek. Silently, he hoped she wasn't in one of her talkative moods tonight because he had another woman on his mind.

"Hi, baby. How was your day?" Bolinda asked, sounding bubbly. She was casually sprawled out on the California, king sized, canopy bed in the master suite on the first level of their huge house. Wearing a black lounging set on her size eight body, she had vacation brochures spread out all over the bed from Disney World in Florida, to Niagara Falls Resort in Canada, all the way to the Wisconsin Dells. They'd been discussing this trip for the last two months, and she was determined they would make a decision tonight, considering that the Thanksgiving holiday was less than a month away.

"It was all right," Desmond responded, sounding perturbed. He threw his suit jacket on the bed and walked in the master bathroom, loosening his necktie. Desmond wasn't up to hearing this foolishness right now. He was too busy plotting on how to see Lisa for a late dinner tomorrow evening.

"I was hoping we could go through the brochures tonight and finalize a few things. The kids have been asking about where we're going, and my parents are requesting we come visit them. What would you like to do, sweetheart?" she asked, following her husband into the bathroom. Desmond was standing at the toilet handling his personal business when she walked in.

"Actually, I've been thinking. Things are starting to pick up at the office, and there's a conference in San Diego the weekend before Thanksgiving that I really would like to attend. It's going to focus on some of the latest developments in dermatology. Famous doctors from all over the world will be speaking at this seminar. If I want my practice to continue growing and thriving, I need to be at this key event," he said, zipping up his pants, turning to face his wife. Desmond headed for the double sink to wash his hands.

"I know you're not trying to get out of this trip, Dez. This whole vacation was your idea just two months ago. Now you're talking about going to a conference instead of spending time with your family. What will the children think?" she inquired, giving him an intensifying stare.

"The children are used to going on vacations without me. It's no big deal to them. As long as they get to shop and have fun, it's all good."

"What about me, Dez? You know I don't like traveling without you," she stated, flapping her hands at her side.

"I'm sorry. I can't pass on this opportunity because you're insecure about traveling alone with the kids. You know, they're teenagers. It's not like they're little babies you have to look after anymore. Just go somewhere they can be free and you can spend time at a spa or something like that, B.," he said, waving a clean hand in the air, demonstrating his irritation.

Releasing an exasperating sigh, Belinda knew it was useless arguing with her husband once he'd made up his mind about not going somewhere. A drastic change like this in his personality could only mean one thing. It was the thing Belinda regretted the most about being married to the flamboyant Dr. Desmond Taylor. The one thing that could make her lose her strong reasoning skills, causing her emotions to fly wildly out of control. Her husband had undoubtedly met a new floozy whom he wanted to spend time with while his family was away on another extended vacation. It wasn't that bad when the kids, Justine and Jesse, were younger. They had a lot of fun traveling with her to national amusement parks, museums, and fancy resort hotels. But now that they were both teenagers, they had their own activities they wanted to participate in, which didn't include mommy dearest. So traveling alone with them had become an unpleasant experience for Belinda.

"Well, since you don't care anymore about where we're going, I'll just take them up to my parents' home in Michigan. They're getting on up in age. It'll do them good to visit with the kids for the Thanksgiving holiday."

"Yeah, that's a great idea. Why don't you go ahead and make reservations for that, B.?" he asked, turning toward his wife. "Be sure and tell your folks I said hello and send my best," he added, hugging his wife, placing a light kiss on her raised forehead.

Belinda was holding her peace for now, but she knew exactly how to get to the bottom of this. *My mama didn't raise no fool. I pity the hussy who thinks she can mess with my man.*

They walked out of the bedroom together arm in arm. "What's for dinner, baby?"

"Oh, I had Ms. Rodriguez make all of your favorites: smothered pork chops, brown rice, asparagus with butter sauce, and fresh brewed lemon tea."

"Well, then, what are we waiting for? Let's eat," he stated, leading the way into the formal dining room. Belinda stared at his back imagining she had daggers to throw at his cheating heart.

CHAPTER SEVEN
(DESMOND'S WIFE)

Belinda stepped out of the oval-shaped whirlpool bathtub, dried herself off with an extra-plushy cinnamon-colored towel, and slipped on the white-laced nightie she reserved for special occasions. If some prostitute was trying to take her man, she needed to give him something he could feel tonight. Taking her time, she slathered on the creamy Fashion Fair brand lotion Desmond liked because it didn't contain much fragrance. Letting down her long relaxed hair, Belinda shook her head from side to side, and then fluffed it out with her fingers. Looking in the bathroom vanity at her glowing sable skin she'd thought was once upon a time undesirable to men, Belinda smiled as she remembered meeting her husband for the very first time.

She had been visiting at the home of a friend in New Haven, Connecticut. Belinda had just graduated from Harvard Business School and was still living there when she flew down to visit her college friend, Antonia, who'd just tied the knot with a young doctor, named Montgomery Ayers. They were having a private reception at their home and Belinda was just one of their many house guests. Standing at the bar outside on the patio waiting for the bartender to mix her another martini, Belinda's eyes focused on Desmond the instant his tall frame floated through the double French doors. Wearing an Armani black formal suit, he eyed her blue satin slip dress all the way down to her matching blue slippers. He immediately approached her and started a conversation with her, and she held his undivided attention all through the rest of the evening. For the next six months after that, they called each other every day and took turns flying back and forth to visit one another on the weekends and holidays. Desmond couldn't seem to get enough of her dark chocolate skin—he devoured her faster than hot cocoa every chance he got.

However, their steamy romance almost came to a screeching halt when Desmond revealed that he'd accepted a high paying position to work in Dallas, Texas, with a noted dermatologist. Two months later, Belinda's determination to keep track of her man caused her to hastily pack up everything she owned and move to Dallas, too. She had managed to convince her employers to transfer her job so she could be in the same city with the man she loved. Amazingly, within the next four months, she'd planned an incredible wedding ceremony, and they were on their way to Nuptial Island.

Now, here she was fighting to keep her lackluster marriage in tact with all of her feminine powers. Stopping at her oversized walk-in shoe closet, she stared at the hundreds of shoes of every style separated by color and stacked from the floor to the ceiling. Pulling out a pair from the red section, she chose patent leather pumps with a peek-a-boo toe. Slipping into her favorite pair of four-inch "hooker" high heels, Belinda admired her profile in the full length mirror. Wearing sexy shoes to bed had become her trademark way to let Desmond know when she was in the mood for love. And they always had to be red in order to match her polish, regardless of what color her lingerie was. With a standing weekly appointment at the nail salon, Belinda's fingers and toes always had a fresh coat of Opi brand polish.

Entering the dimly-lit master bedroom, Belinda sashayed her smooth hips over to the right side of the bed. Desmond was propped up on four pillows reading a *Money* magazine wearing his red, silk Oscar de la Renta pajamas with the top open. Sliding under the thin, white satin sheets, Belinda scooted over in the bed until she was right beside her husband. Extending her right hand, she clasped the magazine, pulling it away from him.

"I have a far more engaging activity planned for you tonight," she panted, feeling her body temperature starting to rise already. Throwing her hair back to one side, she gave Desmond the seductive look he'd come to know so well.

"And what could that be?" he asked, folding his hands over his flat midsection. Desmond knew exactly what Belinda had in mind, but he figured it wouldn't hurt to play along with the game. Besides, he needed this release tonight just in case his potential new lover wasn't ready to go all the way on the first date.

"Well, first I thought we'd start with this," she teased, giving him a long passionate kiss. Searching for the passion that she knew Desmond possessed, Belinda found his lips searching for hers in return. Sliding off his pajama top with both hands, she tossed the garment to the foot of the bed. Carefully unsnapping his pajama bottom, Belinda slid her right hand underneath his underwear until she felt him. One thing about it, her man was well-endowed, and that was part of the problem. That was the main reason so many women were always trying to seduce her husband. They could tell from the front imprint of his tight fitting pants that the doctor had it going on in the bedroom.

Moaning from Belinda's gentle strokes, Desmond asked, "What was the second thing on your mind?"

Belinda responded by placing another passion-filled kiss on his lips while climbing on top of him. This was her night and she wanted to be in control. Belinda continued kissing downward until reaching the tip of his twinkling pedicured toes. Then she made her way back up to about midway his body, where he was waiting patiently for her.

Minutes later, she was out of the white nightie and the red "hooker" pumps. She was driving Desmond wild like a 380-horse powered race car. Just when she was getting ready to shift into fifth gear, he began sputtering out of gas. Knowing she'd better get hers real fast, Belinda threw her head back, and tightly squeezed her feminine muscles. She climaxed at the same time as Desmond, and then collapsed on top of his glistening chest.

After that, Belinda tried to give him another round of sexual activity, but Desmond wasn't interested. Turning his back to his wife, he drifted off to sleep with thoughts of being with Lisa underneath the sheets. It was a vision which he was determined to make come true as soon as possible.

***

Belinda tossed her long straight black hair out of her face as she rolled over in the bed. She'd just finished making love to her passionless husband. *At least he could have tried to fake some emotions for once.*

Remembering a time when they would passionately sex each other all through the night, she released a sigh of frustration. Now they would normally do it only when she initiated it or offered to give him a special treat like she had done tonight. And they would only do it one time before he rolled over and fell asleep, making no further attempts at closeness. If she wasn't hot enough to get her fulfillment before he did, then that was too bad. He would just leave her hanging without any sense of remorse. Desmond didn't see anything wrong with getting his sexual gratification and leaving Belinda wanting for more affection from the man whom she was desperately trying to hold onto with all of her strength.

George and Julia Hines, Belinda's parents, had always taught their daughter to put her husband's needs above her own. "The rewards will be worth the effort," she remembered her mother saying on more than one occasion. Being her mother's child, Belinda respected the words of wisdom passed on to her from a seemingly happily married woman. But Julia Hines was a woman far from having a real love story. She just knew how to put the best on the outside for the entire world to see while she dealt with the heartache and pain of a philandering husband. "It's important to maintain one's appearance. Having wealth and not having to ask anyone for anything is all that matters," her mother said.

Well, I've got the wealth, but I'd be a lot happier if I had an attentive man sleeping with me every night. I just need to find out who this latest slut is and deal with her in the same manner I've dealt with all the others. Dez is a wonderful husband when he's not distracted by some gold digger trying to take my place. No one will ever be able to fill my shoes. And every time somebody tries, I put my pointed toe shoes up her behind so fast, she crawls back under the rock from which she came. I can't wait to meet my latest challenge.

Belinda fought away sleep by thinking about the joys of her splendid lifestyle, courtesy of Dr. Desmond Taylor. She enjoyed spending her days with pampered rich friends getting spa treatments, having lunch at overly expensive restaurants, shopping for the latest designer clothing, and fulfilling her pointed toe shoe fetish. Belinda had a passion for shoes that couldn't even be matched by Patti LaBelle, the diva claiming to have over three hundred pairs of shoes in her closet. Well, Belinda was sure she had double that amount in her custom made closet dedicated to showcasing her foot attire. And the amazing thing about it was that they were all pointed toe shoes, sandals, and boots in every color by every significant designer known in America and abroad. It was a way of life that only a fool would walk away from or allow to be taken away from her. *My mama didn't raise no fool. I know how to keep my man.*

Eventually, Belinda began giving in to the drowsiness with the front of her body pressed closely against Desmond's back side. Her right arm was wrapped around his waist in the spooning position. Placing her left ear to his firm back, listening to his soft breathing in and out, she wondered what and whom her husband was dreaming about.

Fighting sleep with worry, Belinda began thinking of how she'd first learned about her man's infidelity during their second year of marriage. Belinda's mind recalled Allison Dennings. The young, twenty-year-old, white female was a community college student who'd dared to invade the sanctity of their marriage bed. She'd truly been the youngest and the easiest one for her to dismiss from their lives. The child was so foolish thinking Desmond would leave his wife and baby son for her that she called Belinda on the telephone, providing all the details of their sordid affair. Taking the information in stride, Belinda met with Allison at the apartment she claimed to share with Dez, and offered her enough money to make her disappear to another country. She knew the girl was only looking for a meal ticket out of the South, somewhere far away from her almost destitute white trash family. So Belinda provided her with the funds which she happily accepted, and then got out of Dodge with a quickness that same week.

What was it the child had told Belinda sitting at the round dining room table in that crammed-up, one bedroom apartment on Saxton Street? "Desmond and I are in love. He said he's leaving you. So you might as well go ahead and divorce him now and save yourself some embarrassment."

"Oh really," Belinda replied, not believing her diamond-studded ears. Leaning over the table into Allison's face, she stated, "Listen, you cheap, white, garbage bag. Desmond is not leaving his wife, child, and happy life for the likes of you. You're simply some easy stuff on the side. Now take this check, get a new life, and don't ever contact my husband again," Belinda continued, sliding a white envelope containing a one hundred thousand dollar check across the small table.

Allison carefully opened the envelope, keeping her eyes on Belinda's oval shaped face and smiling fuchsia painted lips. She grabbed her chest as she counted and recounted the zeroes. "Oh my, you must really love Desmond," she gasped, her pale face reflecting her shock.

"He's mine, and I'll do whatever it takes to keep him. Now do we have a deal or not?"

"I'll be out of here in two days. You won't ever have to worry about seeing me in this city or state again for that matter."

Since that time, Belinda had vowed to never pay money for another woman to leave her man alone, but to take a more personal approach to dealing with his indiscretions. Usually, that meant confronting the enemy and threatening them with some form of bodily harm, which was normally enough to scare away the majority of them. But every now and then, she'd meet a few who didn't give up that easily and she had to deal with them accordingly. Like Meena Pierce, a middle-aged, Korean, travel agent with skinny legs, who thought she seriously had a chance at taking Desmond away from his family. Well, Belinda simply followed them to their hideaway location, waited until they were gone out for a night on the town, and bribed the super to let her into the apartment wearing leather gloves. She took the woman's small dog, a pretty white poodle, ran a tub full of bath water, and drowned the poor animal. After calling Meena the next day, hearing her distraught cries through the telephone receiver, Belinda let her know what time it was. That was enough for the heifer to permanently stay away from her husband.

After scaring Meena away, Belinda's marriage eventually returned to a state of happiness for the next eleven months, until she suddenly began to notice some significant changes in Desmond's behavior. Over the course of the next fifteen years, Belinda learned how to recognize the three telltale signs when her husband was definitely up to his old deceitful tricks. For one, he stopped wanting to go on vacations with them, even if they'd spent months planning something together with the children. He'd insist on her taking the trip alone with the kids, claiming he'd join them later, which he never did. Then, he would suddenly stop wanting to sleep with her as often as they had before and wouldn't spend as much time trying to stimulate her when they did make love. And finally, he would adamantly claim he needed to spend more time at work training new employees or attending out of town conferences at a moment's notice, like he'd done tonight.

Desmond had cheated with women from all races and nationalities, making him an international male whore. Although he'd worshiped her dark skin when they first met, Belinda was sure her husband had a preference for the fairer-skinned sex. Most of the women Desmond courted had been white, Korean, Italian, or a combination of cultures. She could count the number of real black women he'd been with on one hand, and none of them were as dark-skinned as Belinda. Anyway, she was sick of the light and the white hoochies trying to take her fine brother man.

Drifting to sleep, Belinda wondered what the new interest in Desmond's life looked like compared to her. Feeling certain she'd find out in the upcoming weeks, Belinda gave in to slumber, thinking of a scheme to clip the newest snag nail invading her marriage. *I can't wait to get this one out of the way so we can get back to being happy again. Eventually, he'll get tired of these no good unsophisticated women and realize what he has at home. After all, you can buy ass, but you can't buy class.*

CHAPTER EIGHT
(THE FIRST DATE)

When she woke up the next morning, Lisa was amazed at how well the topical cream was already working. Her neck and upper arms were no longer red, and there were just a few bumps left from where she'd scratched so hard. Although Lisa felt fine, she decided to stay home another day since she wanted to be well-rested for her first dinner date with Dr. Taylor tonight. By ten o'clock that morning, she couldn't stand the idea of going another second without hearing his voice.

Lisa punched in the numbers to his office, and counted while she waited for the receptionist to pick up the telephone. "Hi, this is Lisa Bradford. I'd like to personally speak with Dr. Taylor, please."

"The doctor is with a patient right now. I'll be happy to put you on hold while I inform him that he has an incoming call."

"That will be fine, thank you." Less than a minute later, Desmond answered the line.

"Hello, Dr. Taylor. This is Lisa Bradford. I'm calling to let you know my skin looks a lot better this morning, thanks to you."

"Oh, well, I'm happy to hear that. Thanks for calling me."

"I'd also like to know where you'd like to meet for our dinner date tonight."

"I'm sorry, but I'm with a patient right now. Please give me a number where you can be reached, and I'll call you right back."

Lisa gave Desmond her cellular telephone number. Within ten minutes, he was calling her back just like he'd promised.

"Hi, Ms. Bradford, I've been waiting for you to call. I've already made reservations for two tonight at 8:30 at the Monarch Restaurant. It's inside Hotel ZaZa. How does that sound? "

"I'm not familiar with that place. I've only been in town for a little over a month, you know?"

"No, I had no idea. It's just north of downtown, among many of the city's best restaurants, shops, and museums. It's guaranteed to be a sumptuous experience which you will never forget. The facility is spectacular. So are we on?"

"We certainly are. I will meet you inside the restaurant at 8:30 tonight. I'll be wearing a red dress that's guaranteed to impress," she replied, laughing cunningly with the doctor.

"I'm looking forward to meeting you there. Now I have to get back to work if I intend on meeting you on time. By the way, I'm calling you from my cellular phone, so you should have this number on your caller ID. In case you need to call me back, please dial this number."

"Yes, I have it. Thanks for giving me your private digits. Good-bye."

Lisa flew to her closet, pulling out the sexiest, red, low-cut, halter-neck dress in her wardrobe. She wanted to make sure she made a grand entrance into the Dallas high-life tonight. The Tracy Reese gown cost Lisa almost a full month's salary, but it would be worth it tonight to see her red dress light up in Desmond's emerald eyes.

Later that evening, Lisa pulled up to the hotel's entrance in her silver Chrysler PT Cruiser, handed her keys to the valet, and headed to the Monarch Restaurant. After checking her long coat at the front desk, she was shown to a quaint table nestled in the far end of the facility, where Desmond awaited her wearing a sharp charcoal suit with a glimmering tie. Extending his right hand to Lisa, he helped the beautiful woman into her seat across from him.

"I see you found the restaurant okay. Tell me, what do you think?" he asked, knowing from her glowing expression she was tremendously impressed.

"It's the most magnificent place I've ever seen," Lisa replied, taking in the full effect of the upscale facility.

"I calculated that the atmosphere here would be very close to your liking."

"And what makes you think you know what I'd like? I've barely known you for twenty-four hours."

"Yes, but we have a connection that it doesn't take long to make. That's why I've taken the liberty of reserving one of their private suites, so we can spend some time alone talking and getting to know one another better," he said, sounding persuasive and confident he would get exactly what he'd come there for.

"I know you don't think it's going to be that easy to get me into a hotel room, Dr. Taylor. I'm not a twenty-two-year-old you know."

"What is that supposed to mean? I was simply implying that we needed some secluded time together where we can learn more about each other. Somewhere quiet and free from worldly distractions," Desmond replied, playing the perfectly innocent role.

"If I was twenty-two right now, I'd probably be inclined to meet you in a hotel room without a second thought. But at this stage of the game, I'm not quite that eager."

"My dear lady, I was just teasing with you. There's no way I'd reserve a room without discussing it with you prior to doing so. You just passed your first test."

"Oh, so you're testing me, are you?" Lisa asked, giving him a devilish smile.

"Yes, it was just a test to see if you were a desperate woman or not. You see, I can't stand that type of female. But I would imagine that a woman of your caliber and fortitude would never have to be without a man in her life."

"You are so right about that. Now, are you ready to order dinner?" Lisa asked, seeing the waitress walking toward their table.

They enjoyed the next hour together by making small talk with one another. Lisa was careful not to ask him about his family life. She could find out about that on her own. She didn't want him to ever be reminded of his family while he was in her presence. So, instead, she drilled him on his pedigree and medical practice.

Desmond was very comfortable talking about himself and his major accomplishments. He enjoyed dating women who unselfishly catered to his every need. Lisa was playing the attention game by hanging on to every word coming out of his mouth as if it was the gospel according to Matthew, Mark, Luke, and John. She knew exactly when to laugh at his jokes, and how to lean forward just enough to show some of her small cleavage.

Once they finished their fabulous meal and wine, Desmond walked Lisa outside to the valet desk. Retrieving her car keys, Lisa turned toward Desmond, and planted a kiss on his cheek. "Thanks for dinner. I had a great time."

"I'm glad to hear that. Would you like to do it again, this weekend perhaps?"

"You mean you want to come back to this same place?"

"Sure, why not. It's beautiful isn't it?" he asked, glancing up at the towering hotel.

"All right. What time would you like to meet here on Saturday evening?"

"Let's meet earlier this time, say six o'clock. Would you be opposed to me reserving a suite for us this time?"

"That depends on whether or not you're planning to spend the entire night with me."

"And what if I said I would be available to you all night long? Will that be enough for your consent?"

"Tomorrow's Friday, so I'll think about it and call you back in the morning. I'll leave you a text message in your cell phone with my answer."

"Okay. I usually check my private messages before noon. I'll be expecting to have your answer by then."

This time, Desmond kissed Lisa on the cheek before she entered her vehicle, driving off into the night. They both knew what her answer would be in regards to the Saturday evening date. Desmond just had to come up with an excuse for his wife that would allow him to stay out all night.

CHAPTER NINE
(THE FIRST TIME)

Saturday evening arrived, and Lisa checked her car in with the valet attendant. Only this time she went to the black front desk, asking for the suite reserved under Dr. Desmond Taylor's name. She checked her coat in with the desk attendant, asked for directions to the elevator, and proceeded to their home for the night. Making her way to the luxurious room on the top floor overlooking the magnificent skyscraper city, she wondered how her new man would be able to slip away from his wife for an overnight visit. But since it wasn't her concern, she was just happy with the prospect of seeing Desmond's gorgeous naked body in a matter of minutes. Considering that she didn't want to appear too eager, she made it a point to arrive almost an hour late.

Pushing the horrific scene with Hampton Dupree out of her mind, Lisa was ready to enjoy the company of a real gentleman. She thought about showing up on Hampton's job and showing her true colors, but decided she didn't need any enemies right now, especially, a high-powered attorney. Figuring he would have to pay for the broken window in his car, Lisa felt a strong sense of satisfaction for now. Closing her frosted eyelids, she tried to imagine what Desmond was wearing as he waited for her late arrival. Lisa wondered if he'd be relaxing in silk pajamas or in his smooth bare skin. Either way, she couldn't help but smile at the gorgeous images in her head.

At first, she had considered holding out on her new love interest after that fiasco with Hampton, then, she realized that Dr. Taylor was a man who wasn't likely to wait very long for her. So Lisa decided to go ahead and give him a test run at the hippest hotel in the city.

Minutes later, she was exiting the elevator and knocking at the high rise room door. Lisa could hear Desmond's footsteps coming toward her over the soft music playing in the background.

"Hi, I'm glad you could make it. I've been here almost an hour waiting on you. I was beginning to get concerned." Desmond answered the door wearing a Moschino's red printed smoking jacket over a pair of black silk pajama pants. Lisa recognized the sultry smooth R & B sound of Sade singing, "Your Love is King," as she sauntered into the room. He was definitely going to be her king for the night, looking better than any vision she'd imagined earlier.

"It took a little longer for me to get dressed than I thought it would. So do you like my attire?" Lisa asked, modeling her short black sleeveless dress with a deep v-cut in the front and back.

Taking her by the left hand, Desmond spun Lisa around so he could get a full view of her beauty. "Yes, I like it very much," he commented, pulling her into his strong embrace. Wrapping both arms around Lisa from behind, he placed his nose on her neck, and inhaled her fresh scent.

"I like it when you wear your hair up like this. It's very attractive," he mumbled against her scented neck.

"Well, thank you. I see you've already made yourself comfortable. I thought we were having dinner before retiring for the evening."

"We are, but I've decided to order room service. I don't feel like sharing you with anyone else tonight. I hope that's okay with you."

"Well, when you put it like that, how can I resist?" Lisa stated, strutting over to the king size cherry wood bed in her four inch black stilettos. Taking a seat on the red, jacquard bedspread, she sensuously ran her hands over the luxurious textured fabric. Looking up at the mood chandelier with crystals changing color every two seconds, Lisa took in the splendidness of the room from the Picasso prints on the wall, to the flat screen television set at the bottom of the bed. This would definitely be the classiest place she'd ever seduced a man before. If she was going to give her body away, this was undoubtedly the best way to do it—in style where a room cost at least eight hundred dollars a night.

Desmond took care of ordering their dinner, which consisted of salmon with curry pineapple chutney, parsley mashed potatoes with seasoned asparagus tips including a house wine, and chocolate covered strawberries for dessert. He gave the waiter a huge tip, telling him that he didn't need to worry about returning for the trays this evening.

Lisa took her time savoring the meal, making sure to moan in pleasure every time she took a small bite of the delectable food. Intentionally drawing his attention to her ruby painted lips, Lisa chewed several times before swallowing, knowing Desmond was carefully observing her every move.

"You have a very sensual mouth. Are you doing that deliberately to tease me?" Desmond inquired, staring at Lisa's luscious lips wrapped around a chocolate drenched strawberry.

Lisa gave a sexy laugh at his observation and replied, "Of course, I am. I thought you could take a little teasing."

"That's good, because a little teasing is about all I can take. I've thought about nothing but being alone with you since you entered my office on Wednesday morning," Desmond said, rising from his chair. Easing over to Lisa's side of the table, he placed his lips over hers, biting into the other half of the fruit she had clutched between her front teeth. They started chewing and kissing each other at the same time, enjoying the taste of the ripe chocolate coated strawberry, as well as the sweet taste of each other.

Making their way to the bed, they were still enthralled in a passionate kiss. The fruit was completely gone, but they continued feasting on each other's heated lips. With two swift moves of his hands, Desmond was out of his smoking jacket and his silky pants bottom. Lisa was lying on her back against the jacquard bedspread with the skirt of her dress gathered around her waist. Desmond lowered himself over her body. He nibbled on her earlobes, whispering in her ear, "We're going to be the perfect match from this day forward. I've got a lot of plans for us. You'll see what I mean."

"Umh, I like the sound of that," she replied, reaching out to touch his hairy chest.

They made love all through the night in a different position each time until they were both completely satisfied and exhausted. After the third session, they both slept for a few hours until the daylight started creeping in on their slumbering faces. As the sun began to rise, so did Desmond with thoughts of his angry wife waiting at home for him. *I don't know what I'm going to tell Belinda, but I've got to come up with something original. When will she learn that she's just not enough for me anymore? I'll just have to call her on my way home and tell her I had an emergency at the hospital or something. I'm sure she's going to be upset. But she should be used to me staying out all night by now. I'll have to pacify her a little while longer since she's being a dutiful wife and all.*

As they lay wrapped in each other's arms, Desmond mumbled against Lisa's neck, "I've got to get home. It's almost eight, and I need to get going." *I hope you can accept that without making a scene. Even these mature women can act foolish sometimes.*

"When can I see you again?" she asked, lifting his face to hers.

"I'll call you later in the week, and we'll decide what type of arrangement we'd like to have," he stated, sliding his naked body out of bed. *Maybe this will work out nicely after all.*

"Are you rushing home to your wife? Where did you tell her you were going to be last night?" Lisa asked, rising up on both elbows.

"Don't worry about my relationship with my wife. We have an understanding, and so far it's working," he smirked, staring down at her. *Now I hope you don't go getting an attitude. I don't need another woman questioning me.*

"Okay, where have I heard that one before?" Lisa asked, throwing her head back in laughter.

"So, ah, you have a history of dating married men, do you?" he asked, walking down to the end of the bed. Looking back at her smiling face, he stopped and waited for her response. Just as he thought, it didn't take her long to formulate a reply.

"Well, I've dated a few in the past. I find them to be much more attentive and free-hearted, if you know what I mean."

"Oh, I think I know exactly what you mean. I just hope we can come to a suitable arrangement for our relationship." *I wonder how much money this is going to cost me. She should be worth it at least.*

"I think we've already reached a profitable agreement, don't you?" Lisa asked, staring his body down.

"As long as we're both happy, that's all that really matters. I believe I can make you a very satisfied woman. Tonight was just a sample of what I have in store for you. Would you like to meet at this hotel again?" he asked, taking another survey of the suite.

"Yes, I love it here. I'm looking forward to sharing a lot with you, Desmond. Are you going to take a shower before you leave?" Lisa asked, watching his bottom as he headed toward the bathroom.

"Yes, I'm headed there now. Would you like to join me?"

She bolted out of bed before he could change his mind, and rushed to join him in the shower. Lisa wanted to give Desmond something to remember her by under the running water.

CHAPTER TEN
(IT'S ALL ABOUT ME)

Over the course of the next month, Lisa was shamelessly pampered at the stylish uptown hotel almost every weekend through the ZaSpa experience, which included massages, manicures, pedicures, incredible body wraps, and hydro-therapy whirlpool baths while sipping on the house's best wines. It was a soothing sanctuary for Lisa within the secluded shelter of the expansive hotel. She would come alive with a tingling power shower and felt positively cuddly in her Zaza bathrobe on a bed of rose petals with scented candles all around the room. Keeping the radio on their favorite jazz station, the music would fill the large room, essentially adding to the relaxing atmosphere they'd created.

She and Desmond used the same room twice a week, and most of the maids on staff had become familiar with Lisa's demanding ways. She only wanted lavender scented massage oil, Godiva's special milk chocolates on her pillow, and she always had to have an extra set of clean towels. Lisa normally checked in first so she'd have time to go through her ritual before Desmond arrived with his special gifts.

In fact, she was dying to know what he was bringing her this evening as she relaxed across the bed wearing a rose-colored lace and chiffon nightie with molded cups and a swing skirt. She was listening to the sound of Javier singing "Crazy," while smoothing lotion all over her body when Desmond knocked on the door. Springing to her feet, she hurried to the door and swung it open, "Hi, sweetheart. Come on in," she said, walking backwards into the room.

"Hello. I see you've made yourself comfortable," Desmond stepped into the room donning a slate blue suit, taking a leisurely look around. He noticed the fresh cut flowers, the soft music, and the dinner cart in the center of the room.

"Yes, I have, and I have one of your favorites waiting for you. I thought we could have dessert first," she stated, removing the top from one of the covered, silver-plated dishes revealing a raspberry, chocolate chip cheesecake with a separate container of chocolate sauce.

Desmond's mouth began to water at the sight of both treats he was about to taste. He was definitely a chocolate connoisseur—in love with dark, milk, and white chocolates. Desmond always ordered something extra rich and chocolate for their dessert. They had shared chocolate fudge layer cake, chocolate covered fruit, white chocolate strawberry cheesecake, chocolate amaretto pie, chocolate peanut fudge, chocolate raspberry soufflé, and double chocolate pound cake. Lisa wondered how the man could be so fine with the taste of chocolate consistently on his lips. But Desmond made it a point to let her know that he worked out three times a week at the Dallas Athletic Club with several of his friends.

"Dessert might be the only thing we need tonight," he said, staring into Lisa's emotion-filled eyes.

"That's fine with me. Here, let me feed you a slice of this delicious cake. Have you had this before?" she inquired, reaching for the cake cutter.

"Yes, of course, I have. It has chocolate in it, right?" he asked, arching his eyebrows at her as he chuckled.

Flashing him a loving smile, Lisa sliced a thin piece of cheesecake and then held it up to his moist lips. Taking a small bite of the delectable dessert, Desmond moaned, enjoying every chocolate chip he tasted. "Ah, that tastes heavenly."

"Would you like some chocolate sauce poured over the rest of it?"

"No, I'm saving the chocolate sauce for you." Desmond dipped a finger in the warm sauce and licked it off, smiling at his lover for tonight. "You're going to be the real dessert for the evening."

"Umh, I'm looking forward to it," Lisa replied, rising from her seat. Stripping out of her sheer nightie as she sashayed toward the king size bed, Lisa sat down on the side of the bed, and then laid back against the burgundy satin comforter. Closing her eyes, she waited patiently for him to make the next move.

Clutching the handle of the silver container, Desmond eased up from his chair, tipped over to the side of the bed, and nudged himself between Lisa's legs. Drizzling the warm chocolate sauce down the center of her body, he watched Lisa arch her back as the heated liquid touched her silky skin. "Oh, I can't wait to taste every inch of you drenched in chocolate tonight," he breathed.

"Well, what are you waiting for?" she asked, giving him a naughty smile.

Without wasting another word, Desmond poured the remainder of the sauce all over Lisa's petite body. Then, he tossed aside the container as he began ripping off his clothes. He was ready for his chocolate covered lover.

The passionate couple made love in every position Lisa could imagine that night, and every one of them made her feel more powerful. In between each session, they fed each other bites of the raspberry, chocolate chip cheesecake.

Desmond relaxed against the stack of pillows with both hands behind his head. Licking his lips, he still tasted the sweet chocolate on them. "This is the best combination in the world. Being able to indulge in chocolate and sex at the same time is the greatest high I've ever had."

"I'm glad to be here sharing the ecstasy with you, darling. Now, I think it's time for me to return the favor," Lisa stated, reaching for the telephone to call room service requesting more chocolate sauce. It was time to taste his chocolate covered body from head to toe. Licking her lips, she relished the ultra sweet thought.

Lisa was willing to try anything with Desmond, making sure that his needs were always fulfilled, whether hers were or not. It didn't matter as long as he was pleased with her performance and kept coming back for more. It only made her feel in control of her destiny. Desmond was content to let her think she was calling all the shots, but he knew regardless of what happened, he was in control of this situation. Tomorrow, he would decide where they slept, where they ate, and whether or not they had sex, and how long the relationship lasted.

Desmond took Lisa to the most extravagant restaurants, the swankiest hotels, and the best plays and concerts the city had to offer. They attended the Dallas Black Dance Theatre, a modern dance company with a mixed repertory of modern, jazz, African, and spiritual compositions. Desmond loved the arts and the theatre, so they spent time at the museums, ballets, symphonies, and operas. They'd even been to Fort Worth one weekend in the downtown Sundance Square where the sidewalks were crowded with people enjoying the nightlife opportunities. And the shopping sprees had truly been incredible with this man. He would take her to Macy's and let her pick out anything she wanted to wear for their weekend excursions. Money was never an object when Lisa was with Desmond. The man used his credit card as if it had an unlimited balance.

Needless to say, Lisa's designer wardrobe was significantly increasing in size. All of the hottest African-American designers resided in her closet, including Eric Gaskins, Kate Mack, and Lawrence Steele. The amazing thing is that Desmond loved to take her shopping himself. He would take Lisa to the finest boutiques, and then patiently wait while she tried on numerous outfits that she'd proudly walk out and model for her man. He was amused by excitement Lisa displayed by simply trying on a few garments, and that energy overflowed into the bedroom.

Anytime he offered to take Lisa on a shopping spree, he immediately knew what the rewards would be—a completely submissive woman in his bed. She thanked him every way she knew how each time she received a new item of clothing. The thought that he had a wife at home who was willing to do the same intimate acts with him never fazed Desmond Taylor. It was the adventure of having someone new cater to his every need, which positively turned him on, and he was willing to have that desire filled at any monetary price. As long as Belinda never harassed him about his comings and goings, he was a happily married single man, and able to do as he pleased.

Lisa was completely running out of closet space in the small bedroom where she lived with Uncle Johnny and Auntie O. However, being the manipulative woman she was, Lisa complained about this on several occasions to Desmond, emphasizing the fact that she wasn't making enough money to move into her own place just yet. Lisa knew that given some time and lots more sexing, her man would eventually find them a place to call their own.

The major reason Lisa wanted to move was because she was tired of living with Uncle Johnny and Aunt Oretha, who were always talking about the Bible and trying to persuade her to go to church with them on

Sunday mornings. When Auntie O knocked on her door around nine o'clock every Sabbath Day, all Lisa wanted to do was roll over in the full size bed and go back to sleep. She figured as long as Jesus didn't bother her, she wouldn't bother Him with anything either. Of course, she didn't tell her favorite aunt this. She simply made up some excuse for not going each time she was asked to attend the Baptist service with them.

One night while she and Desmond dined on lobster scallions served with red chili coconut sake at the exquisite Abacus restaurant on McKinney Avenue, Desmond dropped a key into Lisa's champagne glass. Showing all the surprise and excitement she could muster, Lisa's eyes widened as she watched the gold key sink to the bottom of her flute.

"What is that you put into my champagne?" Lisa asked, giving Desmond a broad smile.

"It's my latest gift to you, sweetheart. It's time for you to leave your uncle and aunt's house. You need your own place where we can be together without having to go to a hotel all the time. So, I found this nice piece of investment property close to my office. It's a furnished two-story townhouse with two bedrooms and two bathrooms with a full size kitchen. I'm sure you're going to love it," he replied, straightening the silk, navy-printed tie he was wearing along with a blue shirt and Christian Dior navy suit.

"Oh, Desmond," Lisa screamed, jumping into his lap right there at the dining table. She wrapped both her arms around his neck, squeezing him with all of her strength. "Can we go see it right now?" she asked, leaping off his legs. Lisa straightened the front of her Dimmer D'Ursi beige pants suit with patch pockets, downed the remainder of the champagne, and retrieved the key from the bottom of the flute.

Less than thirty minutes later, they were pulling up to a brand new subdivision with gray, brick-front townhomes. Her section was located in the rear of the facility, giving them more privacy away from the noisy main streets.

Lisa was the first one to enter the unit with Desmond trailing behind her, holding onto her right hand. She immediately loved the modern bright colors maintained throughout the complex. The deco-styled living room consisted of an orange Metropolis sofa with uniquely designed line tables, and a colorful area rug. In the dining room, a round, wooden, hand-carved table with four beige cushioned chairs was the center of attention. The full size kitchen was completely stocked with food and beverages from ginger ale sodas to Krug champagne. The master bedroom downstairs showcased a low setting queen size bed built into a wooden wall unit with a full size mirror over the headboard. The master bath was awesome with a Jacuzzi tub sitting in the center of the floor in front of a picture-sized garden window. And finally, the guest bedroom was located upstairs with a full bath of its own.

Lisa was completely taken with her new housing. This was the nicest place she had ever lived, and she wanted to thank Desmond for making it possible.

"Oh God, this place is beautiful!" Lisa exclaimed, covering her open mouth with her right hand.

"It's all for us. This is our own special place where we can be together whenever we want," Desmond replied, pulling her lips to his lips. "You don't have to worry about paying for anything because everything is already taken care of. I even bought you a 46-inch plasma television with an entertainment center for the living room, and a 30-inch flat screen television for the bedroom." Desmond picked up the remote control off the cocktail table, and pushed a button, turning on the new television set. After adjusting the volume to a comfortable hearing level on the smooth jazz music channel, he swept Lisa up into his long arms, carried her into the master bedroom, and laid her body across the bed.

His hands searched for the buttons on her suit coat, and he had all three of them unbuttoned in a matter of seconds. Sliding the jacket off her thin arms, Desmond unhooked the front of her black push-up brassiere. Leaning forward, his puckered lips slid over her plump breasts with ease.

Hastily undressing himself, they were between the copper colored sheets in the throes of sexual desire within a matter of minutes. Filling each other to the brim with their love making, they soaked the sheets with their body sweat.

Lisa drifted off to sleep in Desmond's muscled arms with her head resting against his hairy chest. Thinking she was closer to realizing her life long dream, Lisa felt secure and loved for now. *With a little more time and cunningness, I'll have the incredible mansion he now shares with a worthless wife. It shouldn't take too long for him to see that he deserves to be with someone like me permanently.*

CHAPTER ELEVEN
(NOVEMBER)

"Desmond, the kids and I will be leaving next weekend before Thanksgiving and returning the weekend after the holiday. I've decided to take them up to Michigan to visit with my parents for the full week," Belinda stated, tying the sash around her royal blue bathrobe. She sat down at the breakfast nook in the front of the bay window across from her husband. Taking a quick sip of her black coffee, she stared at Desmond over the rim of her huge mug. "We'll be leaving for Grand Rapids early Saturday morning. Will you be able to take us to the airport before seven o'clock?"

"Yes, I should be able to do that, and when will you all be returning?" Desmond asked, with his eyes buried in the morning newspaper. He was fully dressed in a hand-tailored, mocha brown suit with polished leather shoes.

"We'll be back on the following Saturday. Our flight is scheduled to arrive here at 5:58 p.m. Will you be available to pick us up, too?"

"I'll be there, Belinda," he reassured her.

"I mean you've had a conference or an out of town meeting every weekend for the last month or so. Are you sure you'll be able to meet us at the airport on our return date on time?"

Placing the paper down on the dining table, Desmond gave Belinda a stern look, making direct eye contact with her. "I said I would be there, didn't I? When have I ever broken my word to you?" he asked, carefully enunciating each word he spoke.

"I don't know, Dez. I was simply asking a question for verification purposes only. My parents want to know why you aren't coming with us. You haven't been with us the last two times we've gone to visit with them. What am I supposed to tell them this time?"

"You can tell them the truth. You're married to a doctor who has his own practice, and a very busy work schedule. You know, this is the time of year when I receive the most business. People want their skin looking picture perfect for the holidays. I'll call them later and personally apologize."

"Sure, Dez. Will you be home in time for dinner tonight?"

"Yes, I plan to be in the house by six o'clock this evening, if that's all right with you."

"Well, you haven't been home that early in quite some time. I'm not sure if I'll be able to handle it. Would you like for me to ask Ms. Rodriguez to make you something special?"

"No, I'm just coming home for a regular meal. There's no need to go to any special trouble," Desmond said, rising from the table.

"Good morning, Dad," Justine said, entering the breakfast room. She gave her father a kiss on the cheek and a quick hug, too.

Seconds later, Jesse entered the room and spoke to his father also. "Hi, Dad. Are you coming to my football practice this afternoon? You've missed the last two."

"Oh goodness, I'd forgotten about that, but I'll be there, I promise," he said, reassuring his only son. "Now I have to get on to work, or I'll miss seeing my first client for the day." Giving Belinda a light peck on the forehead, Desmond left his family sitting at the breakfast table.

***

Belinda, Justine, and Jesse were all packed and ready to report to the Dallas airport terminal early Saturday morning for their non-stop flight to Detroit, Michigan. Desmond packed the six bags into the family's champagne pearl Toyota Land Cruiser Belinda normally drove, and headed to the airport where they arrived an hour and ten minutes prior to the take-off time. Desmond said good-bye to his wife and children at the security check point, then he headed straight to Lisa's townhouse around seven o'clock in the morning.

Unlocking the front door with his own key, Desmond slipped into the house, peeled off his clothes, and quietly slipped into bed beside Lisa's heated naked body. The space next to her was very warm; it felt like he was climbing into a heated waterbed. Turning over to look into her lover's glowing emerald eyes, Lisa smiled. She'd been expecting him to arrive at any second to claim his place in her empty bed. Now he was by her side staring into her eyes. Her body was desperately yearning for this session of morning pleasure. Lisa didn't want to waste time with pleasantries. She just wanted to give him what he'd come to get.

As the electricity from their bodies pulled them together like magnets, Lisa sought out his lips. He'd known she would be waiting, but he never expected her to be this eager to please him so early in the morning. Covering his upper body with soft fluttery kisses, she made a trail down the center of his hairy chest. Singeing with pleasure, Desmond pushed her head even further down until she reached the center of his maleness. Lisa didn't have any trouble consuming his thickness or swallowing his juices as a master plan entered her head.

Knowing his family would be away for the entire week, Lisa saw this as the perfect opportunity to sample the lifestyle of being Mrs. Desmond Arnez Taylor. So as she relaxed in Desmond's arms with the taste of his semen still lingering on her hot breath, she whispered in his left ear, "I want to see your house."

"What? Are you crazy? You know I can't take you there. No, that's out of the question," he stated, responding firmly.

"Come on. Don't tell me you haven't thought about it. Don't tell me you haven't thought about having me in your personal bed?" Lisa smiled, showing her self-assuredness.

"Well, ah. It's not that simple. You see..."

"Why not, your family is out of town for an entire week. You even gave the housekeeper time off, for goodness sakes. I want to see where you live. I need to see the life you have when you're not with me."

"I said no, Lisa," he stated, reaffirming his first answer.

"Please. Please. Please. I promise we won't be there long," she begged, taking the words he was about to say right out of his mouth with a deep fiery kiss. Every time Desmond tried to come up for air, she would delve her tongue deeper into his mouth until she was ready to release him. And even then, she continued biting and pulling on his lower lip.

"That's not going to change anything. I would have to be crazy to take you to my house. What if the neighbors saw you?"

"Come on, your neighbors don't care about who comes in your house. I just want to see your place one time, and I'll never bother you about this again."

Desmond closed his eyes, sighing heavily. He'd never risked taking a lover to his house before, regardless of how safe it seemed to be. However, he couldn't deny that the thought of having Lisa in his personal space was quite tantalizing. Should he throw all caution to the wind?

Lisa was relentless when she wanted something from a man. She wasn't about to give up, especially when she could tell from his silence that he was giving her request serious consideration. Wanting him to make a quick decision, Lisa decided to give Desmond a little bit more motivation.

"Come on, baby, I'll do anything. Just this one time, please," she begged. Lisa sunk her teeth into his left nipple, reached her right hand underneath the sheet, and massaged his soft spot.

"Is that a promise? You won't ask me to do this again?" he asked, eyeing her suspiciously.

Feeling his arousal in her hand, Lisa pressed even more. "Yes, I just want to walk through your house one time, and then we can leave," she replied, holding up her left index finger.

Shaking his head in a slow back and forth motion, Desmond reluctantly gave in to Lisa's request. "I know this is crazy, but get dressed and we'll go."

Bolting out of bed before he could or would change his halfway made up mind, Lisa rushed into the shower, and changed into a sophisticated outfit befitting a doctor's wife. She slipped into a pair of white thong panties and then dressed as if they were headed to an evening at the symphony in a silk ivory long sleeved dress with cut-out shoulders and a flowing skirt. Desmond changed back into the taupe dress slacks and beige shirt he'd worn to Lisa's house earlier that morning.

Filled with excitement, Lisa nervously talked the entire journey to Desmond's house as her mind filled with self satisfaction. *I knew he'd do this. He knows he really wants me to see his mansion where I'll be residing someday. I can't wait to see what the inside of that house looks like. I bet his wife doesn't have a clue about decorating a place like that. This is going to be a great day. Now that his family is out of the way for a while, I can see how it feels to have everything I've ever wanted.*

Lisa's mind was blown from the second they entered Desmond's three story mansion. Her mouth dropped open upon entering the extra wide foyer which was almost large enough to hold her entire townhouse. Looking up at the huge crystal chandelier, Lisa turned around in amazement as she stared up at the three-foot object hanging directly above her head. From the spiraling gold trimmed circular staircase in the center of the entrance area to the recreation room on the third floor, the house was meticulously decorated in rich burgundy and deep green colors with huge African-American antique and contemporary paintings lining almost every wall. Lisa couldn't believe there was even an elevator on the back wall next to the den to save her from climbing stairs. And in the backyard, there was a waterfall behind the Olympic-sized swimming pool with indigo colored water, as well as a heated spa tub.

"Oh, Desmond, this is an incredible house! I can't believe you actually live here," Lisa exclaimed, leaving her mouth open and uncovered, reaching out to touch the deep green antique satin curtains covering the double French doors.

"It's only a house, sweetheart. What we have is far more important than this," he answered, taking Lisa by the right hand.

Desmond led her up the steps to the third floor first. He showed her the two tastefully decorated guest rooms with their private full-sized baths along with the recreation room, which contained a pool table. Moving on to the second floor, he showed Lisa both of his kids' bedrooms and their two bath areas. Finally arriving back on the first floor, Desmond showed her the second master bedroom first. Then, after guiding her through the remainder of the house, which included a living room, a den, a media center, his office, dining room, breakfast nook, and an oversize kitchen, they ended up in the main master bedroom. By this time, Lisa was ready to try working her feminine wiles on him again.

Wrapping her hands around his neck, Lisa gave Desmond an enticing kiss on his quivering lips. Although he was a bold man, he'd never been daring enough to have another woman in his house before. This was the line he had promised himself to never cross. However, his nervousness was gradually changing to arousal with the taste from each of Lisa's fervent kisses. As she started leaning downward toward the California, king-sized bed covered with a beige cashmere comforter, Desmond snapped his head up. "Let's do it somewhere in the house I haven't tried before," he whispered.

"And where would that be?" she asked, taking in their surroundings. "This is a very big house."

"Come, take my hand, and I'll show you," he commanded, reaching for Lisa's left hand. Desmond led her into the gigantic master bathroom, walking across the gold-colored marble floors. When they reached the beige toilet seat, he abruptly stopped, taking Lisa into his arms for another hunger-filled kiss before removing both their clothing.

"What is it you want me to do? I'll do anything for you," Lisa cooed, leaning away from him, staring into his lust filled eyes.

"Turn around," he suddenly commanded. Lisa turned her back to him, spread her legs over the toilet, and balanced herself clutching the top of the commode with both hands.

Their love rhythm started out slow and easy, but minutes later, Desmond and Lisa were thrusting against each other's perspiring bodies. With an intensity matching that of two canines in heat, they brought each other to a sizzling climax in minutes.

After retrieving his pants, Desmond reached out for a green towel hanging on the other side of the sink. "That was wonderful. I've never experienced anything like that in my entire life. You are an awesome woman," he said, still panting for breath. Lisa simply smiled as she absorbed his compliments. She was used to being praised for her sexual powers and relished every comment she'd ever received.

Desmond wiped his body down and then handed the towel to Lisa. He crept out of the bathroom, leaving her alone to clean up. Straddling the bidet, Lisa turned the water on, gently washing away their mixed fluids. Then she walked across the room to the brown, wicker dirty clothes hamper in the corner. While dropping the soaked towel into the basket, Lisa suddenly had another menacing idea. Instead of sliding her white thong panties back on, she dropped them on top of the dirty towel she'd just placed in the hamper. *This will be a nice little present for his wife*, she thought, lowering the lid to the basket. She turned to look in the mirror, ran her fingers through her tousled hair, and then stepped out of the room wearing a sinister smile.

As they walked out of the master bedroom hand in hand, Lisa thought about the calling card she'd left for Desmond's dumb wife. Hopefully, she would at least be smart enough to figure it out and leave him so Lisa could be the next Mrs. Taylor. Without giving it any further thought, Lisa squeezed Desmond's strong hand and pranced through the front door feeling like Cinderella leaving the ball.

CHAPTER TWELVE
(THE SPYING GAME)

Meanwhile, Belinda Taylor had checked into a ritzy hotel across town where she would be residing for the next seven nights. "All right, Mrs. Taylor. We have your suite ready for you now. I'll get someone to help you with your luggage. Please enjoy your stay with us," the receptionist stated, admiring the black, two-piece, pants suit Belinda wore. She handed Belinda the green key card to her fifth floor room.

"Thank you," Belinda replied, leading the way to the elevator carrying only her Christiana paisley print handbag.

Instead of getting on the airplane with her children, she told them goodbye at the boarding gate, stashed the ticket in her purse, and headed to the rental car booth. Belinda had given great thought to hiring a detective, but then decided it was best to conduct her own investigation. Anyway, she wanted to see firsthand what was going on; she didn't want some stranger giving her pictures of events which had already transpired. Besides, she didn't have anything better to do than trail behind a cheating husband who she always caught in the act.

"All right, kids, tell your grandparents I said hello and send my love. If your father calls, just tell him that I'm out with friends. I'll be here working on a big surprise for him, okay? So it's very important you not let him know I'm still in town." Belinda hugged her two children, not paying attention to their curious glances, and watched them board the jet to Detroit. Knowing Desmond would never call her parents' home to check on their arrival, Belinda could call him from anywhere on her cellular telephone, and lead him to believe she was in Michigan with the children on vacation. *Thank God for modern technology.*

Belinda rented a silver Mercedes Benz CLS so she would blend in with the other expensive cars in her high-class neighborhood while she spied on her own house. She parked down the street so she would have a clear view of her driveway, turned off the ignition, and relaxed her head against the leather headrest.

Knowing her meticulous husband, Belinda figured he'd come back home sooner or later and change before going out to meet his mistress. And then, she'd follow the sweet talker to their little hideaway or rendezvous location. Wearing a pair of black shades and a broad hat covering most of her face, she fixed her eyes on the front door. Finally, after waiting over an hour in the morning sun, she saw Desmond pull up into the circular driveway with a light-skinned, red-headed female in the Land Cruiser beside him. She couldn't believe her eyes. *This fool is out of her mind! She's riding in my luxury car and about to enter my multimillion-dollar house! If I had a gun, I'd burst up in there and shoot her dead!*

But Belinda waited patiently in the car for over an hour before they emerged through the front double doors walking arm in arm. Desmond was carrying his brown leather overnight bag in one hand while his other arm was wrapped around the gloating female. Shifting in her seat, Belinda desperately wanted to storm over there and slap that stupid grin off the woman's face, and then give them both a piece of her irate mind.

As soon as they pulled away from the curb, Belinda started her car. Trailing behind at a safe distance, she followed them to Arcodoro Restaurant on Westheimer where they sat outside on the terrace enjoying their late Italian lunch. An hour later, they emerged from the dining facility, heading to Lisa's place of residence.

Belinda watched them enter the townhouse and close the front door before driving away. *Now that I know where the fool lives, I don't have to waste anymore time following behind them like a sick puppy. I can check back on them later today. Right now, I need to get home to see what really happened in my house. I never thought Desmond would lose his mind like this over a hussy like that. She must have really put something on him for him to have her up in my house that way.*

Heading straight to her mansion, she stomped into her master bedroom filled with blinding rage. After tossing the covers all over the bed, looking for evidence of their sexual escapade, Belinda rushed into the master bathroom where the amorous smell of sex hit her dead in the face. With the familiar scent of her husband's semen filling her flaring nostrils, she checked the marble counter for signs of their sexual tryst. Then, following her strong nose, Belinda marched over to the laundry hamper thinking she would surely find dirty towels containing body fluids.

Raising the lid of the wicker hamper, Belinda was horrified at the sight filling up her stretched eyes. There at the very top lay a thin pair of white thong panties. Knowing immediately they didn't belong to her, she snatched up the delicate garment with two fingers, threw them in the bedroom fireplace, struck a match, and burned them to ashes. *I'm going to kill that nasty heifer!*

Belinda weaved through the evening traffic in her rented vehicle at an alarming speed. Blinded with rage, she almost side-swiped a car one time while changing lanes. She was rushing to get back to the hotel room so she could start working up a plan to eliminate her newest arch nemesis. Since she didn't have any friends she could share this part of her life with, Belinda settled for talking to herself. *Obviously, this home-wrecker doesn't have any idea whose family she's messing with. Desmond's never brought a woman into our home before—I'm sure of that. This slut must really have him wrapped around her finger to make him act this foolish, jeopardizing everything we have. He's never gone this far with any of his other distractions. She needs to be dealt with quickly and severely. I'm not going to put up with no crazy mess like this. If she thinks she can get away with leaving her dirty drawers in my face, she's going to learn a valuable lesson.*

Believing this latest fling was a serious threat to her marriage, Belinda began thinking of a scheme that would remove Lisa Bradford from both of their lives. She had never considered taking anyone else's life in the past, but Belinda was so intimidated with the gall of this woman coming up in her house and leaving a pair of nasty drawers for her to find, that she was bordering on insanity. Pacing the floor for hours, Belinda felt it would take drastic means to get a fool like that away from her man. Thinking of all the schemes she'd used in the past, Belinda dismissed all of them. *This woman has to be bold beyond bold, but she just doesn't know that she has met her match now. When I'm done with her, she won't have anywhere to go but to the streets where all whores belong. I'm going to ruin her life for good. Her days of cheating with married men are about to come to an end. I promise her that.*

With that thought in mind, Belinda spent the next four days and nights dreaming of getting her revenge on her husband's latest conquest. Belinda followed Lisa everywhere she went, from the grocery store, to the hair salon, to the nightclub, and back to her townhouse where she met with Desmond sometimes late in the evenings. Following Lisa to the bar one night where she was still employed as the part-time manager for her uncle, Belinda strolled into the bar wearing a sapphire dress suit just to have a look around. She simply walked through the facility, taking in the atmosphere of the place, then turned around and walked back out. *Just like I thought, she doesn't have anything going for herself but a good looking body. We'll see how long that lasts.*

Chapter Thirteen
(Lisa's Game)

Pulling up to the gray, brick, bi-level townhouse, Desmond pressed the button to close the top to his Porsche convertible, and then turned off the motor. He sat still for a few minutes enjoying the cool crisp evening. This was definitely his favorite time of day when the sun was just setting over the orange, smoky-looking horizon. Exiting his low riding vehicle, he briskly stepped up to the front door and rang the doorbell. Although he owned the place and had a personal key, he usually pressed the doorbell to let Lisa know he'd arrived, just in case she was on the telephone or handling other business.

Desmond's eyes almost popped out at the sight of the lovely vision greeting him at the doorway with wavy reddish hair flowing over her shoulders. Taking in her barely clad body in a Banana Republic, pink, cashmere blend, lacy cardigan over a stretch, lace camisole with matching boy-cut panties, he let out a breath of pure happiness. "I hope you don't answer the door like this for everyone," he stated, crossing the threshold, and closing the door.

"No, I don't. You just happen to be a very special person. I want to make sure you feel appreciated," she responded, taking his hand, leading the way to the master bathroom, making sure her bottom moved with each sensual step she took. Modeling a pair of pink, Manolo Blahnik pumps and a double-stranded, crystal necklace, she oozed whip appeal.

Desmond had learned from past experiences that the other woman was always willing to make herself accessible to him. Not only did they do everything within their power to make him feel welcomed, but they answered to his every call. And being the kind, considerate gentleman he was, Desmond was eagerly willing to take advantage of their desperate situations. There was just something about being with a new vixen that excited him.

The sound of John Legend's latest release filled the air, along with the rose scented candles floating in the bubbly bathwater. "Did you do all of this for me?" Desmond asked, flinging his hands open, faking a look of surprise.

"Of course, it's for you, darling. After you called to tell me you were on your way, I put this little surprise together for you. I want you to have a smooth relaxing evening as I wash all of your cares away," she cooed, unbuttoning his white shirt.

"You know I like these nice pants you're wearing, but you don't need them tonight," she teased, tugging them down to his ankles as he stepped out of them.

Slipping himself into the garden bathtub, Desmond held on to the sides with both hands. Lisa carefully soaped up the bath sponge and began bathing him from his neck all the way down to his long skinny toes. She gently washed between each digit and then rinsed them off. With his feet sticking out of the bath water, Lisa gave him an invigorating foot massage before devouring each of his moist toes between her heated lips. As pleasure consumed his body, Desmond moaned for his lover to continue her assault on his tender feet. He'd had women to do outrageous things to please him, but he'd never had anyone to lubricate his toes with her mouth. It was an ecstatic feeling he craved more with each passing second. *Ah, this is the life*, he thought. *Having a woman like this to literally worship at your feet is every man's desire.*

Taking Lisa by the hand, Desmond pulled her into the tub with him. She didn't mind getting wet as she nestled her body on top of his.

Minutes later, Desmond reclaimed his clothes, walked into the bedroom, and started getting dressed. "What are you doing?" Lisa asked, looking surprised.

"I'm going home. I came by to tell you that my family is due back tomorrow. I need to get some things done around the house before their arrival."

"What? Are you kidding me? You're just going to leave? You're not spending the night?"

"I'm sorry, but I have to go. Belinda asked me to do some things around the house before she left. I haven't done them because I've spent all of my time with you."

"I don't give two cents about Belinda! How dare you even mention her name to me?" Lisa retorted.

"Well, that's too bad! She's my wife and the mother of my children. My family is very important to me."

"I thought I was important to you."

"You are, Lisa, but I really can't stay with you tonight. I have to get home."

"Please don't leave me like this. Let's just make love one time and then you can go," she begged, throwing herself into his arms.

"I told you already. I have to go," he replied, pushing her away.

"Bump you, Desmond!" she shouted, slapping his face.

No woman had ever hit Desmond. He had to teach her a lesson that she would never forget. His face was burning with rage as he raised his hand.

Lisa realized her mistake and tried to move out of harm's way, but wasn't quick enough to avoid Desmond's backhand across her face. Caressing her stinging red cheek, Lisa began crying as she fell back onto the bed.

"Don't you ever touch me again!" Desmond exclaimed, glaring down at Lisa's tearstained face. "My family comes first, and you're second. Do you understand that?"

"Yes! I understand! Now get out!" she screamed between her tears, holding a hand to her face.

Desmond finished buttoning his shirt, tucked the tail inside his pants, and hurried to the front door. Just as his hand touched the doorknob, Lisa called his name. He thought about leaving without acknowledging her voice when he turned to see Lisa walking up behind him.

"I'm sorry for hitting you, Desmond. I had no business slapping you across the face like that," she mumbled.

"It's okay. I'm sorry for striking you, too. I've never hit a woman in my life. It won't happen again."

"Let's both forget about this, all right?"

"It's forgotten. Now I really have to go," he stated, opening the door to leave. Lisa grabbed his neck, pulling him closer to her pounding heart. She placed a passionate kiss on his lips as Desmond returned her intensity.

Moments later, Desmond tore himself away from Lisa's embrace and headed to his vehicle. He never noticed his fuming wife in the parked Mercedes across the street as he entered his car and sped away.

Belinda pulled off behind Desmond, swearing at the whore she'd seen kissing her husband. "She's going to get hers real soon. I promise that," she mumbled to herself. "Her pitiful fate is going to be sealed by me. I'm going to teach her a lesson about messing with married men."

Desmond arrived home, heading straight to the master bedroom, removing his clothes along the way. When he opened the door to the master bedroom, he was shocked to find Belinda resting against a stack of pillows in the center of the bed, wearing a black sheer negligee. "Wha— What are you doing here?" he asked.

"I live here, don't I?" she replied, smiling at him.

"Yes, but you're not due home until tomorrow. Where are the kids?"

"Oh, they're still in Detroit. I took an early flight home so we could have a night together before they arrive."

"Listen, Belinda, I'm really not in the mood for..." Belinda was out of the bed, wrapping her arms around his waist, and consuming his mouth in a deep kiss before he could complete the sentence.

"I'm not taking no for an answer tonight, Dez," she cooed, slipping out of her lingerie.

Desmond didn't know what had come over his wife. He saw something in her eyes besides desire; he just couldn't tell what it was. But after the rough exit from Lisa, he was ready to be taken away with pleasure again. So he returned her fiery kisses with some of his own as he made a trail down her scented neck. Pushing her back on the bed, he took the time to remove his own clothes before joining his smiling mate.

***

Meanwhile, Lisa lay in bed alone, dreaming about the man she was going to marry someday. She visualized them standing on the sandy white seashore exchanging wedding nuptials with both of them wearing pure white outfits. Her long full tail dress was flowing in the wind as they stood holding hands across from a beautiful setting sun.

She could hear the minister reciting the marriage vows they were to take, feel the light breeze across her face, and smell the salty ocean water. Lisa even heard the rhythmic island music playing in the background as she was holding a colorful bouquet with one hand and clinging to her fiancé with the other. She could see her smiling face on this magnificent day, but when she looked over for Desmond's face, it was blurry and out of focus.

Sitting up in bed, Lisa gasped for air. It scared her that she wasn't able to clearly see Desmond's face. *Oh, well, he's definitely the man I'm going to marry. His face will become clearer in my dreams with time. We're going to have a fabulous life together. I'm sure of that.*

CHAPTER FOURTEEN
(A COLD WINTER)

"There is a cold front expected to come through the Dallas-Fort Worth area on this Wednesday afternoon. It's going to be a dreary-looking Thanksgiving Day tomorrow. Although there isn't any rain in the forecast, there probably won't be very much sunlight either." Lisa listened to the news coming over her car radio. She had called into her job earlier, telling Uncle Johnny how she wouldn't be in to work that evening and she wouldn't be joining them for dinner tomorrow either. As much as she hated disappointing her Aunt Oretha, Lisa saw this as her big chance to impress Desmond with her minimal culinary skills. So, she headed to the Kroger grocery store to buy a small turkey to prepare for them to share over the holiday.

Wearing a pair of sharply-creased Calvin Klein jeans with a pale blue, pullover sweater, Lisa entered the supermarket with a grocery list in her right hand. Pulling out a shopping cart, she rushed down each aisle. She was planning to prepare a small turkey with cornbread stuffing, a green bean casserole, and a chocolate pecan pie. Thanks to Aunt Oretha, she had a list of all the ingredients she needed to pull off the meal.

Desmond had become Lisa's whole life. She didn't have any friends whom she could name, and she hadn't spent much time with her aunt and uncle since moving out of their house to live with her married lover. A few of the women at the club had tried to befriend Lisa, but she was usually so abrupt with them until they would eventually stop trying to be her friend. She would sashay into J's Bar and Grill on most days and the few evenings she worked, look over the books, maybe serve a few drinks, and then stroll right back out the front entrance barely speaking to anyone as she made her way out. Since Lisa really didn't need the money anymore, it didn't matter what the other employees thought or said about her behind her back as long as they obeyed her orders whenever she arrived at the bar.

Lisa left the grocery story carrying three bags of food, including a premium bottle of merlot for their private Thanksgiving celebration. She hadn't told Desmond she was planning to cook for him at her place. Lisa was hoping to surprise him with a tempting meal when he showed up to take her out to eat tomorrow night. Lisa knew there wasn't a black man alive who would turn down a home-cooked meal. Although she wasn't much of a cook and wouldn't have to be if she married Desmond, she wanted to show him that she had some other skills outside of the bedroom. So, Lisa sailed homeward in the dark, not paying any attention to the silver Mercedes that had been trailing her every move for the last four days.

Turning onto a lone street, Lisa headed to the rear of her subdivision. Belinda was loosely following behind her enemy when Lisa stopped at a four-way stop sign after the other vehicle to her right had already stopped. Just as the other car pulled away and passed in front of Lisa's vehicle, Belinda saw the opportunity of a lifetime and decided to put an end to this witch's life right then.

After doing a quick check of her surroundings, she didn't see any other cars in sight. Swallowing her slight nervousness, Belinda pressed the accelerator to the floor and rammed into the back of Lisa's car, causing the PT Cruiser to leap forward into the center of the crossroad.

Making a rather quick recovery, she shifted the Mercedes into reverse. Belinda backed up and then fled the scene of the crime without any remorse. *Happy Thanksgiving! I hope you rot in hell!*

***

Lisa woke up in an ambulance with her whole body aching from the awful pain she was experiencing. The back of her head felt like it was about to explode, both her legs were flaming like she'd ran through hell's fire, and she could taste the bitter blood seeping down her throat. Lifting her head, she tried to speak to the paramedic hovering over her. After receiving instructions to keep still and relax her head, Lisa lost consciousness again until she arrived at the Dallas Southwest Medical Center where she was rushed to the Emergency Care Unit.

"Hi, Ms. Bradford. Can you hear me?"

Lisa opened her eyes to see a young black male doctor with a neatly trimmed afro and a mustache, staring at her face. "I'm Dr. Thomas. Can you hear me, Ms. Bradford?" he asked again.

"Yes, I can hear you. Where am I?" she asked, sounding drowsy.

"You're at the Dallas Southwest Medical Center. You were involved in a car accident. Do you remember what happened?" he asked, leaning his long body over closer to her face.

"No, not really. I remember being at a stop sign in my car. Then, I felt this jolt like a truck hit me from behind."

"Yes, ma'am. We believe that's what happened. Someone rammed into the rear of your vehicle. Are you in any pain?"

"My head hurts, and both my legs are throbbing in pain around my knees. I can't move either one of my legs."

"All right, we're going to take you down to x-ray and try to find out exactly what's going on. Try to stay conscious for me, and we'll have a diagnosis for you in no time."

"Thank you, doctor. Is my face — is my face injured?"

"No, it's not. You have a slightly bruised lip, but that's about it."

"Okay, doctor, thank you so much," Lisa replied, sounding relieved that her precious good looks hadn't been ruined.

"Would you like for us to contact your family or next of kin?" he asked.

"Ah, yes," she replied, giving them the telephone number to Aunt O's house.

Less than an hour later, two male orderlies wheeled Lisa's bed back into the emergency examination room. "All right, Ms. Bradford, the doctor will be in shortly to explain everything," the short stocky one stated, pushing her bed against the wall.

"Thank you both for everything," Lisa replied, lifting her head, making eye contact with the attendants.

"No problem, ma'am. Take care of yourself and hang in there," the other one stated, smiling as they both rushed out the room.

Within a few minutes, Dr. Thomas' long body was standing at the side of Lisa's hospital bed, staring down at her with a serious look on his handsome face. "Ms. Bradford, I'm sorry to inform you that both of your legs were broken in the car accident. We looked at your x-rays and they show us where both legs are broken in two separate places. We have two highly-skilled surgeons on staff here who will have to perform surgery right away."

"What?" Lisa asked, looking wide-eyed and stunned. "What are you talking about? You mean to tell me both of my legs are broken, doctor?" she asked, hoping she'd heard wrong.

"Yes, I'm sorry. Apparently, you were hit from behind with such force that your knees jammed against the lower part of the dashboard, breaking both legs in two separate places. Surgery is our only option if you ever hope to walk again."

"Oh, God, no! This can't be happening to me!" she screamed, covering her red cheeks and eyes. Tears poured through Lisa's fingers.

"Please, calm down, Ms. Bradford. Your blood pressure is very high and we're doing everything in our power to get control of it. We can't perform surgery until it comes down significantly."

Lisa lowered her hands and wiped the tears from her eyes with a Kleenex tissue she pulled from the box on the nightstand beside her bed. Blowing her nose, she peered up at Dr. Thomas' somber face. "I'm sorry, doctor. I know you're doing your best," she said in a weak voice. "What is it I need to do?" she asked.

"I just need you to relax because the only problem right now is with your blood pressure. It's running extremely high at 200/136. As soon as that comes down a bit, we'll take you into another room to get you prepped for surgery, which will take approximately ten hours to complete. If everything is normal after a couple of days of observation, you'll be released to the rehab facility for extended care. With two broken legs, there's no way you'll be able to live on your own for some time. They have excellent physical therapists there who will be able to assist you in regaining the use of your legs."

"And just exactly how long will that take?"

"Honestly, I'm not sure. It just depends on how hard you're willing to work."

"Oh, believe me, I'm willing to work very hard, Dr. Thomas."

"Well, then, you may be able to go home in a couple of months or so. We'll see. Don't you worry about anything right now, okay? Let's try to get you down to the surgery room as soon as possible. The two bone specialists have been called and they're in the process of preparing for your operation. I assure you that you'll be in very good hands," he stated, using an optimistic tone as he patted the back of her right hand.

"Yes, doctor," she replied. Although she was still sniffling, Lisa tried to sound brave. Her mother, Sadie, had taught them to be strong and tough when faced with adversity. This was only a test of her strength. A test she was going to pass with flying colors. *And if I ever find out what fool is responsible for me being in this predicament, he or she will have plenty to pay for temporarily taking away the use of my legs.*

Giving in to the anesthesia flowing through the mask while lying flat on her back on the operating table, Lisa's mind wandered to a happier time. It was a wonderful time when she had full use of her slim legs and they were wrapped around the fine torso of Desmond Taylor, the most attractive man she'd ever met with a body to rival even that of D'Angelos', the sexy R & B crooner. The medicine man had been a perfect gentleman, taking her to the finest hotels and restaurants, buying her fabulous designer clothes, taking her on romantic weekend excursions, and paying her high mortgage every month. *Desmond, I love you. I can't wait to get through this so I can see you again. We're going to be so happy together once you realize how much you love me.*

CHAPTER FIFTEEN
(RUDE AWAKENING)

Lisa woke up early the next morning wondering where she was. Suddenly remembering she was still in the hospital recovery room, she turned her head to the right, opened her brown eyes, and peered directly into the green eyes of Desmond Taylor standing over her dressed in a burgundy Sean John velour jogging suit. Even with her blurry vision, Lisa would have known Desmond from his fresh clean scent. Her heart suddenly filled with gladness upon realizing her lover was standing by her side in this time of need. She tried to smile, but her lips felt numb. Blinking the drowsiness from her tired eyes, Lisa observed Desmond was giving her a strange look. His eyes were widened, forehead wrinkled, and his mouth was slightly gaped open. When she tried to open her mouth to ask him what was wrong, she gravely slurred her words.

"Lisa, your face..." he started, but was unable to complete the sentence. Becoming upset just from the horrible look on Desmond's face, she was trying to concentrate on the words coming out of his mouth. It sounded like he was saying something about her face, but Lisa was confused and couldn't comprehend exactly what he was saying right then.

"Lisa your face...your face is twisted! It's kind of droopy and twisted to one side! You look terrible! I have to get out of here!" he exclaimed, backing away and almost tripping over the chair beside her bed.

"Desmond, no! Please don't leave me! Please don't go! I need you Desmond!" she tried to say, sitting up in the bed wearing a white hospital gown, but it came out as jumbled words of pleading, which he rudely dismissed. Desmond just continued looking at Lisa like he didn't know who she was or where she had come from. He continued putting one leg behind the other, backing out of the hospital room. Easing the door open, he slipped through the smallest possible opening, trotted down the hospital corridor, and headed out to his red Boxster Porsche. There wasn't any way on this Earth he wanted to be associated with a disfigured woman.

When the police found Desmond's telephone number in Lisa's wallet last night, they called informing him Lisa had been involved in a car accident. Yet, he decided to wait until this morning to come visit her. After all, there was nothing he felt he could do for her, so Desmond remained in the comforts of his home until this morning. He'd expected to come in the hospital and see Lisa's usual pretty smile staring back at him, but instead he saw her contorted lips trying to speak.

From now on, Lisa Bradford was damaged goods and there wasn't any room in the good-looking doctor's life for any woman who wasn't perfect in his eyes. Seeing Lisa's once beautiful face, drooping and curving to one side, had caused him to exit the hospital room in a state of panic. It was definitely easy for him to walk away because it wasn't like he was in love with her or anything close to that. She had just been a simple diversion from his lackluster marriage. Belinda had stopped being able to satisfy him years ago. If it wasn't for that thing she did with her mouth, he would have left her shortly after their second child was born.

Frantically reaching for the remote control to the nurses' station, Lisa pushed the red button summoning help. She made loud gurgling sounds deep in her throat during her desperate cries for assistance. In no time flat, one of the registered nurses, Judy Carter, came bursting through the door asking if she was all right. But Lisa could only moan and point at her mouth, which was construed toward the left side of her face.

"Calm down. Calm down, now," Nurse Judy begged, holding Lisa's arms down at her side. "Don't worry. The doctor is on his way. He'll be here any minute."

Lisa collapsed in tears. Leaning her back against the stacked pillows, Nurse Judy held Lisa's right hand until the doctor arrived a few seconds later.

After careful examination, Dr. Thomas sat down on a stool beside Lisa's hospital bed. Using his best professional bedside manner, the doctor spoke calmly. "Ms. Bradford, I'm sorry to inform you that you have suffered a mild facial stroke. A stroke is an interruption of the blood supply to any part of the brain, resulting in damaged brain tissue. Now, high blood pressure is the number one reason for most strokes. After we reset your right leg last night, your blood pressure went up again, and we've been unsuccessful at getting it down to within a normal range all night. Do you understand what I'm saying?"

Lisa nodded her head, indicating she understood Dr. Thomas. Tears rolled down her rosy, freckled cheeks as she carefully listened to the doctor's statements. Lisa couldn't imagine why this was happening to her, and she couldn't understand why Desmond would flee from her side like he'd done.

"In general, cerebral neurons from the left side of the brain send their signals to brainstem neurons on the right side of the face and right-sided cerebral neurons go to brainstem neurons on the left side. However, the facial nerve is somewhat unusual in that the fibers that spread to the upper face, the muscles around the eye and the forehead, come from cerebral neurons on both the right and left side of the brain. Basically, if you can raise both eyebrows, the facial nerve is still intact, meaning that since you had a stroke involving the left side of the brain, your lower face is paralyzed. Are you still with me?"

Lisa nodded again, showing she was listening intently to Dr. Thomas' words. She raised both eyebrows, and released a sigh from the left side of her mouth. As hard as she was trying to concentrate on the doctor's words, Lisa was wondering about when she'd see Desmond again. She'd never forget the disgusting look in his eyes like he'd seen a monster in her room.

"Now, what you're probably wondering right now is how we're going to treat this. First, we're going to put you on blood thinners, such as Heparin and Coumadin which are both commonly used in the treatment of strokes. You will also receive a prescription for analgesics, also known as pain killers, which will probably be needed to help control your severe headaches and the pain in your legs. And you will be placed on an anti-hypertensive medication in hopes of reducing your high blood pressure. As soon as you're released from the hospital, you'll be admitted to a rehab facility for speech and physical therapy." Dr. Thomas looked up to see a tall medium-built staff nurse entering the room. He immediately recognized the face of Oretha Bradford rushing to Lisa's outstretched arms.

"Oh baby, how are you doing? I just signed on for duty and thought I'd come check on you this morning. How is she, doctor? Is my niece going to be all right?" Oretha asked, sitting on the bed, cradling Lisa to her bosom. Lisa felt like a weak, fragile baby, clinging to her aunt's arms.

"Yes, we think she's going to be fine, but she's got some work ahead of her. She will be placed on several medications, and be referred to speech and physical therapy as soon as possible. If everything goes well, she may be released in a few days."

"Thank you, Dr. Thomas, for all your help. I'll be on duty in this unit for the next few days, and I'll be able to keep a close watch on her myself. It's always nice to have family with you when you're in the hospital," she stated, looking at Lisa. "Don't you worry, baby, you'll be back to your pretty self in a few weeks. The main thing is to never give up hope. I'm going to call my prayer group right now, and we're going to start sending up the timber before the sun goes down."

"Well, Ms. Bradford, it sounds like you have the right lady on your side." Dr. Thomas smiled at the determined look on Oretha's face. He didn't have any doubt that he was in the presence of a praying woman with a direct line to the Master, just like his late grandmother, Olivia Thomas, had. If that woman, God rest her soul, ever prayed for you and you didn't get well, then it was just your time to go.

Dr. Thomas exited the room, leaving Oretha alone with her crying niece. Tears streamed down Lisa's face from her tightly closed eyes as she held on to Oretha's hand. "Now it's going to be all right," her aunt stated, easing down onto the hospital bed. "I promise you, it's going to be all right."

Tears continued streaming down Lisa's face as she tried to mumble something to her aunt. Oretha squeezed Lisa's hand even harder, and used the other one to rub her heaving back. "Now you calm down. I don't care how bad it looks, you have to have faith, baby. Ten years ago, the doctor told me I had cataracts in both my eyes. I went to see two or three specialists and they all told me the same thing. In fact, they all predicted I'd be blind in a few years if I didn't have laser surgery or take eye drops for the rest of my life. Well, I didn't do either one. I called my prayer warrior friends, and we all got down together on our knees. Plus, I started praying morning, noon, and night for my healing, which is what I still do everyday. It's been ten years, and I'm still seeing fine."

Oretha pulled a few tissues from the box on the nightstand and wiped Lisa's face. Placing her hand under Lisa's chin, she stared into her red eyes and said, "Let's pray together right now."

Closing her eyes, Lisa listened to her aunt praying for her like no one had ever done before. Every word from Oretha's emotion-filled mouth caused Lisa to shiver, squeezing her aunt's hands even tighter. Lisa had never known the power of a praying woman, but she was certainly about to find out. As she relaxed her mind to concentrate on Oretha's words, the tears continued to escape from her closed eyelids. All the hurt from every failed relationship she'd ever had was beginning to come back to haunt Lisa, but she couldn't keep her mind off the greatest love of all. *I have to get better so I can call Desmond without sounding like a mumbling retard on the phone. No wonder he gave me those disgusting looks. I probably had drool coming from my mouth. He'll never want me again if I can't even speak properly. I'm going to work hard in therapy and do whatever it takes to keep my man.*

CHAPTER SIXTEEN
(FEBRUARY)

I need you to walk alone to the end of these rails," stated Cynthia, Lisa's physical therapist, standing to the right of her client. Lisa lifted herself out of the wheelchair, grabbed the railing, and pulled up. Standing between the two six foot rails, she placed one foot in front of the other, and screamed out in pain. Still, she took another step before collapsing.

"It's okay. I've got you," Cynthia said, clutching Lisa's tiny waist. "That was good. Now let's try it again. I know it's painful, but you have to keep trying." She had been Lisa's chief motivator since the first day of rehabilitation. Being a trained professional, she knew just how far to push her clients.

"All right," Lisa replied, biting her bottom lip. She was determined to reach her goal today. Forcing her legs to cooperate with her mind, Lisa gritted her teeth in pain, and then took five more steps before collapsing against Cynthia at the end of the railing.

"That's what I'm talking about! That's exactly what I'm talking about. You did it!" Cynthia shouted. Lisa had been walking well with the crutches, but now it was time for her to move on to the next level. And regaining the strength in her legs was the only way to accomplish such a milestone.

"Thank you for helping me," Lisa stated, sounding out of breath. Cynthia helped her turn around, starting the journey back to her wheelchair. With each painful step, Lisa pushed herself harder to make it back to her seat. Cynthia wheeled her back to her room and helped Lisa into the bed so she could rest awhile.

Three months had passed and Lisa was on her way to a sparkling New Year recovery at the Texas Physical Rehabilitation Facility. The leg casts had been removed, and she was able to walk with the aid of crutches or a cane while dealing with the hurt in both legs. The pain killers that had worked so well in the beginning were doing very little to stop the throbbing aches Lisa felt in her legs right this minute.

The muscles in her face, through intensive speech therapy and extensive facial exercises, had almost returned to normal. Lisa was almost able to speak clearly without stuttering or fumbling over simple words.

Unless you knew exactly where to look in her face, you wouldn't be able to tell she had suffered a stroke a couple of months ago. She was doing much better, but not well enough to speak intelligently with Desmond. Lisa wanted to wait until she was perfect again before contacting her perfect man. There wasn't any way that she'd ever want to see again that disgusting look in his eyes like he had at the hospital. She was confident that the next time they met, he'd be so impressed with her looks there wouldn't be any way for him to resist her charm. Still, given the circumstances, Lisa hadn't been able to resist calling him daily just to hear his voicemail message while she panted for him over the phone.

When Lisa looked in the mirror at her reflection, she gently smoothed her hands over her face, thanking someone up above for sparing her life. If Auntie O was correct, Jesus was responsible for bringing her this far without any additional complications.

Only, Lisa really didn't know what to do because she'd never learned very much about God and going to worship services when she was a child. Her mother, Sadie, hardly ever took her and Jenna to church, unless it was Easter Sunday when they got to show off their pretty new dresses or at Christmas time. Other than that, they never saw the inside of a church, and there was certainly never any talk about Jesus or praying to God for anything. Her mama always said she provided them with whatever they had, and didn't no man have anything to do with it unless she slept with him. And Sadie sure hadn't spent any nights with Jesus in her bed.

Sundays were their days to sleep in and rest up for the following week. By the time they all got up around noon, most of the day was already gone. Then, they would spend the remainder of their time ironing clothes for the upcoming school and work week and cooking Sunday dinner. Sadie loved to eat, but she made sure she and her daughters remained slim by not overeating and staying away from most sweets.

Lisa grew up without having any moral guidelines. Therefore, she was free to live her life any sinful way that she pleased, just as her mother had. They made their own rules and never worried about the consequences of not pleasing a higher power.

Reminiscing about all the men she'd been with in her life, Lisa realized most of them had been married with families. Thinking about her past and the pain she'd caused so many wives and children, Lisa wondered how she could ever possibly turn her life around. This was the first time in her life Lisa had considered that, maybe, she wasn't a very nice person. She had naturally assumed for forty-two years that all women were as heartless and cunning as she was. Now at this stage in her life, she was beginning to ponder her values.

If this God really did save my life, why did He do it?
Lisa didn't know where to go for answers because she'd never read a Bible verse as far back as she could remember. They didn't even have a Bible in their house as a child growing up in Lake City, Florida. Whenever they did go to church, she and Jenna would sit there beside Sadie, listening to the preacher read one or two Bible passages before going into a tirade of screaming and jumping around the church like he was running over hot coals with bare feet. Then, the older women would start shouting and fanning like their flesh was on fire. And the next thing Lisa knew, they were passing out in the aisles. She never understood what that was all about and until now, Lisa didn't really care.

Almost an hour later, Lisa woke up to a friendly face. "Hi, Lisa." Auntie O was smiling down at her. "How are you?"

"I'm feeling okay, Auntie," she mumbled.

"I just came by to check on you and to pray with you if you don't mind."

"No, I don't mind," Lisa replied, closing her eyes. Aunt Oretha clasped both of Lisa's hands and bowed her head to pray.

After praying for several minutes, she lifted her head and smiled at Lisa again. "Everything is gonna be all right. You know that don't you? God is looking out for you."

"Thanks for coming, Auntie. I appreciate you praying for me." Lisa had to admit she felt something as Aunt Oretha held her hands in prayer, but she couldn't figure out what it was. *Maybe it's just the medication that's making me feel strange.*

CHAPTER SEVENTEEN
(DRUG ME)

Lisa was sitting up on the examination table in Dr. Thomas' office at the end of another follow-up visit. As she finished closing the top button on her Chaus lavender blouse, the doctor informed Lisa it was time to make some changes in her medical prescriptions. Unfortunately, she wasn't quite ready to handle this news.

"Dr. Thomas, I'm still suffering from mild headaches and pain in my legs. Can you please extend my prescriptions for another month?" she asked, batting her eyes at the male physician. She wasn't ready to come off her pain medications just yet.

"You know, you're going to probably have to deal with some level of pain for the rest of your life, Ms. Bradford. I've already lowered your dosages as much as I can. I think it's time for you to try making it without any pain medications. I don't want you to become addicted to anything," he replied, showing concern.

"Oh, no, don't worry about that. I just think that in another month with continued exercise, I'll be in a better position to live without the medicine. I'm getting stronger everyday."

"Yes, I can see that. I'll keep you on the low dosage for a few more weeks, and then we'll see how you can manage without it, all right?" He scribbled on a sheet of paper and handed it to her.

"Sure, Dr. Thomas," she replied, taking the prescription from his hand.

Lisa wasn't happy with his decision, but she would have to live with it for now. Since she had very little tolerance for pain, she popped a pill whenever the slightest discomfort occurred in her body. Lisa was used to feeling good and wanted to feel like her old self again. Those pain relievers caused all of her problems and stressors to temporarily go away. But as soon as the smallest pain returned, she swallowed another pill, providing her with immediate relief again.

With the help of an assistant physical therapist, Lisa made it back to her room in the rehab center. "Thanks for helping me. Could you see if Ms. Fountain has signed in to work yet?"

"Yes, ma'am," the young man replied. "I'll check on that right away. Is there anything else I can do for you?"

"No, thanks. I'm just waiting to see Ms. Fountain."

"All right, if she's signed in, I'll let her know you're waiting."

"Thank you very much," Lisa replied, easing herself to the side of the bed. She was tired after her doctor's visit and needed to rest.

A few minutes later, Lisa's main physical therapist, Cynthia Fountain, a twenty-six-year-old African-American single mother with two children, entered the room acting like her usual cheerful self. Her positive attitude had been instrumental in Lisa's rehabilitation. She worked full time and spent at least three or four hours each day in Lisa's company. She'd been through two financially draining divorces and was literally scuffling to make ends meet on her current salary. Just when she'd gotten back on her feet after the first divorce, Cynthia married another man whom she thought had money. As things turned out, he didn't have anything but a long list of debts. Then, she ended up co-signing for new loans, hoping to help him get back up on his feet. So, when they ended up in divorce court, and he left town with his other woman, she was left paying his multitude of bills. Yes, she had been played for a fool.

After listening to her patient cry every night, undoubtedly over a guy, Cynthia shared her man troubles with the heartbroken woman, hoping to help ease her pain. She wasn't the first woman who had been a fool for love or fallen into the "married man syndrome," and she certainly wouldn't be the last. So, over the course of Lisa's first month in rehab, they began developing a bond which was something amazingly new for Lisa. The only friends Lisa ever had were the two college roommates, Jolene and Ranetta, she'd left behind in Jacksonville, Florida, after graduating from college over twenty years ago. She'd reconnected with them during the short time she lived and worked in Jacksonville prior to moving to Dallas. But she hadn't communicated much with either one of them since the day she'd been forced out of the urban city.

Lisa hadn't made any friends since arriving in Dallas, either. Making it a point to stay away from women, the only female she was close to was her Aunt Oretha and a few of her church friends who'd stop by their house every now and then to chit chat. So when Cynthia showed an interest in being friends, Lisa gradually opened up to the extremely helpful younger woman who was very knowledgeable about the drugs she'd been taking for almost three months. In Lisa's vulnerable state of mind, she was finally ready to accept another female as her friend.

Considering she was still having severe headaches and pain, Lisa wasn't responding to the lower dosages Dr. Thomas had prescribed for her, and openly complained to her new friend.

"Cynthia, I don't know what I'm going to do now since the doctor has cut my pain prescription. My head and legs are still bothering me. Dr. Thomas is sending me home tomorrow, and I'm still in pain," Lisa said, rubbing her vibrating forehead. They were sitting on the side of Lisa's bed.

"I tell you what, these doctors don't know everything. You'll be better off going directly to a street pharmacist anyway. I have a connection who might be able to help you out if you're interested," Cynthia whispered, looking around to make sure the coast was clear.

"Are you talking about going to a drug dealer? Girl, I'm not that far gone. I just need something a little stronger to help me out until I'm completely healed."

"No, I'm talking about a pharmaceutical representative who can get the same tablets you're taking from the doctor at your full prescription strength. Dr. Thomas is just trying to cover his own butt by lowering your dosage. He's afraid you're going to sue him or something if you don't fully recover. Anyway, I've got your back. There's no reason for you to be walking around in pain if you don't have to."

"Yeah, but are those drugs safe? How can I be sure about what I'm taking?"

"They're safe. I told you, they're the same pills you're taking now but at the full strength like you had before. I've known this guy for years. He works for a well-known pharmaceutical company that gives him free samples to hand out to his doctor clients, but he sells some of them on the side for the right price to needy people in your position. Either he'll give you the same drug or an alternative one, which will be just as strong as your prescription. I'm telling you, he knows what he's doing."

Lisa was leery of using street drugs but considering the fact she wasn't used to pain and Dr. Thomas was not giving in to her whining this time, it seemed like a feasible alternative. She also trusted Cynthia's knowledge regarding medicine and her overall physical care. The woman had been by her side during some of the most humiliating moments in her life—wiping the drool from the side of her face when Lisa didn't even know it was there, making sure she took her pain pills on time, and providing her with extra pillows so she was comfortable during the many nights she'd been in the rehabilitation center. Not to mention the countless times Cynthia had helped her use the portable potty during the night. Now, that was real humiliation.

Cynthia helped her get around in the wheelchair everyday, and then once Lisa was strong enough to start trying to walk again, she encouraged Lisa through the physical therapy program, pushing her to bend her knees, and consoling her when she cried out in pain. So if she couldn't trust Cynthia, who could she trust? Dr. Thomas would never be able to identify with what she was going through as a woman accustomed to living a carefree painless life. She desperately needed to secure those drugs before being discharged from the hospital tomorrow. If that meant going to a crooked pharmaceutical salesman, then so be it. At least her hands wouldn't be dirty by using Cynthia as the middle man. Yeah, this was just the break she needed right now, and since Cynthia was willing to be a friend in need and help a sister out, it was only proper to give her the business.

Lisa rationalized this really would be the best alternative for her. She'd only take the pills for another month, she told herself. By then, the pain should have subsided enough for her to deal with the lower dosage or none at all. But right now, she needed her old life back, along with her old man. She desperately wanted to return to her two-story townhouse and Desmond's arms. Since her speech had dramatically improved lately, she'd been incessantly calling Desmond and leaving voice messages. Lisa was still obsessed with him and knew he'd be coming around to visit her as soon as she was released and living in their playpen again.

Being absent from him had only made her want him more. Now that she was beautiful, walking again, and finally had her proper speech back, Lisa believed things would return to normal once they were in each others' arms. Although he hadn't returned any of her phone calls, Lisa firmly believed Desmond would respond to the good news regarding her release. She couldn't wait to call her lover and let him know she'd be home in the morning. Both of their lives would finally return to normal. And if Cynthia came through like a true friend, she'd really be feeling fine when she walked out tomorrow.

"Thanks, Cynthia. I appreciate you helping me out, girl. You know, I consider you my friend, and I haven't had very many of those during my life."

"Look, I like you a lot, and I understand what you're going through. I try to help out women in your same predicament. A lot of sisters have been through exactly what you're experiencing and you can't always rely on the doctors around here to provide the proper medication. So don't worry about this. When you leave here tomorrow, you will have enough pain medicine to cover you for at least another month, and since a therapist will be coming by your house everyday to help you, she'll be able to monitor your intake."

"I wish you were available to do my home care at least for a little while. Are you sure we can't work something out?"

"No, I'm sorry, but I have so many patients here depending on me that I can't provide any type of home services. But the therapist assigned to help you is really good. I think you'll be pleased with her."

"I really hope so. I just can't wait to get back to my townhouse. I'll be much more comfortable there with plenty of room to stretch out in my own space."

"Well, I'll be happy to see you released from here. But you have to promise me one thing, though."

"What's that?"

"You can't tell anyone about our arrangement. Please promise me you'll keep this between us. You know, I could lose my job and my license behind this if my supervisors find out."

"I know, I know. I would never tell anyone about our agreement. I just appreciate you helping me out at a time like this. If it wasn't for you, I don't know how I would be able to deal with this pain once I'm home. By the way, how much is it going to cost me to get a month's supply of pills?" Lisa asked, thinking that no price would be too great to have her beautiful, pain-free life back. They worked out the monetary details, and Lisa gave Cynthia a check large enough to seal the deal right there.

"I promise you, I'll have this ready for you by the time you check out in the morning," Cynthia stated, rising from the bed. "Now let's get you tucked in for a nap because you have a physical therapy session coming up in about an hour."

Lisa leaned back against the pillows propped up against the headboard. Closing her eyes, she began pondering what the next day would bring. *I can't wait to get out of here tomorrow. I'm going to feel brand new once I get those full prescription pills in my system. It's going to be so exciting to see Desmond's face again. He didn't need to be seen around these nosy people anyway, but we'll be fine as soon as I get out of here.*

CHAPTER EIGHTEEN
(HOMEWARD BOUND)

"All right, Ms. Bradford, we have all of your discharge paperwork completed. We just need you to sign a few papers at the main nurses' station, and you'll be on your way home," Dr. Thomas said, smiling down at the patient he was about to release from his care.

"Thanks for everything, doctor. I'm happy to finally be leaving this place," Lisa stated, sitting in the wheelchair completely dressed in jeans and a long sleeve printed blouse. She scanned the room, checking to make sure she hadn't forgotten anything.

"Do you have someone coming to pick you up this morning to make sure you get home safe?" he asked.

"Oh yes, my aunt should be here at any second. She's giving me a ride to my place. I'm telling you, I can't wait to get home either."

"I'm sure you can't. Anyway, I need to see you in my office for a follow-up visit in about two weeks, okay? In the meantime, you will continue with your daily physical therapy. If you have any problems, feel free to call my office at any time."

"No problem, Dr. Thomas. I'm looking forward to seeing you then. Right now, I just want to get out of here. It feels like I've been hospitalized for a whole year."

Dr. Thomas laughed at Lisa's exaggeration. Then, he looked up to see Cynthia rushing through the doorway. "Good morning, Dr. Thomas, and good morning, Lisa," Cynthia said, greeting her friend.

"Hi. I was beginning to wonder whether or not you would make it here before I checked out," Lisa stated, sounding concerned because Cynthia was late coming in.

"All right, I'm turning it over to Ms. Fountain from here. She will assist you in completing these papers and check you out." Dr. Thomas patted Cynthia on the shoulder as he was leaving.

As soon as he closed the door behind him, Cynthia turned to face Lisa. "Well, I wasn't able to meet my connection last night, so we had to meet this morning before I came in. I'll give you your package once you're checked out. Let me wheel you out to the front desk and get everything taken care of for your discharge." Cynthia grabbed the handles of Lisa's wheelchair and pushed her down the hallway to the discharge desk.

Aunt Oretha pulled up in her cool vanilla sedan, stopping at the glass sliding doors. She waited for Cynthia to wheel Lisa outside. Fastening her brown, suede jacket, she rushed to Lisa's side. "Looks like I made it here just in time. Are you all set to go?"

"Oh, yes, I've got the discharge papers right here in my hand," Lisa replied, waving the folded documents.

"Do you need any help?" she asked Cynthia.

"No, ma'am, I've got it. I just need you to open the car door for me."

"No, problem," replied Lisa's aunt, reaching for the door handle.

Cynthia helped Lisa get situated into the beige leather seat, then she pulled a gift wrapped present out of her coat pocket and placed it in Lisa's lap. "Here's your package, girlfriend. Call me if you need anything else," she said, giving Lisa a close hug.

"Thanks for being a friend, Cynthia. Let's keep in touch. I'll call you in a few days once I'm home and settled in."

"Hey, that sounds great. Maybe we can have brunch or lunch together sometime. I'd like that."

"I promise to call you. We'll work something out real soon," Lisa stated, easing her body into the front of her aunt's car. She waved at Cynthia as they pulled away from the rehab center, thankful she had made a helpful friend.

Shaking her head, Cynthia stood there watching the light-colored sedan until it disappeared around the corner. She honestly felt bad about deceiving Lisa, but at this point, she didn't have much of a choice. She had bills to pay and gorgeous women like Lisa would always have a man to take care of them while she struggled with feeding two children after two divorces.

Hopefully, if Lisa called her within the next couple of days, she would be long gone with a new start in another city far away from here. Cynthia would be away from these whining patients who were constantly vying for her attention. She would be able to give her children the life they deserved in a place where they could be a happy family. In a few hours, she would have enough money to make her dreams come true. *Sorry, Lisa.*

Cynthia pulled out her cellular phone before reentering the hospital and dialed a familiar number. Since no one answered the call, she left a message. "The package has been delivered. We need to meet later today. Call me back right away."

CHAPTER NINETEEN
(A DIABOLICAL PLAN)

"Good afternoon, may I get you another cup of coffee?" the waitress asked, staring down at her customer.

"Yes, thank you. I'll have one more cup, please." Cynthia was sitting in a corner at the small diner around the corner from the rehabilitation center. With both of her legs nervously twitching, she ordered a second cup of fresh-brewed decaffeinated coffee. Closely watching the door and her Jennifer Lopez watch, she knew her accomplice should be arriving any minute now with her money. She hadn't risked her job and license just for the sake of friendship. How stupid would she be to have done that?

It was the first and last time she'd ever do anything like this. With a hundred thousand dollars in her bank account, all of her problems would be resolved. It was worth it for only a few weeks work where she only had to do her regular job and befriend some snobby woman in the rehab center. It didn't take her long to say "yes" to the deal she'd been offered that day when she was leaving work. A dark-skinned sister approached her wearing some type of expensive designer suit that Cynthia would have to work three months to afford. Anyway, the mysterious lady asked her if she had a few minutes to talk and offered to buy her a cup of coffee at this very shop.

Thinking the stranger was a relative of one of her patients, Cynthia agreed to meet with her.

At first, their conversation started off as a normal one, like two old friends who had met up together after years apart. They ordered their drinks and made small talk for a few minutes. Cynthia kept smiling at the woman, waiting for her to get to the point of their meeting while admiring her exquisite attire. She knew this woman had money and lots of it from the shiny diamonds she wore on almost every finger of both hands. The lady told her that she knew someone who was admitted to the facility, but she wasn't related to her.

"Excuse me, what did you say your name was again?" Cynthia asked the smiling woman with the perfect teeth.

"My name is Ms. T, and I know everything about you. I know how you're struggling with your life right now, and I'm willing to help you out if you'll help me."

"What is it that I can possibly help you with?" Cynthia asked, sounding curious, leaning across the table on both elbows. For the next hour, she listened to Ms. T. tell her all about her own business and how she was there to rescue her. Cynthia was about to leave in disgust when the rich woman casually mentioned that she could earn the sum of one hundred thousand dollars.

"And just who would I have to kill for that kind of money?" she asked, jokingly thinking how this woman had to be crazy even though she looked perfectly sane.

"I'm not asking you to kill anyone. No, I would never ask you to do that. However, there is this one patient you have whom has tried to ruin my life for no worldly reason, and now I need to return the favor. All I'm asking you to do is substitute her current drugs for one of a much higher dosage, so she can become addicted to it once she's discharged from the facility."

"Whoa lady, you've got to be kidding. Why would you wish that on anybody?"

"I told you, she tried to ruin my life. Now I want hers to be ruined. And in the process, you can have a new start wherever you want to go. I'll buy you and your kids a first class ticket to anywhere in the world and give you a hundred thousand dollars in cash."

Cynthia couldn't believe this woman was actually serious, that she would want to devastate another human being in such a manner. But once she found out who the patient was that Ms. T. wanted turned into a junkie, it didn't take long for her to put two and two together. Her newest patient, Lisa Bradford, was certainly a handful. Cynthia knew the snobby woman she'd been assisting at the rehab center had made a mortal enemy through her checkered past.

"I'll have to think about this for a minute. This isn't something I can take lightly."

"And neither can I," Ms. T stated with determination in her voice. "I need to know whether or not we have a deal right now. I have ten thousand dollars in my purse I'm willing to give you as a down payment. If you can say "yes," it's yours to take with you today. All you have to do is gain her trust, make sure she stays on the pain medicine, and then give her the substitute drugs once she checks out of the center."

Cynthia stared at the woman with her mouth slightly opened. Ten thousand dollars alone was enough money to get most of her financial problems cleared up. All those creditors could stop calling her house every other hour during the day trying to catch her in one place. She could take the other ninety thousand dollars in a few weeks, invest it in some prime real estate property, and not work for a whole year. Then, she could buy a small cottage out in the country where her children would be free to run and play. She had to think about her babies first, because they deserved to have what she never had, a house with a loving parent.

Contemplating the offer before her, Cynthia compared her life to Lisa's. Sure, Ms. Bradford would become addicted to the drugs, but she'd be able to get into rehab and turn her life around eventually. On the other hand, this was a once in a lifetime opportunity for Cynthia that she wasn't going to pass up. She didn't know what Lisa had done to the attractive woman sitting in front of her, but the lady was willing to pay handsomely for her revenge. With all things considered, Cynthia didn't hold any obligations to either one, so she decided to take the prosperous solution. She was tired of working overtime every day just to be able to pay the necessary bills, and then being too tired to help her children with their homework at night because she had to soak her swollen feet.

"All right, I'll do it," she relented, holding out her right hand for the money she'd been promised.

Now here she was today, sitting in the same seat she'd been in on that day, waiting to receive the remainder of her hard-earned money. It had been difficult trying to stay friends with a fire cat like Lisa Bradford, who fussed and complained about everything. The lady couldn't stand a stab of pain for more than two seconds. But Cynthia hung in there, smiling at Lisa and being attentive to her every need. After all, she was going to be rewarded handsomely for doing so. She would look at Lisa growling at her, imagine dollar signs in her eyes, and return her frown with lips turned upward.

Checking her watch one more time, she looked up into the face of Ms. T walking toward the table wearing a navy suit, carrying a leather attaché case. "Hi, Cynthia, how are you today?" Belinda Taylor asked, sliding into the booth beside her accomplice.

"I'm fine. I've been here waiting on you for the last fifteen minutes," Cynthia replied, irritated the woman had made her wait. She didn't even know her partner's real name, and that's exactly how Cynthia wanted it to remain. The less of a connection they had to each other, the better it would be in the long run.

"I'm sorry, but I got caught up in traffic. Now that I'm here, let's talk business. I understand you have completed your mission?"

"Yes, I have. Ms. Bradford checked out of the rehab center today with a bottle of pills strong enough to turn her into a drug fiend within the thirty days it will take her to complete the supply."

"Okay, I'm happy to hear that. Ms. Lisa Bradford is finally going to get what she deserves: a life on the streets with the other lowlifes. It'll be a cold day in hell before she dreams about sleeping with another married man. She'll be too busy scouring the streets looking for her next hit to think about taking somebody else's husband."

"Look, I just want my money so I can get out of town, all right? You'll have your revenge on Lisa soon enough. Let me have my money so I can be long gone by the time she realizes what's happened to her. The way she's been popping pills, it won't take a month for her to be calling me for another supply."

"And since you won't be available to help her, she'll have to hit the streets on her own. I can't wait to see how beautiful she looks then. Anyway, here's the rest of your money," Ms. T stated, sliding the leather briefcase over by Cynthia's feet.

CHAPTER TWENTY
(LISA'S TEMPER)

Lisa made it home safely with Aunt Oretha's help after stopping at the grocery store to restock her bare refrigerator. She was able to use one of those motorized shopping carts to zip around the store beside her aunt. Knowing she probably didn't have any salvageable food at home, she stocked up on bread, cold cuts, fruit, and a variety of juices.

"We have a little surprise for you," said Aunt O. They were only about a block away from Lisa's building.

"What?" Lisa asked. Her mind was racing with thoughts.

"You'll see as soon as we get to your place."

Pulling up beside Lisa's newly repaired PT Cruiser, Oretha turned the engine off, and plastered a smile on her face. She turned to Lisa and said, "Your uncle and I took care of everything with the insurance company while you were away. It's good as new."

"Oh, Auntie, thanks so much." Reaching across the seat, Lisa hugged Oretha the best she could.

"Well, of course, it'll be awhile before you can drive. But, at least, it'll be here when you're ready."

"I know. Just knowing that I have my car back is a big relief. I can't believe I didn't think about it the entire time

I was gone. Thank you guys so much. I really appreciate everything."

"You're welcome, Lisa. I drove it over here myself. The insurance adjuster didn't give us any problems. And your uncle made sure the body shop fixed it right. Now, let's get you inside so I can get these groceries out the car," Aunt O stated, placing a hand on the door lever.

Entering the townhouse with the use of a walker, Lisa stopped in the living room for a second to savor the feeling of being home. Since she'd gotten comfortable with using the walker, she preferred that to those hard crutches she'd started out using in the rehabilitation center. Making their way to the kitchen, Lisa took a seat at the dining room table while her aunt started putting the groceries away.

"Would you like for me to fix you some soup or maybe a good meal?" Oretha asked, opening the refrigerator door.

"No, Auntie O, that's all right. I'll be fine."

"I don't mind, you know. It wouldn't take long to make you something hot."

"No, really, I'm fine. I want you to go home and enjoy the rest of your day off. Thanks again for coming to pick me up."

"All right. Since you're determined to get rid of me, I guess I'll be moving on. I'll call later on this afternoon to check on you."

"That sounds good. Maybe I'll be ready to eat something hot by then. But for right now, I'll just fix me a sandwich and be happy."

Lisa said good-bye and hugged her aunt while standing in the kitchen. Then she hobbled to the living room in search of her leather jacket. With the pain pounding in her head, she just wanted to get to the bottle of pills Cynthia had supplied her with.

She ripped open the gift box, grabbed the bottle out, and made it back to the kitchen sink. After filling a small glass with tap water, Lisa popped two capsules in her mouth. Being that she was weak, tired, and exhausted, she decided to lie down and rest while the medicine took effect on her.

About an hour later, Lisa woke up to the sound of the doorbell ringing. Still in a daze, it took her a few minutes to gather her bearings long enough to realize she was home in her bed. Making her way to the door, Lisa's heart began to race wondering who was on the other side. She had a slight tingling sensation telling her that it could be Desmond, and somehow he knew she had made it home. Picking up her pace using the walker, she pulled the door open with a wide smile on her face. Lisa stepped outside, looking around to see a glimpse of the man walking away from her townhouse. When she turned around to reenter the living room, Lisa noticed a letter attached to the doorknob.

"What the...is this?" she asked out loud, clutching the eviction notice in her right hand. From what she read, Desmond had sold her home, and the new owners were giving her thirty days to vacate the premises. *This has got to be some type of mistake. There's no way...*

Lisa's head started spinning. She felt the anger rise from her heart and rush to her brain. Lisa tried to think of a logical explanation for what was happening, but the all consuming rage was preventing her from thinking clearly. She felt a sharpness thumping in her temples. Then Lisa heard her heart pumping against her chest cavity so loud it sounded like a drum being beaten directly into her ears.

Stepping back inside the living room area, Lisa slammed the heavy door behind her. Her entire body was nervously shaking as she recalled Desmond's telephone number. *He has to get this straightened out today. There isn't any way I'm leaving the house I've been dreaming about seeing again. It's bad enough that he hasn't returned my phone calls and now this is ridiculous. But first, I need something for this headache.*

Being consumed with madness and pain, she rushed to the kitchen counter, reached for the medicine bottle, and popped two more capsules into her mouth without using water. After swallowing, Lisa began walking toward the master bedroom when a sudden spell of dizziness caused her to become faint. Holding onto the walker with both hands, Lisa felt herself losing consciousness as her thin body began sliding down onto the cold tiled kitchen floor.

***

Since Uncle Johnny had been trying to call Lisa for the last thirty minutes, he decided to swing by her house. His wife had already told him she'd dropped Lisa off at home over an hour ago, so he was wondering why she wasn't answering the telephone. Uncle Johnny had meant to come with Oretha to pick up Lisa from the hospital this morning, but then remembered he had a doctor's appointment for a colonoscopy which he'd scheduled two months ago. Anyway, he figured it wouldn't take long to stop in and check on his niece.

Oretha had called him on his cell phone and given him the correct address and house number. Looking up from the piece of paper he'd written the information on, Johnny verified that he was in the right location. Then, he recognized Lisa's silver PT Cruiser parked in front of the building. Noticing that the curtains were pulled, he thought Lisa was probably inside sleeping and started to drive away.

Without thinking about it anymore, Uncle Johnny stepped out of his Lincoln Town Car, rang the door bell, and waited several minutes for someone to answer. He was about to walk away when suddenly he got an eerie feeling. He reached out, turned the unlocked doorknob, and pushed the door open. Taking one step through the doorway, he called out to his niece, "Lisa! Lisa! Are you in here?" As soon as he made a couple of more steps through the front door, he saw Lisa's thin frame sprawled out on the kitchen floor. Her head was turned to the side, and her hair was covering her whole face.

"Oh, my God! Lisa! Lisa! Can you hear me?" Uncle Johnny cried, running to her side. Bending down on his knees, he gently turned Lisa over onto her back. Pressing his thumb against the veins on her small wrist, he tried to get a pulse but couldn't tell if she had one or not. He pulled out his cellular phone and punched in the emergency response telephone number for help.

Uncle Johnny stayed with her until the ambulance arrived. He was praying to God that his niece was still alive.

CHAPTER TWENTY ONE
(PSYCHIATRIC WARD)

Lisa woke up the next morning confined in a small hospital room on the psychiatric floor with a locked door and a painful headache. With her weak body slumped down in the bed, she lifted her head up as far as possible, surveying her sterile surroundings. Lisa opened her mouth to cry out for help, but her throat was too dry to make a sound. Throwing her head back against the pillow in exhaustion, Lisa closed her eyes, praying for the pain to subside between her ears.

Pressing the red button on the emergency remote control, she summoned the floor nurse.

"Yes, may I help you?" the voice asked.

Lisa mumbled something, and the voice replied, "I'll be right there."

When the nursing attendant entered the room, Lisa pointed to her throat, indicating she needed a drink of water. "Oh, I'll get you a full pitcher of water right away," she stated, grabbing the empty container from the nightstand. The young lady made a quick exit out of the room in search of crushed ice and cool tap water.

Moments later, the nurse returned carrying a blue pitcher. "Here you go, Ms. Bradford," she stated, smiling down at her new patient.

Lisa noticed from her badge that the nurse's name was DeeAnn, and she was actually older than she first appeared to be. Her braided hairstyle gave her a youthful flare.

Nurse DeeAnn walked to the foot of Lisa's bed, pushed a few buttons, and the bed began to rise. Then, she moved the tray in front of Lisa and poured a small cup of water.

Gulping the water down as fast as she could, Lisa stared up at the woman assisting her, wondering why she was back in the hospital. "Don't worry. The doctor will be with you in just a few seconds. She'll be able to answer all of your questions. If you need anything else, just press the buzzer again," the nurse explained when she recognized the questioning look on her patient's face.

A few minutes later, Lisa heard a loud clicking sound. Opening her eyes again, she saw a thin, average height, walnut brown woman enter the room wearing a white lab jacket. The middle-aged woman appeared to be a doctor and stared at Lisa from behind a pair of thick black glasses. She carried a clipboard filled with papers in one hand and a black ink pen in the other one.

Standing about a foot away from Lisa's bed, the woman identified herself. "Good morning, Ms. Bradford. My name is Dr. Elizabeth Hopson, and I'm a psychiatrist. You were admitted to the psychiatric ward this morning after being treated for an overdose of drugs. We found high levels of an illegal narcotic in your bloodstream. Are you a habitual drug user?" she asked, moving closer to her patient.

"No, no, I thought I was taking pain pills."

"I see, and were these pain pills prescribed by your doctor?" she asked, looking over the top of her glasses.

Lisa didn't know how to respond. She simply stared at the woman looking terrified, wondering what type of illegal drugs the doctor was talking about. Suddenly remembering she'd gotten the supply of pills from

Cynthia, Lisa kept her mouth closed. She couldn't focus on what the doctor was saying anyway because the pounding in her head was getting worse.

"Please, please, my head is killing me. I need something for the pain. Doctor, please give me something for the pain," she cried out.

"All right, Ms. Bradford. I'll have the nurse bring you something shortly. I really need to review your medical records very carefully before I can prescribe anything for you. I understand you were just dismissed from our rehabilitation center this morning. Is that correct?"

Lisa simply nodded her head as she continued staring at the doctor. She needed a little more time to process what was happening before she started talking to anyone.

"I have to inform you, Ms. Bradford, that we have to keep you here under surveillance for the next seventy-two hours. Then, you'll be released from our care and free to return to your home. But while you're here, you will have to attend at least two counseling sessions with me. Do you understand everything I have said?"

"Yes, thank you, Dr. Hopson," Lisa replied, thankful the doctor would be honoring her request for pain medicine. She would have to worry about the counseling sessions later.

"I'll be back to check on you later today, after you've taken your medicine, to set up a time for our first meeting tomorrow."

Lisa simply nodded her head, acknowledging she was in agreement with Dr. Hopson. She was too weak to even try whispering any more words. The only thing she really wanted right now was relief.

Minutes later, another nurse entered with the prescribed pain medicine and a hot lunch. Lisa downed a pill with one sip of water and turned her nose up at the bland food. Closing her weary eyes, she drifted off to sleep, wondering what type of illegal drug Cynthia had given her. Thinking the one woman whom she'd decided to trust in over twenty years had drastically let her down, Lisa felt the anger rising in her stomach. Then, remembering she had made the mistake of taking her medicine twice in a short period of time, she cursed to herself. *How did I let this happen?*

CHAPTER TWENTY TWO
(DR.'S OFFICE 1)

The next day, Lisa was wheeled, by the male attendant, to Dr. Hopson's office on the third floor of the hospital in the psychiatric unit. Lisa tugged at the white cotton robe hanging loosely over her hospital gown. She had her red, wavy hair brushed back into a long flowing ponytail and wore a solemn look on her face. Lisa really wasn't up to talking with some shrink about her personal life but if it was going to help her get released from this crazy place, Lisa knew she would have to play the part.

The attendant stopped the wheelchair directly in front of Dr. Hopson's marble-topped, wooden, hand-carved desk and politely excused himself. "I'll be back for you in about an hour," he said to Lisa. She simply nodded, acknowledging she'd heard him before he left.

"How are you feeling today, Ms. Bradford? Do you mind if I call you Lisa?" Dr. Hopson asked, flashing a warm smile.

"I feel okay, and you may call me by my first name."

Lisa surveyed her neutral-colored surroundings and surmised that Dr. Hopson was probably an earthy woman who naturally enjoyed helping others. Her immaculately maintained space looked more like a European furniture showroom than a physician's office. She even had a solid wood taupe electric fireplace in the corner with a hand carved front. And the burgundy multicolored woven jacquard drapes added a warm feeling to the atmosphere. Everything looked as if it had been explicitly selected by an interior designer or expressly designed for the psychiatrist. Lisa momentarily forgot she was sitting in a hospital facility.

"Is there anything I can do to make you feel more comfortable? Would you like to sit on the sofa?" Dr. Hopson asked, pointing to the green, cloth sofa across the room.

Lisa turned to look at the barely used couch and decided it would be more comfortable than sitting up in a wheel chair for the next hour. So she replied in her sweetest voice, "Yes, I would like to sit over there if you don't mind."

"No, I don't mind at all. Let me help you," the doctor replied, rising from her seat behind the wooden desk.

She pushed Lisa's wheelchair over to the sofa and helped her get out. Relaxing her back against the soft cushions, Lisa crossed her ankles and folded her hands in her lap while admiring the Jones New York, blue skirt suit her new doctor was wearing. Judging from the gray around her temples and the few age lines around her eyes, Lisa estimated Dr. Hopson had to be somewhere in her fifties or early sixties. And according to her well made-up face, perfectly manicured fingernails, and coiffed haircut, she was definitely a sophisticated lady.

"Let me get my digital tape recorder and we can get started," Dr. Hopson stated, returning to her unique desk to retrieve the digital machine, a pen, and a note pad. When she returned a few seconds later, Dr. Hopson took a seat in the solid brown armchair beside the sofa, and crossed her thin, short legs.

"Now that we're both comfortable, I would like to welcome you to our first session together. As I told you yesterday, you're required to have at least two sessions with me before I can authorize your release. So I'll meet with you again tomorrow and then you will be free to go, all right?"

"Yes, I understand. What is it you want to talk about?" Lisa asked, giving the doctor an apprehensive look.

"Well, first of all, I need to give you some ground rules before we officially get started. I have to inform you that everything that's said here today will be held in the strictest of confidence. I only ask that you be honest with me and rest assured you will not be judged by me in any way. I'm here to listen to whatever you're willing to share. Do you have any questions for me before we start?"

Lisa lowered her eyes, shifting her body on the sofa. "I was just wondering why this is necessary. I mean I'm not crazy or anything close to that. I just took an accidental overdose of pain pills."

"Can you tell me how you happened to take an accidental overdose of an illegal drug?"

"I thought I was taking legal medicine. You see, my doctor cut my pain prescription and a friend of mine offered to help me out by securing alternative drugs from a pharmaceutical representative. I took a couple of pills when I got home from the rehabilitation center yesterday morning and laid down. When I woke up about an hour later, someone had posted an eviction notice on my front door. I flew into a rage and the headache returned. I forgot that I had already taken a dose of medicine and swallowed two more pills. All I can remember after that is trying to make it back to my bedroom before blacking out."

"Do you know the pills you took were three times stronger than your original prescription? You're lucky to be alive."

Lisa stretched her eyes, dropping her lower lip. She couldn't believe what Dr. Hopson had just said. "So if she was supposed to be a friend, I would hate to meet one of your enemies."

Closing her mouth, Lisa lowered her eyes to the floor. She knew the risks of using a street drug dealer, but she'd been so desperate for the pain to subside that she'd gone against her better judgment. Now, here she was in a meeting with a psychiatrist who thought she must be some lunatic.

"I was a fool for believing in her. I just wanted the pain to end. I was ready to get back to my life."

"I see. Sometimes we make irrational decisions when our bodies are in disarray. Why don't you tell me about the life you were so anxious to return to? Tell me about Lisa Bradford."

Lisa turned away, staring out the window, shaking her head. She finally responded, "You don't want to know what I've been through in the last three months. My life has been a living nightmare."

"Then let's talk about your life prior to the car accident, which started all of this. I'd like to hear about your childhood. Where did you grow up?"

"I was born and raised in Lake City, Florida. My parents, James and Sadie were married shortly after my sister, Jenna, was born. Then, two years later, I was born."

"Tell me more about your parents. What type of work did they do?"

"My father worked in the post office all his life. He was a postal delivery man. And my mother worked as a secretary for a private insurance agency."

"How was the relationship between you and your parents?"

"We had a very happy life until they divorced when I was four-years-old. My sister and I both took it very hard after my mother told us daddy was moving out to live with another woman."

"Did your mother actually say your father was moving in with another woman?" the doctor asked.

"Yes, she did. As a matter of fact, he moved right across the street from us to live with Della, one of my mother's closest, single friends. It seems he took that being neighborly thing a little too far."

"That had to be a difficult time for your family, wasn't it?"

"I was only a child, but I do remember my parents used to have a party every other Saturday evening. The original sound of rhythm and blues would be blasting over the stereo. And since both my parents were crazy about Ray Charles, his distinctive voice is the main one I recall. The cheap liquor would be flowing from glass to glass. All the neighbors would come over and gather around that little card table we had tucked in the corner of the den and play spades or gin rummy all night long. They were having a good time laughing and talking smack, until one night, my mother caught Ms. Della playing footsies under the table with my daddy and all the floodgates to hell broke loose."

"Do you remember exactly what happened?"

"I'll never forget that night as long as I live. Mama snatched that long-haired "Tina Turner" wig off of Ms. Della's head so hard she fell back in her chair, hitting the hard floor with a resounding thump. Anyway, mama jumped on top of Ms. Della and proceeded to give her a good, ole-fashioned whipping like she'd stole something. It took three men to pull mama away from that woman's bald head. Then, she and daddy fought off and on for the rest of the night. The next day, Ms. Della had two black eyes. Daddy packed up his two suitcases and dragged them across the lawn to her house." Lisa had a faraway look in her eyes as she easily relayed the details from her childhood.

"How long did they live across the street from your family?"

"Oh, they didn't stay together in that house for very long because mama was over there harassing them everyday. About a month later, they moved across town in a two-bedroom house. He married Ms. Della a year later, less than two weeks after divorcing Sadie, and she never got over it or him."

"What do you mean by that statement? Are you saying that your mother never remarried?"

"No, she didn't ever get married again. She took advantage of every man who crossed her path after my father left. She talked about daddy everyday and what a low-down, dirty scoundrel he was for leaving her with two kids for a slut whom she thought was a friend. She made it clear that she'd never be a fool for another Negro in this life."

"How did you react to your father's actions?"

"I was totally devastated. My father was the light of my world. He treated my sister and me like real princesses. Every Halloween, he would dress us up in our pink gowns, put furry crowns on our heads, give us a magic wand, and take us trick or treating to every house in our neighborhood." Lisa smiled from just recalling that fond memory of the first man in her life.

"I see. You really adored your father."

"Yes, he was a great man. But after he remarried, he stopped coming around to visit us once his new wife became pregnant. It was as if we didn't exist anymore," Lisa stated, her voice trailing off the last sentence.

"And how did that make you feel, Lisa?" Dr. Hopson leaned in closer to her client.

"It hurt me. It hurt me to know that my father was taking care of his other children better than us. They lived well while my mother scuffled to provide for us." Lisa's voice rose slightly, showing her irritation. It took all the strength she had to resist the tears that were beginning to swell in the corner of her sore eyes.

"Okay, let's move on. What can you share with me about your relationship with your mother? Are you two close?"

"I've been in the rehabilitation center for three months with two broken legs and neither she nor my sister has been to see me. What does that tell you?"

"Well, it certainly answers my question. When was the last time you spoke to your mother?" Dr. Hopson scribbled a few notes on the pad she was holding. Then she returned her attention to Lisa's frowning face.

"I think it was when I first entered the rehab center. She probably called the first week I was there, and I haven't heard from her or Jenna since."

"How do you feel about that? Have you tried to contact them?"

"No. Why should I? I'm the one who's been in that awful place fighting with pain everyday. I don't care if they never call me again."

"What type of relationship did you have with your mother growing up?"

"It was okay, I guess. It's nothing that I want to brag about. She worked hard to make sure we had what we needed. She just didn't have time to show us much affection because when mama wasn't working, she was busy entertaining her gentlemen friends."

"Did your mother do a lot of entertaining?"

"It depends on what you think is a lot. She would come home on Fridays, change into sexy clothes and make us clean up the house for her company. There was a different lover man there every Friday and Saturday evening. Most of the time they stayed home, but occasionally they took her out."

"What did you and your sister do while your mother was busy entertaining?"

"Mostly, we tried to stay out of her way, which was fine with me. I couldn't stand most of the ugly dogs she brought home anyway," Lisa stated, sounding disgusted.

"Why? What was wrong with the men she dated?"

"Well, most of them were sexual perverts, to say the least. I was barely twelve-years-old when one of her suitors offered me money just to touch my breast. That ole fool was crazy. I snatched that ten dollar bill out of his hand and ran to my room. I didn't want his crusty, wrinkled hand on me."

"Did you tell your mother about that incident?"

"No, no. She probably wouldn't have believed me anyway. I just took the money and took off. I knew he wouldn't tell her if I didn't."

"Did your mother ever date any decent men you would approve of?"

"Yeah, she had a few guys who were pretty nice to us. But those were the ones she got rid of real quick. Mama said the last thing she needed was a weak man lapping around our kitchen."

"Since this is what occurred at your house every Friday and Saturday, tell me what you all did on Sundays. Did your mother ever take you to church?"

"Oh yeah, we usually went on Easter Sundays. She would dress us up in frilly lace dresses and take us to Shiloh Baptist Church down the street."

"Was that it? Was that the only time you ever went to church?"

"Doctor, my mother was too interested in other social activities to worry about taking us to church. She spent her energy on preparing us for the debutante balls and other high society events she really couldn't afford. I think she wanted us to feel like we were just as good as the other girls in town."

"I see, so religion wasn't discussed in your house. Did you all ever pray together?"

"Not really. I can't say that I ever saw my mother praying," Lisa replied, trying to remember if this was a true statement. "Why are you asking me about religion?"

"It's just a routine question. I like to know all about my patient's background. If you're not comfortable with it, we can move on to something else before our time is up," Dr. Hopson eyed Lisa for a response. Lisa simply nodded, indicating she wanted to move on. Talking about religion wasn't high on her priority list right now.

"All right, I'd like to know about your past. Are you close to any other family members? How did you end up here in Dallas?" Dr. Hopson queried Lisa, hoping for some sign of emotion besides bitterness.

"It's a long story, but I'll give you the short version. I lived in D.C. for almost twenty years. Then, I moved to Jacksonville, Florida, to help out with my elderly aunt. I stayed there a couple of years before moving out here with my uncle and his wife."

"That's interesting. Why did you leave Jacksonville? Did your aunt pass?"

"No, she's still living but... I lost my job and decided to move out here for a change of scenery," Lisa replied, not wanting to give too many details regarding her abrupt departure from Florida.

"I see, and what type of work do you do?"

"I worked in the computer software industry in D.C. and Jacksonville. Since I've moved to Dallas, I've been working with my uncle at his lounge. He needed a night time manager, so, I've been helping him out until I can find something in my field."

"Our time is almost up for today, Lisa," Dr. Hopson stated, glancing down at her gold watch. "I'm looking forward to meeting with you tomorrow. If everything goes well, you can schedule several follow-up visits with me."

"I don't think that will be necessary. As you can see, I'm a normal human being who made a mistake. I need to get out of here and back into rehab for my legs."

"Well, we have one more session before you'll be approved for discharge. I'll see you tomorrow at this same time," Dr. Hopson replied, rising from her seat. She walked over to her desk and pressed a red button, signaling the nurse on duty to come escort her patient back to her room.

Lisa sat quietly with her hands folded across her lap, as if she was in deep thought. Dr. Hopson had raised questions and emotions inside her that she thought were gone forever. Now Lisa was feeling all of the tremendous hurt she'd felt growing up without a father and a very emotionally distant mother. But mostly what she felt right now was a great deal of anger toward a woman she'd trusted with her life. Lisa was determined to find Cynthia and make her pay for what she was going through.

"Oh, let me help you." Dr. Hopson turned to see Lisa struggling to rise from the sofa. She rushed to Lisa's side and clutched her right arm.

"I'm all right. I can do it myself, doctor." Lisa stretched out both hands and grabbed the wheelchair arms just as the nurse entered the room.

Dr. Hopson watched as Lisa was wheeled out of the office and felt her heart leaving along with her new client. The doctor realized she was dealing with a woman who had never known the ways of the Lord. Right then and there she lowered her head, whispering a silent prayer for guidance and patience with Lisa. She couldn't blame the woman for her actions if she's never known or been exposed to Christian principles. While Dr. Hopson never tried to force religion on her patients, she considered herself a spiritual doctor as well as a caring psychiatrist. Just from the few minutes she'd spent with Lisa Bradford, Dr. Hopson knew the hurting woman needed Jesus.

Stepping behind her desk, Dr. Hopson turned on her Dell laptop computer and began composing a list of support centers and groups Lisa could join after her release. She made sure to put a few church-based facilities on the list, including the one offered through her small church, New Hope Baptist, on Martin Luther King, Jr. Boulevard. *Maybe, just maybe, she'll choose one of these spiritual groups to start her recovery. I pray so.*

CHAPTER TWENTY THREE
(DR.'S OFFICE 2)

Lisa felt a little better about having a second visit with Dr. Hopson today. Yesterday, the doctor had made her feel very comfortable, and Lisa was surprised at how she'd opened up with the woman enough to talk about her childhood memories. Although she didn't have any expectations as far as psychotherapy was concerned, it really felt good to speak with someone who wasn't being judgmental or preaching to her.

"Hello, Lisa. How are you feeling today?" Dr. Hopson was all smiles as she greeted Lisa wearing a royal blue short sleeved suit while sitting behind her desk.

"Hi, Dr. Hopson. I'm doing well. I've sort of been looking forward to our visit today."

"Oh, that's nice to know. I'm very happy to hear that. Would you like to sit over on the sofa again today? I think you'll be much more relaxed over there," she stated, walking around her desk.

"Yes, that would be fine."

"All right, let's get you over here, and we'll be ready to start our session," she replied, pushing Lisa across the room.

Minutes later, Lisa was lying on the sofa with her ankles crossed, and Dr. Hopson was seated in the armchair beside her. After pressing the record button on the digital recorder, she started their second session.

"Okay, Lisa. I appreciate you sharing some of your childhood with me yesterday. I just need to ask you a few more questions about that, and then we can move on to the more current events in your life."

"Sure, doctor. What else would you like to know?" Lisa asked, turning to face the physician.

"You stated yesterday that your relationship with your parents changed after they divorced. Can you tell me more about how this affected you?"

"I just know my mother became a mean and bitter woman. She hardly spent any time with us anymore. She barely ever laughed or smiled, and she didn't want anything to do with my father or his new wife. Then to make matters worse, my dad stopped coming to visit us because my mom treated him so badly when he did come around. He used to take us over to his house, but after Della became pregnant, those visits soon ended, too. I've never developed a relationship with my half sister and brother. I guess he couldn't support two families, so he made a decision not to spend any money on us either."

"I see. Now tell me about your relationship with your sister, Jenna. How did you two get along together?"

"We got along fine. We weren't really close either, but just sort of tolerated each other. I always thought she was too mild and easygoing. Although she was the older one, she acted younger than me. She became shy and withdrawn, while I became bold and outgoing. I couldn't wait to leave Lake City after I graduated from community college, while she's never had any desire to attend school or leave that boring country town."

"Why do you think you and Jenna are so different when you've basically had the same childhood experiences?"

"I have no idea why she's stupid enough to stay in that hick town with mama. I guess Jenna is just not motivated enough to want more like me."

"Does she live with your mother? Has she ever married or had children?"

"She stayed with mama for about a year after she graduated from high school, then she moved in with her boyfriend. She had two kids with him and then they broke up. Jenna put him out after she caught him cheating with another woman in the apartment she was paying for. Since then, she's had several guys move in and out, but she's never gotten married. Both of her girls are almost grown now and still living with her."

"Do you have a relationship or any type of contact with her daughters?"

"No, not very much. I've only seen them a few times in their lives. I don't go home too often and they never came to visit me in D.C. or Jacksonville."

"Okay, let's move on, Lisa. I'd like to know more about your personal life or your love life, if you will. What type of men are you attracted to?"

Lisa wasn't sure if she was ready to share this part of her life with a stranger. However, she decided that since she probably wouldn't be seeing the nosy doctor again, why not have fun and be completely open with her. So, Lisa spent the remainder of the session telling the psychiatrist about her many failed relationships, beginning with the high school instructor whom she had an affair with for over a year. Then, she relayed her numerous exploits with countless married men whom she'd tried to lure away from their wives, to no avail. Finally, Lisa ended with her most recent fiasco with Hampton Dupree, thinking this would surely surprise the sophisticated woman who had dared to enter her risqué world.

"Lisa, I notice you've been involved with a great deal of married men in your life. In fact, you seem to be the most proud of those relationships. Have you been intentionally trying to date attached men?"

"Well, I hadn't given it much thought, but I think I like the thrill of dating married men. After all, if they were happy with their wives, they wouldn't be sniffing behind me. They're much more attentive and more willing to spend money on me. I would say I've had some of my best experiences with men who were committed to other women," she responded with a sinister smile crossing her lips.

Dr. Hopson leaned forward in her seat, narrowed her eyes, and asked, "Do you think that's normal, Lisa? Do you consider that as appropriate behavior for the average single woman?"

"I've never considered myself average by anyone's standards, Dr. Hopson. I do what pleases me. I do whatever makes me happy, and rich married men know how to make me very happy."

"Have any of these men's wives ever confronted you regarding their husbands?"

"No, I don't think most of them ever found out except for the one in Jacksonville, and she was a religion freak and didn't dare do anything but pour a glass of tea on my white dress when we met for lunch."

"Do you know how she found out about your affair with her husband?"

"I believe she asked Michael about us and then the silly fool confessed and told her everything. So the next day, she invited me to lunch, and she ended up spilling a glass of tea on my dress. I lost my temper and tried to get at her, but the heifer got out of there too fast for me to do anything."

"Have you ever thought about the consequences of dating these men? What if one of their wives decided to do more than this particular wife did?"

Lisa looked at the doctor and shrugged her shoulders. "I don't worry about that happening. They should be worried about confronting their husbands instead of worrying about me. It's not my fault if they want me."

"If these men really want you, Lisa, why hasn't one of them left his wife for you?" Dr. Hopson asked, making direct eye contact with Lisa.

Rising to a sitting position on the sofa, Lisa narrowed her eyes at Dr. Hopson before speaking. "I just haven't found the right one yet, that's all."

Dr. Hopson leaned back in her seat, clasping her hands together. "I hear what you're saying, Lisa. Based on what you've told me today, I believe I'm ready to make a diagnosis for your condition."

"Oh, really, doctor. Just what exactly do you think is wrong with me?" she asked sarcastically.

"I believe you're suffering from a mental condition referred to as a Personality Attachment Disorder, or PAD. This normally occurs when a child has issues separating from one or both parents and ends up attaching themselves to unhealthy relationships. In your case, you were detached from both parents at an early age, which increased your chances of developing this disorder."

"What are you talking about?" Lisa asked, squinting her eyes at the doctor.

"What I'm saying is that you're looking for someone to give you the affection you didn't receive from either of your parents after they separated. So you keep attaching yourself to unavailable men who you think will fill that void in your life. Can you follow my logic?"

"I'm not sure what you're saying, but you may have a point. I just never gave much thought to the fact that I like dating married men."

"It's my goal to help you become aware of your negative behavior and assist you in making appropriate changes to live a more fulfilling life. Now, there are basically three ways that this specific condition is normally treated. I recommend we use a combination of medicine, counseling, and group therapy for an unspecified amount of time. I know you may not be able to see this right now, but your irrational behavior has caused you to take an overdose of an illegal drug." She paused for a second. "I also recommend that you contact NAMI and Narcotics Anonymous."

"What are they, and why do you think they're necessary?"

"The National Alliance for the Mentally Ill is a national organization dedicated to helping people suffering from your type of disorder and other mental illnesses. They have a website where you can read about what services they have to offer, and Narcotics Anonymous is a support group for people who are addicted to narcotics. They also have a website where you can log on to and find out where they have local meetings. What do you think?"

"This is just a lot for me to digest right now," Lisa stated, shaking her head. "There's still one thing that's bothering me, Dr. Hopson."

"Okay, what is that?" she asked, looking directly at Lisa.

"You said that I need medicine. Well, I'm not comfortable taking any more drugs after this episode. What if I become addicted?"

"Well, you'll be taking anti-depressants, and they are not addictive. So you don't have to worry about that. I'll also give you a list of other local support groups you can contact. Hopefully, you'll find one you'll be able to fit into. Is there anything else that you're concerned about?"

"Not right now. I'll give this some thought and get back with you after I'm discharged. I just want to get out of here and back to my life."

"I understand what you're saying, Lisa. I just want you to know that I'm here for you, and I sincerely hope you'll continue your therapy sessions with me. I'm sure I can help you overcome your disorder if you're willing to make a commitment to seeing me at least once a week for the next six months or so. Are you ready for that? Are you ready for a new life?"

Chapter Twenty Four
(June)

Four months later, Lisa had moved back in with her Uncle Johnny and Aunt Oretha. Although it had been a long, hard path, she was walking on her own without the aid of crutches, a walker, a cane, or pain killers. That bad episode with the illegal drugs and spending seventy-two hours in a psyche ward was all Lisa needed to get back on the straight and narrow.

Although she'd tried to track down Cynthia Fountain, the corrupt physical therapist was long gone by the time Lisa came around searching for her. When she called the rehabilitation center asking about Cynthia, she was informed that the well-liked physical therapist had resigned the same day Lisa was checked out of the facility. Then, a trip to Cynthia's apartment proved that she'd moved on to another city. At first, Lisa was determined to hunt the woman down by hiring a private investigator, but after inquiring about the price of such services, she changed her mind. She decided that as long as Cynthia stayed out of her way, they'd both be safe.

Now, Desmond was a different story. Lisa had lain awake many nights, tossing and turning, contemplating the best way to get revenge on him for abandoning her in the hospital. She was still traumatized from the memory of the horror in his eyes when he initially saw her contorted face. That was honestly the one thing about the good doctor she'd never forget—how he'd backed away from her as she lay in a hospital bed suffering from a facial stroke, longing to be held in his arms. And on top of that, he had the audacity to have Lisa evicted from her townhome. Yes, he had to pay for his sins. If only she could come up with the perfect plan for his punishment, all would be well with Lisa. Of course, she was still calling his cell phone occasionally just to see if he'd eventually pick up or had the number changed.

At first, she'd thought about telling his wife, but figured it would be too easy and probably wouldn't hurt him a bit. Chances were, Mrs. Taylor already knew a good-looking successful man like Desmond could never be faithful to one woman. And Lisa was wise enough to know she definitely wasn't the first woman he'd cheated with and neither would she be the last. *Shoot, I wouldn't doubt if he's laying up with somebody right now.*

Then, it crossed Lisa's mind to hire someone to physically harm Desmond. She'd even gone as far as researching sites on the Internet which offered those types of services. It was amazing to Lisa what people would do for the right amount of money. *Maybe they could mess up his face or break his legs just so he'd know how it feels to be disfigured and have people back away from you. Then again, that plan would only work if I had the funds to hire the right criminal for the job. But still, I can dream of Desmond experiencing just one-tenth of the pain I've endured. Somehow, someway, I'm going to make it happen. I can't let him get away with this. No man has ever treated me this badly.*

Of course, Auntie O was driving Lisa crazy with all her spiritual conversations about how Jesus had saved her life and how she should be thanking the Lord for his grace. Just like now, Lisa was trying to watch an episode of "Grey's Anatomy" on television while her aunt carried on about how prayer changes things. *Why do older people always want to talk about Jesus?*

Lisa just smiled and pretended to follow along with her aunt. Then, when Auntie O took a deep breath in between sentences, Lisa came up with a good reason to slip out of the living room. "Auntie, I'm really tired. I'm going to my room for a minute," she stated, rising to her feet. Lisa headed to her bedroom for solitude and laid down for over an hour.

The smell of Oretha's home cooking finally caused Lisa to stir from slumber. Following the aroma to the kitchen, Lisa took a seat at the small round table, wearing a pair of denim shorts and a pink t-shirt. Her aunt stood over the stove checking the tenderness of the chicken with a fork. She stuck the sharp fork into the breast several times before returning the glass pan to the heated oven. Oretha wiped her hands on the yellow printed apron covering up her blue sundress while she spoke to Lisa.

"Yeah, child, I tell you. You have a lot to be thankful for. I prayed for you every night you spent in that hospital bed. I called everybody on my prayer list and asked them to send up some timber. I tell you the truth, God is good. That's why I praise Him in the morning when I rise and every night before I lay my head down, because if I don't wake up the next morning, I want my soul to be with Jesus."

This was more than Lisa could take. She had forced herself to go to the sanctified church with her aunt a few times, but she found it extremely hard to stomach the dancing in the aisle, the loud music, or the speaking in tongues the sisters did when they got happy. She'd never seen folks carry on like that in the few Baptist churches she'd attended. Uncle Johnny normally came up with an excuse not to escort his wife to church on Sunday and so did Lisa. *I've got to get out of here before I suffocate. Can't I just have one day of peace without all the religious talk.*

"Ah, Auntie, I need to go get changed," Lisa stated loud enough for her aunt to hear as she was rising from her seat. "I'm meeting with my psychiatrist today at three, and I need to start getting ready." Lisa had been committed to meeting with Dr. Hopson once a week since her release from the psychiatric ward. She didn't agree with everything the doctor said, but Lisa was beginning to understand more about this Personality Attachment Disorder she supposedly had.

"Child, I told you. You don't need that psychiatrist. All you need is Jesus, baby. If you get on your knees and humble yourself to the Lord, He'll bring you out of darkness into the light. He's the best psychiatrist in the world, do you hear me?"

"Yes, I hear you," Lisa replied, thinking on her feet. "Thanks for fixing me something to eat on your day off," Lisa uttered. Auntie O offered her assistance, but Lisa turned her down stating, "No, you stay here and finish dinner. I can make it to my room alone."

"Are you sure? It's no problem, now."

"I'm sure, Aunt O, I can make it on my own. I'll be back to eat before I leave."

"All right, baby. I'll have this chicken done along with some yellow rice, green beans, and homemade gravy by the time you return." She smiled at Lisa making her way through the kitchen doorway. "I think I might make your uncle a peach cobbler to go along with dinner."

"Yeah, he'll love that, auntie, and so would I," Lisa yelled back.

Oretha watched Lisa's thin body disappear around the corner as she closed her eyes, praying in silence. *Lord, please touch this child and show her that You are the way. She's like a lost babe wandering through the woods. She just needs the direction that only You can give her.*

Lisa returned to her neatly made up bedroom, and eased down on the foot of her bed, pondering what she'd wear to see the doctor today. Looking up at the colorful outfits hanging in her closet, she couldn't make up her mind. Lisa was trying to concentrate on her possible attire when suddenly other thoughts began floating through her mind. The same type of thoughts that she'd had during her hospital stay when she began to think about Jesus and why He'd spared her life. *Maybe there is something to what Auntie is saying after all. I've been through so much in the last six months—maybe God is trying to tell me something.*

CHAPTER TWENTY FIVE
(UNDERSTANDING IS MELLOW)

"Dr. Hopson, I think I finally understand why I always fall in love with married men," Lisa began, using a low solemn voice. She was stretched out on the green, cloth sofa in the doctor's high rise office with her soft hands gently folded over her small chest. The back of her head was relaxed against a foam pillow with her long wavy reddish hair falling about her light freckled face. Lisa's beaming brown eyes were staring up into a fixed place in the ceiling as if she was in a hypnotic trance, visualizing scenes from her childhood that had probably haunted her subconsciousness for most of her forty-two years.

"After my father left my mother when I was four years old, he married another woman a couple of weeks after their divorce was final. My mother, Sadie, became a bitter and cold person while his second wife, Della, shined like an eternal ray of happiness." Lisa paused, swallowing hard. "I can remember being so angry at my father for leaving us. He turned my whole world upside down. Then when he stopped coming to visit us after he had other children, I felt like I wasn't good enough for anyone to love. So I've always imagined, doctor, that if I could get a married man to leave his wife and family for me, then that would prove I was worthy of happiness, too. I thought maybe — just maybe, I would stop falling asleep every night with anger raging inside of me."

With a bewildered expression, Lisa turned to face the sensible psychiatrist she'd come to trust over the past four months, "Do you think that's sick? Am I that crazy, Dr. Hopson?" Lisa asked, refusing to let a single tear fall from her batting eyes.

Taking note of her client's childlike voice, the salt and pepper-haired psychiatrist leaned in closer to Lisa's left ear. Softening her normally serious expression, she curved her rose-painted lips upward, and stated in an honest, straightforward tone, "I've never thought you were crazy, Lisa. You just need to learn how to value yourself without basing your happiness and self-worth on a man, whether he's married or not."

"But how can I do that? You can't teach an old dog new tricks, can you?"

"Well now, I'm glad you asked that question. It just depends on how bad the old dog wants to learn," she replied, adding a light laugh after her statement. Leaning back in her brown cushioned armchair, Dr. Hopson pulled on the lapel of her off-white suit jacket. Relishing the progress her newest client had made in such a short period of time, she pressed her thin lips together. At that very second, one of her favorite sayings drifted through her mind. *God is good all the time and all the time, God is good. There might be some hope for Miss Lisa LaRaye Bradford after all.*

Suddenly, Lisa sat straight up in the sofa, coming out of her self-induced trance. She blinked her teary eyes several times as Dr. Hopson continued. "I've told you from the first day that you entered my office, Lisa; you have to make recovery your number one priority. Anger will eat even the strongest person alive."

"I understand that now, doctor, and all I want to have is a man of my own."

"Well, I don't think you're asking for too much. But, you know, a good man is hard to find. My husband passed away six years ago, and I haven't found anyone who can come close to taking his place."

"Really? How long were you married?" Lisa asked, sounding intrigued. Dr. Hopson had shared very little of her personal life during their weekly sessions. She would ask a few questions during the hour, but she mainly let Lisa talk about her childhood and her negative feelings regarding her parents.

"Oh, I was married for almost thirty years. We were very happy together. My husband and I have two grown children and three grandchildren," she replied cheerfully.

"You were married for thirty years. How did you manage to live with one man for so long?" Lisa asked in amazement.

"It took a lot of energy and innovation to really make it work. We were both very determined to stay together and raise our children as a family. So I know exactly what it feels like to have a man of your own."

"That sounds great, but I can't imagine sleeping with one man for that long," Lisa replied, shaking her head.

Dr. Hopson eased her head back, letting out a slow but hearty laugh. "Well, I've heard that before. All I can do is repeat what I said a minute ago, a good man is hard to find. And a hard man is a very good thing to have."

"Well, all right, Dr. Hopson!" Lisa laughed along with her psychiatrist. She was finally beginning to let go of the anger that had held her hostage for so long. Lisa was proud of the fact that she'd continued her visits with Dr. Hopson. Although the lady was just slightly older than Lisa, she had a wealth of knowledge and great wisdom to go along with her doctoral degree.

"Lisa, you've made a lot of progress in the few months we've been meeting. I'm so happy you decided to continue your therapy with me. Have you checked out any of the support groups from the list I gave you?"

"I've looked at a few of them, but I just haven't been able to make a decision yet. Most of them are church-based, and I've never been much of a churchgoer, you know."

"Well, it's never too late to start. Why don't you just choose a few, make an initial visit, and then make a decision about which one you'd like to attend on a regular basis? I tell you what. I'll write down three right now. I want you to visit at least one of these before our next visit, okay?" Dr. Hopson gave Lisa one of her stern looks. While they had become very comfortable around each other, the doctor knew when to be serious with her client.

"Sure, I think I might be able to do that, if you insist."

"Well, I insist, and I can't wait to see which one you choose," she stated, secretly hoping Lisa would choose her favorite choice on the list, New Hope Baptist Church. They had formed a group, New Outlook on Everything in Life (N.O.E.L.), over three years ago for the mentally ill and depressed. In fact, her nephew, Antwan, was one of the co-founders and the main leader of the eleven member group. Ever since he had that nervous breakdown on his corporate job over three years ago, he'd become one of the strongest local advocates for mental health support groups. Dr. Hopson hoped Lisa would find her way to the New Hope Center and to Antwan because he would take good care of her. She knew her nephew had a kind heart, and he would be able to give Lisa the spiritual guidance she wasn't able to offer as her psychiatrist.

Dr. Hopson wrote down the name of each group along with the location, and a contact telephone number. She quietly escorted Lisa out of her office on a wing and a prayer. That was the best she could do for now.

Chapter Twenty Six
(Lisa Meets Antwan)

Lisa arrived at the traditionally-designed, red brick church almost an hour early. If Dr. Hopson insisted she visit one group this week, this one would have to do. Actually, this was the only place a real person had answered the telephone when she called yesterday to confirm the meeting day and time. The casual male voice with a Caribbean accent had informed her that the group met on Thursdays at 7:00 p.m. in the church's cafeteria area, located in the rear of the church.

As Lisa glanced down at her silver Citizen's watch, she noted it was only a few minutes after six. Looking around the rear parking lot, she noticed there were quite a few cars scattered about. So she decided to go inside, and see what was going on before the meeting officially got started.

Just as Lisa entered the entranceway, she spotted the ladies room to her right and decided to check out her appearance before anyone noticed a stranger in the building. Since she wanted to appear conservative, Lisa chose to wear a white blouse and a medium-length black skirt along with a pair of kitten-heeled, black, cloth mules. She still had her face made-up, only she chose to wear a bronze toned lipstick instead of her usual bold reddish color.

Stepping out of the rest room, Lisa wandered down the hallway toward the sound of voices when she felt someone tapping her right shoulder. Turning around to face the person with a calm-looking face, she surveyed him from head to toe in one quick glance. "Hi, may I help you? Are you looking for someone?" the young male asked, sounding like the Caribbean voice she'd briefly heard yesterday. There was a certain caring tone to his voice she felt, even over the telephone lines. He spoke with the melody of a poet. He wasn't exactly the tall and attractive type she normally went for, but he was adorable in his own way. Lisa could tell he had a strong muscled build from the outline of his shirt, and he was slightly taller than she was with eyes and skin the color of midnight. And the brother smelled like a bottle of fresh cologne, something floral with a woodsy top note. She couldn't identify the scent, but it was very appealing and slightly familiar.

"Hi, I'm Lisa Bradford. I'm here for the N.O.E.L. support group. I called yesterday."

"Oh, it's nice to meet you, Lisa," he said, extending his hand to shake hers. "I'm Antwan Saunders. I'm the one you spoke to yesterday."

"Great! I recognized your voice. I love your accent." *But you're definitely too dark for me.*

"Thank you. I'm from Trinidad. Did you find the place okay?" he asked, with white teeth sparkling against his brown lips, which curved upward into a unique smile.

"Yes, I did, and I know I'm early. I just decided to come on in and have a look around."

"No problem. In fact, I'll be happy to give you a tour of the church while we're waiting for the other members to arrive. I assume you haven't been here before."

"That would be correct."

"Well, this is the reception hall where we'll be meeting tonight," he stated, pointing toward the open doorway.

"Let me show you around, and then we'll come back here. I'll tell you a little bit about the history of the church while we walk around," he said, taking Lisa's forearm. They walked together throughout the huge building as Antwan gave her a guided tour. Lisa indulged herself in the special treatment, hanging on to his every word as he escorted her from one room to another. She'd never heard a voice that sounded as calm and sexy as his. He seemed to be a completely relaxed man who was happy with his smooth brown skin, short kinky hair, and the world around him. Fitting snugly into a pair of neatly pressed Lee jeans, a blue short-sleeved shirt, and brown loafers, Antwan glided across the floor as if he didn't have a care in the world. Lisa silently wondered why this clean cut man, seemingly in his mid-thirties, would be in a recovery group with her.

Lisa couldn't believe she was actually feeling some type of attraction to this unattractive man she'd just met. She definitely had never dated anyone this young or dark-skinned before, yet there was something about the way his eyes glistened when he spoke to her that caused a slight tingling in her lower abdomen. "This is one of the oldest Baptist churches in the city. It was completely renovated about ten years ago when the current pastor came on board. They even added onto the back of the building," he stated, closing the door to the sanctuary. Leading the way down the long corridor, Lisa's eyes followed his graceful movements as she listened in silence to the history of the magnificent church. She hadn't visited many church houses, but this truly surpassed anything she'd ever witnessed. The balcony alone was bigger than most of the small churches Lisa had visited during her childhood.

Finally, they were back at the reception room and now there were at least ten other people of both genders and varying ages in the large room. Although it was a predominately African-American congregation, there were a few Caucasians in the mix. A circle of twelve folding chairs were placed in the center of the cafeteria area. There was a fold-up table covered with a white tablecloth in the back of the room set with refreshments, and a few people congregated around it. Making his way to the center of the room, Antwan clapped his hands to get everyone's attention.

"Good evening, ladies and gentlemen. If you all will take a seat, I'd like to go ahead and start our meeting for this evening."

As the room quieted down and people started moving into the empty seats, Antwan raised his voice again. "We have a visitor with our group tonight. If you all don't mind, let's give Ms. Lisa Bradford a hand clap for joining us tonight."

The room exploded in applause as Lisa walked to the center of the circle to stand beside Antwan. She was already enjoying being the center of attention as she flashed a cute smile and waved a hand in each member's direction. "Lisa, why don't you take a seat by me and let everyone introduce themselves to you?"

Minutes later, Lisa knew something about everyone in the group of four men and seven women who were present, except for Antwan Saunders. He remained seated as he turned to face Lisa, cleared his throat, and then proceeded to speak. "I started this program over three years ago with my good friend, Daphne. She and I were co-workers at Smithdine, Incorporated, for almost ten years when I suffered a nervous breakdown. I was handling over two hundred accounts a month, bringing in over a million dollars a quarter for the company, and my boss was still riding me about doing more. One morning I woke up, and I just couldn't get out of bed. I had lost the use of all of my bodily functions. I thought I was going to literally die when my mother showed up at my house after five o'clock. Thank God, one of my co-workers called her because I didn't show up for work. She knew I'd never called in sick before and became concerned. Well, my mother found me in the middle of my bed crying like a baby. My entire body was shaking. That's when she notified the mental hospital to come and get me.

A few months later, I was well enough to go back to work, but I just didn't have the same zest for working like I'd had before. So about three months later, I quit my job, and founded this group at New Hope Baptist Church with Daphne, who supported me through my horrible ordeal at the mental facility. We decided to name this group New Outlook on Everything in Life, N.O.E.L., because that was exactly what I needed. I needed a new outlook on everything in my life!" Again, the group exploded in applause.

"We started this support group to help depressed people, alcoholics, drug addicts, or anyone else in need of a life-changing experience. It doesn't matter what your problem is because the doors of the church are always open to anyone who will come."

Lisa was amazed at the depth in which Antwan had honestly relayed his story. As all eyes turned to her, she was still mesmerized by the cadence of his soothing masculine voice. Realizing everyone was waiting on her introduction, she forced herself to regain composure. Lisa coughed into her hand several times, stalling for a few more seconds when suddenly the words came to her.

"My name is Lisa Bradford. I was referred here by my psychiatrist. Last month I was admitted to the mental hospital because I took an accidental overdose of pain medicine. You see, I'd been involved in a car accident where both of my legs were broken, and I suffered a mild facial stroke. The pain was so great that I became addicted to the prescription drugs I was using. For the last four months, I've been trying to make it completely on my own without the use of medications, but it's been extremely hard. My psychiatrist felt it was time for me to join a support group so I could share my experiences with other individuals. So I thank you all for letting me visit your group," she said, fiddling with her hands.

"Welcome to our group, Lisa. We're happy you decided to join us this evening," Antwan began. "You could have been anywhere else in the world tonight, but you made a decision to be here with us. Thank you for coming." Antwan flashed a genuine smile at Lisa. He could feel all of the pain pouring out of her thin body. Somehow, he felt there was more behind those beautiful brown eyes than she wanted to let on. When she smiled back at him, his heart started racing with the speed of light. He hadn't felt this type of attraction for anyone since his recovery. Was he ready to share his life again after losing so much?

Lisa only took a few more minutes to share the remainder of her ordeal. It wasn't too hard after hearing what some of the others in the group had been through. She considered herself fortunate by the time she'd heard some of the other stories relating to addiction and depression. One gentleman, Steven, even related how he had contemplated committing suicide after his uncontrollable stint with bipolar disorder. And although Lisa found it hard to relate to him, she did sympathize with his heartache.

The meeting lasted an entire hour. Finally, everyone was ready to pitch in with helping Antwan clean up the facility. Lisa picked up a few cups and dumped them in the garbage at the same time Antwan threw in a few plates. "You don't have to hang around for kitchen duty. We can handle this," he stated.

"I don't mind," Lisa replied.

"Listen, since you're not in a hurry. I would like to talk with you for a few minutes and get to know you a little better," he stated, matter of factly. "I'll be done here in just a second. I'll meet you outside on the bench, okay?"

"Sure, I have a few minutes to spare." Lisa wished immediately that she'd replied differently. *What am I thinking? This guy is definitely not my type. Sure he's decent looking, but he's way too short and dark for me. I hope he doesn't think I'm the least bit interested in him.*

"Good night, Ms. Bradford," Daphne stopped to speak to Lisa as she was leaving the building. "It was a pleasure having you with us tonight." She was slightly taller than Lisa, and looked to be about a size ten or twelve. Daphne wore a cropped "all business" styled haircut with a navy suit and matching pumps.

"Oh, please, call me Lisa and thanks for having me. The pleasure was all mine."

"I hope you'll join us again. I could tell Antwan was delighted to have you with us, too," she stated, eyeing Lisa for a reaction.

"Well, I enjoyed meeting everyone."

"All right. Hopefully, we'll see you again next week now that you know where we are. Have a good evening," Daphne said, before turning to leave.

Minutes later, Antwan joined Lisa on the wooden bench outside once everyone was gone. He sat down, crossed his legs, and smiled at the beautiful vision before him. Antwan had been taken with her freckled face and beaming eyes the second she turned around when he tapped her on the shoulder.

"Ah, this is my favorite time of evening. When the sun is setting like this on a warm clear day, it reminds me of Trinidad."

"How long have you been living in the states?" she asked, crossing her leg in his direction.

"Oh, I've been here now for several years. Are you from Dallas?" he asked, stretching both arms out along the back of the bench.

"No, I was born in Florida. I moved out here in September to visit my family and get a fresh start with my career."

"You moved here in September, and then you had your car accident in November. That means you haven't had much time for working."

"Well, I work for my uncle. I also live with him and his wife. So I'm doing okay."

"That's good. Now tell me, how do you feel about your first meeting?"

"It wasn't exactly what I expected. I'm happy with the way things turned out though."

"I see, and just what did you expect?" he asked, laughing lightly.

"I don't know. I guess I expected to see a bunch of crazy-looking people. Luckily, everyone here tonight looked sane enough."

He laughed even more at that reply. "Oh, so you thought you were going to see a bunch of crazy people, huh?"

"No, no, I didn't say that."

"But that's what you just implied."

"I'm sorry. I didn't mean anything by that comment. I just had reservations about coming here tonight, that's all."

"I can certainly understand that. So how long did you say you've been seeing the psychiatrist?"

"It's been four months, and she's really been a lot of help. If it wasn't for her, I'd probably be back in the hospital or the mental facility. But she's really been patient with me."

"I understand what you're going through. You know, I saw a mental health counselor for almost a year after my bout with depression. My mother was also instrumental in my recovery. She visited with me almost everyday and would never let me feel sorry for myself."

"That's great. What about your friend, Daphne? Was she a lot of help, too?" Lisa didn't know why she asked that question. She didn't care about his relationship with Daphne. Yet, it was too late to take the question back.

Antwan narrowed his eyes at Lisa before answering, "Yes, she was. She has always been a good friend. She and I go way back as co-workers."

"Well, anyway, I need to get going," Lisa stated, rising from her seat, swinging the black purse over her shoulder.

"Why, do you have a husband and kids waiting for you at home?"

"No, it's not that," Lisa replied, laughing at his inquiry. "I'm single with no kids, and that's just the way I like it."

"Oh, really? You mean to tell me you wouldn't like to have a man with two or three kids waiting for you when you get home and maybe a hot meal on the table?"

"Let's just say that — I didn't say all of that."

"I understand. I didn't mean to pry into your life. It's just that you're such an attractive woman. I figured you must be married or at least have a boyfriend."

"Right now, I don't have either one of those, and I'm not looking."

"Wow! You really know how to encourage a guy."

"I didn't mean to shoot you down. I've just decided to work on me for a while."

"Hey, there's certainly nothing wrong with that. I'm not looking for a wife either. I just want to thank you again for joining us tonight." Antwan extended his hand to Lisa for a friendly handshake. "I hope this won't be your last visit with us. Please feel free to join us next week," he said, showing his genuine smile again.

"Oh, thank you all for having me. I'll try to make it back next week," Lisa replied, heading toward her silver Chrysler convertible. *I'll give it some serious consideration. I just can't get too attached to you because you're certainly not the man I'm looking for. I need someone with a lot more money than you have.* Suddenly, Lisa remembered that she'd forgotten to ask one of the most important questions in the book of dating—what do you do for a living?

Oh, well, it doesn't matter, she thought, as she saw him straddling a Harley-Davidson motorcycle in her rearview mirror. *My goodness, he doesn't even have a car.*

Antwan strapped on his safety helmet as he watched Lisa pull out of the parking lot with her convertible top down. She seemed like a nice lady, but he could tell she was carrying more than a nice leather purse on those pretty shoulders. He was used to seeing women like that in the group meetings, and he had successfully avoided them. *Women that beautiful with baggage can only mean trouble. And that's the one thing I'm not looking for.*

Even as those thoughts invaded his mind, Antwan secretly hoped he'd be staring into those lovely eyes again next week. *She'll be back. I'm sure of that.* He gunned the powerful engine, then took off in the opposite direction on his big black Harley.

Antwan loved the feel of the cool wind on his body as all thoughts of Lisa flew from his mind. Besides, he'd made a promise to himself to never date anyone from the group sessions. And that was the one promise he planned to keep regardless of how his heart was fluttering.

Chapter Twenty Seven
(Another Meeting)

Lisa debated all day whether or not she wanted to go back to the N.O.E.L. support group meeting tonight. The storm clouds were rolling in, and she didn't care much for getting her designer clothes wet. Even though the weather channel reported only a forty percent chance of rain, Lisa could feel a change in the atmosphere. Only, she couldn't tell if it was from the impending weather or the apprehension she felt about returning to another group session where she'd come face to face with the alluring Antwan Saunders again.

In the past week, she hadn't been able to get the glowing smile of the dark-skinned man out of her mind. She'd even told Dr. Hopson about the peculiar-looking stranger she'd met at the first meeting. "Well, it sounds like the young man might be interested in you. Why don't you give him a chance?" the doctor had asked.

"I don't know anything about him except that he's one of the co-founders of the group. He might not even be employed for all I know. I mean he gets around on a motorcycle. How much money can he have?"

"Is money the only motivating factor for you, Lisa?"

"Right now, considering how broke I am and the fact that I had to move back in with my uncle and his "preachy" wife, I'd say that money is a very motivating factor."

"Sometimes we have to look for other motivators when dealing with new people. What other personable qualities did you see in him?"

"I noticed he seemed to be very relaxed and comfortable with himself. I admired that."

"Oh, you did? Did you tell him what you thought?"

"No, of course not. We just had a short casual conversation, that's all. I wasn't trying to compliment the man."

"All right, I suggest you go back for at least one more meeting before you write off this group. It sounds like this might be a good venture for you."

"I agree with you. Everyone there was really open with each other. They made me feel very comfortable and normal."

"You are normal, Lisa. You just went through an episode in your life where you needed help to get past it. We've all experienced that at some point. Now, I'm looking forward to seeing you again next week so you can tell me more about Antwan Saunders."

"Okay, I'll see you next week, but I seriously doubt if I'll know anymore about him because he really doesn't interest me," Lisa snapped. She didn't have any intentions of learning more about Antwan. She already knew he wasn't the man she wanted to own, and that was all she needed to know. His genuine smile and smooth chocolate skin wouldn't be able to persuade her to think any different. A man without money wasn't worth dealing with.

Now, she was in her bedroom, removing several designer outfits from her closet, debating about what to wear to the meeting this evening since she had officially decided to go. Although she told herself that she wasn't going because of Antwan, her subconscious body knew better and encouraged her to dress accordingly. So she eased into a form-fitting, pink sundress with a v-neck and draped a printed shawl over her shoulders. Considering her life was almost back to normal, Lisa decided to slip on a pair of pink, high-heeled sandals that she's bought on sale last week at the mall. The gorgeous, wedge-heeled, ankle strapped shoes called her name the second she laid eyes on them in the Macy's store window.

Once she was fully dressed, Lisa checked her make-up in the mirror and spritzed on some of her new favorite designer perfume by Davidoff. Inhaling the smell of the sweet fragrance, she felt like the queen bee leaving the beehive for the evening as she made her way to her vehicle. She decided not to let the top down this evening because she didn't want to mess up her perfectly set reddish curls.

Lisa wasn't as early arriving this week as she had been last week. Neither was she nervous about attending the second meeting. The group members had made her feel comfortable and welcomed, which she appreciated.

"Hi, I see you decided to join us again." Daphne greeted Lisa at the door wearing a huge smile. "I love that dress you have on. That color is perfect on you."

"Thank you, Daphne. You look great this evening, too," Lisa replied, returning her broad smile. She admired the slick, black suit with the extra-long white, collar blouse Daphne wore tonight.

"We're about to get started. I saved you a seat next to me in the circle."

"Really? How did you know that I was coming?" Lisa asked, furrowing her eyebrows.

"Oh, you might say that I just had a feeling you'd be back to join us," she stated, moving her eyes toward Antwan. He'd been checking the door every few seconds looking for Lisa Bradford to walk through. Finally, he exhaled as he caught sight of her walking toward him in a killer pink dress.

Lisa smiled as she approached the sitting Antwan slouched down in his seat. He straightened up as she neared him and returned her warm smile. There was something in his eyes that reflected a caring soul. She didn't know what it was, but he had the most intensive stare she'd ever seen. Lisa took a snapshot of him in her head wearing a beige, linen shirt with a pair of matching pants, and then glanced away from him.

Extending his hand to greet Lisa, he said, "Hello, I'm glad you decided to join us again this evening."

"Thank you," she replied, shaking his hand. Again, Lisa sat beside Antwan as he began the meeting. Taking in his entire presence, she was close enough to smell his scent, the same warm inviting fragrance, which she recalled him wearing last week. Every time he shifted in his seat, she inhaled his masculine aroma which was making it difficult for her to concentrate on what was being said during the hour-long session.

Lisa remained silent during most of the meeting, preferring to play the observatory role. She observed the way Antwan maintained control as the group leader. He made direct eye contact with each speaker. He always had a comment to let each person know how he was familiar with their background and that he cared about them.

"Now, I'd like for everyone in the group to tell me something they have learned tonight. I'll start with Lisa here," he stated, turning to his left.

Lisa wasn't exactly ready to speak, but she managed to conjure up a few words. "Well, I've learned that it's important to share your life experiences with other people," she began, placing her hands in her lap. "No matter what you're going through in life, there are other people in the universe who are having similar problems or emotions. When I first met with my psychiatrist, I didn't think I needed treatment. I thought my life and the way I was living was okay. Now I'm beginning to reevaluate some of the choices I've made. Anyway, I appreciate being here tonight and listening to everyone. I know I haven't done much talking, but I think I've learned a lot about myself from just listening to you all," she said, glancing around the circle of twelve members before her eyes rested upon Antwan's dark pupils. He touched her hand and whispered, "Thank you, Lisa," before moving on to the next member.

CHAPTER TWENTY EIGHT
(THE ICE PRINCESS)

As soon as the group session ended, everyone started saying their good nights and hurrying to the building's back exit. It had been thundering throughout the entire meeting period and any second now, the sky was going to burst wide open and shower them all with summer rain. "Hold on, I have to run to the ladies room. Can you wait for me one minute?" Lisa asked Antwan. He nodded his head, indicating he would wait for her by the exit door.

Darting into the women's bathroom, she handled her private business, and then checked her appearance in the mirror. When she opened the door to see Antwan waiting in the same spot she'd left him, Lisa smiled.

"Oh, thanks for waiting on me. I see everyone has left...," she started saying, right before she tripped on a snag in the carpet and tumbled toward Antwan. Luckily, he reached out his arms and broke her fall.

"Are you all right?" he asked, easing her into his embrace.

"I'm fine, but I think I might have twisted my right ankle a little bit. It's hurting some."

"Here, let me help you to a seat so I can take a look at it." Antwan assisted Lisa in sitting in one of the cushioned folding chairs. Then, he bent down and unsnapped the right ankle strap on her shoe. "Show me where it hurts."

"Right here is aching," Lisa replied, rubbing the outside ankle.

"It doesn't look swollen, but I'll go get a little ice to put on it. Stay here. I'll be right back. Don't move, okay?"

"I'm not going anywhere."

A few moments later, Antwan returned with a small ice pack from the refrigerator freezer. Taking a seat beside Lisa, he gently lifted her smoothly shaven leg onto his lap. Placing the ice against her ankle, he leaned back in his seat. "I think it's all right," she stated, feeling embarrassed. "I'll just take my shoes off and walk to the car. We need to get out of here while the weather is still decent."

"Let's keep the ice on it for a few minutes just to be sure. Why are you wearing heels anyway? Didn't you break both your legs less than a year ago?"

"Yes, I did, but I really missed wearing my high heeled shoes. I figured that I would be okay for a couple of hours, especially since I'd be sitting down at the meeting. Besides, this is a wedge heel; I didn't think it would bother me."

"You women amaze me. You'll risk your health for a pair of high heeled shoes. That's unbelievable."

"Hey, I can't help it if I love the things. My legs are fine. I was ready to give it a try."

"And you see what happened. Your body was not ready for them."

Antwan removed the ice, but he continued massaging her ankle with his tender fingers. Lisa could barely tell he was touching her because his strokes were so light. Since she definitely didn't want to become enchanted with this man, she jerked her leg away from him.

"I think it's fine. Let me see if I can stand on it," she stated, taking off the second shoe so she could stand even on both feet.

"How does that feel? Does it still hurt?" he asked, standing with her.

"No, no, it's fine. I can make it from here. Thanks for the ice and the ankle massage," Lisa said, clutching her shoes in one hand just as the thunder clapped in the sky. "Whoa! It's about to get ugly out there. We better get out of here."

"You're right. Let me grab the keys off the table, and I'll walk with you to your car."

The lightning flashed, lighting up the entire outdoors, and suddenly the rain was thumping against the glass door like a hail storm. "We're too late. We might as well sit back down. Hopefully, it'll slack up in a little bit," Lisa said, walking toward Antwan.

"Well, if I'm going to be stuck in a thunder storm, I couldn't think of a prettier person to be with," Antwan said, using a deep tone.

"If I didn't know any better, I'd think you orchestrated this whole scenario."

"Ha! Ha! I would have if I could have. I think the big guy is just smiling on me this evening. He knew I wasn't ready for you to leave."

"And why weren't you ready for me to leave? You barely know me."

"Ah! Ha! That's just the thing. He knows I want to know you better so He made a way for us to be alone in His house together."

"That's right. I'd almost forgotten we were in a church," Lisa said, taking a look around the abandoned facility.

"This is one of the safest places to be during weather like this. Of course, I wouldn't mind being in here even if the sun was shining outside. I love being in church. What about you?"

"Nah, I'm not much of a churchgoer. I've never spent a lot of time in church."

"I sure have. My parents believed in going to church all the time. My father was a minister in Trinidad, so we went to church three or four times during the week and then we had service most of the day on Sunday. When I was a child, I hated it. But as I became older, I began to enjoy going to service on a regular basis."

"My mom never took us to church unless it was Easter or Christmas."

"You're kidding me. That's almost unbelievable for me."

"Well, it's how I was raised. What do you do for a living, Antwan?" Lisa couldn't think of a better time to change the subject. She surely didn't want to get into a discussion about the church or her family life.

"Ah, I see, you want to change the subject. That's fine. I own a bookstore downtown. It's called the Black Experience Book Shop, and I've been in business for almost three years. After I had my depression episode, I left my corporate job and decided to find a more rewarding career."

"How did you come up with the name for your bookstore?"

"It's something that just came to me from — I don't know where. All I know is that I wanted it to be more than a black bookstore. I wanted it to be a black experience. The name sort of came from that thought. You know, I carry more than just books in the store. I sell cards, gifts, music, and various art works from the local artists."

Lisa was mesmerized by his soothing voice. He was a powerfully strong man with convictions that she could hear in every word he so eloquently spoke. "I like it, although, I'm not much of a reader. I can't remember the last time I actually read a book or a magazine."

"I love to read. I read absolutely everything I can get my hands on. That's why I opened the bookstore. I finally wanted to be able to do some of the things I enjoyed doing. The corporate money wasn't important to me anymore."

That was enough to bring Lisa back to her senses. If a man didn't love money, there was no way he could ever love her. "I think the rain has slacked up enough for me to make it to my car," Lisa stated, looking out past Antwan. "I can put this shawl around me and make a dash for it."

"Was it something I said?" he asked, looking baffled. "I thought we were having a nice conversation here. You haven't told me about your career."

"I just want to get out of here while the rain has slacked up some. It's probably going to get worse later on. Besides, I'm not working in my career right now. I used to be a software designer before I moved here, but I've been working as the night manager at my Uncle Johnny's club and lounge. He needed someone right away, and I needed a job. I haven't been able to find anything in my field, so far, especially since I'm just now getting back up on my feet."

"I understand. It's hard moving to a new city and trying to find employment. The computer software field is very tight right now and most industry positions are on hold due to the political state of this country."

"Right. Anyway, I'm going to try and make it out of here while I can. I might get a little wet, but that's okay."

"Sure, no problem. I'll hold the door for you while you make a run for it. Be careful and don't hurt your ankle again."

"I'll be fine. Thanks again for everything," Lisa said, turning away from Antwan. He held the door open while she raced out into the pouring rain and watched her jump into the silver PT Cruiser. Rewinding their conversation in his head, he tried to remember the exact point where he lost her total attention. *It had to be the reference that I made to the corporate money not being important to me anymore. So that's it. She wants someone with gold. Well,*

I'll just have to see about that. There has to be more to that intelligent mind than the love of money.

CHAPTER TWENTY NINE
(AUGUST)

Almost two months had passed, and Lisa was still attending her group meetings every week. Although she was undoubtedly attracted to Antwan, she'd managed to keep him at bay except for the one evening they'd spent together at the Dallas Museum of Art over two weeks ago. Lisa was hurrying out at the end of a session when Antwan stepped in front of her before she could reach the exit door. "Excuse me, Lisa. I was wondering if you might be interested in going with me tomorrow night to see the Gordon Parks exhibit at the Dallas Museum of Art. It's called "Half Past Autumn." I heard it's a spectacular show. Would you like to go see it?"

"Ah, I've heard about that show. I understand they're supposed to have roughly 130 of his photographs that were produced between 1930 and 1997."

"Oh, so you do like art," he stated, raising one eyebrow in surprise.

"Yeah, I love Gordon Parks. He's a legendary photographer. I've always admired his unique work. I'd thought about going by myself, but since you're asking, the answer is yes. I'd love to go with you."

"Oh, great. I can pick you up around seven if that's okay."

"Yes, that's fine, as long as we take my car."

"Excuse me, why do we have to take your vehicle?"

"It's simply because I don't want to ride on the back of a motorcycle wearing a Vera Wang evening gown."

Antwan laughed at Lisa's declaration. "I would never escort you to a museum on my Harley. I do own a car, you know. I just don't like to drive it everyday."

"All right, then, you have a date. I'll see you tomorrow night around seven o'clock," she said, reaching in her purse for a pen and a sheet of note paper to write her address on.

Lisa was pleasantly surprised when she opened the door the next evening to see Antwan standing there gorgeously dressed in black from head to toe. Since her aunt and uncle were both working that night, she was alone when Antwan rang the doorbell.

Inhaling his masculine scent, Lisa recognized his woodsy cologne this time right away. The bold and luxurious scent of Kenneth Cole's Black was already seducing her as it floated across her nostrils. One thing Lisa had always adored was a good smelling man, and Antwan had just soared to the top of her list with this elegant fragrance.

He was standing there looking regal like an ebony king when she invited him to come in for a minute. "You look magnificent this evening, Lisa. That is a beautiful turquoise dress you're wearing. Is that by Vera Wang?"

"No, it's not. It's an original Cavalli. Are you familiar with him?"

"I'm afraid not. I'm really not into name brand clothes. I normally shop at Sears and J. C. Penney's for my casual wear. I haven't worn a suit and tie since I quit my corporate job, except on Sundays."

Lisa shuddered at the thought of shopping at such common stores. "Have a seat, and I'll be right back."

Antwan sat down on the sofa in front of the 40-inch television which was tuned to the VH-1 video channel.

Vivian Greene was there singing about how she was letting some man go because she was unhappy. By the time the video ended, Lisa was back in the living room and ready to go with a flawlessly made up face.

"Do you actually listen to that type of music all the time?" Antwan asked with raised eyebrows.

"Yes, I love that video station. They play really nice music. Why? What type of music do you listen to?"

"Oh, I mostly listen to gospel or jazz. I like Smokie Norful, Fred Hammond, Vickie Winans, and Helen Baylor. You know, mainly the contemporary gospel singers."

"No, I don't know any of the names you mentioned. Are they gospel or jazz artists?"

"They're all contemporary gospel singers. I have Helen Baylor in my CD player right now. We can listen to some of it on the way to the museum if you don't mind."

"Sure. I'm ready if you are."

By the time they returned home from the exhibition show at the Dallas Museum of Art, Lisa had listened to almost the entire CD by Helen Baylor entitled, "The Live Experience." Every song was captivating from "Helen's Testimony" to "The Sea of Forgetfulness," to "More Than a Friend," and "Look a Little Closer;" they all held her attention. Since they were enclosed in a new Audi, it felt like they were at a concert hall listening to her sing personally to them. Lisa had never heard music so beautiful coming from the nine-speaker Bose system of the multi-disc CD player. The two speakers integrated into the headrest delivered a crisp surround sound within the small space. "I can't believe I've never heard any of those songs. I enjoyed every one of them," Lisa stated, as Antwan helped her out of the low-seated car. She'd honestly enjoyed listening to his music.

"Hey, I'm glad you did. Gospel music is so uplifting to me. When I think about Jesus and how He died for us, nothing gives me more joy than listening to music that praises His name. Have you ever thought about joining the church and giving your life to God, Lisa?" he asked, walking to her front door.

"Who? Me? You're kidding, right? I haven't had much experience with Jesus," she replied, taking out the house key.

"Well, maybe it's time you did. From what you've told me about your past experiences, I know He's been there for you whether you realize it or not."

"Thanks for a wonderful evening, Antwan," she stated, opening the door into the living room. "I had a wonderful time."

"Maybe we could do this again. I mean since you had a good time and all. How would you like to go out with me this weekend?" Antwan asked, stepping inside. He gently closed the door behind him as he stared into Lisa's brown eyes.

"Oh, I have to work at the club. Weekends are really busy, and Uncle Johnny needs the extra help during the night shift. Besides, I'm not ready to start dating again on a regular basis. I was already planning to go see the art exhibit anyway, so this really wasn't like a date to me." Lisa noticed the disappointed look on Antwan's face and tried to soften the blow. "I'm sorry if I've hurt your feelings. I just honestly don't believe we're a good match for each other."

"And why is that? Is it because I'm not rich enough or what, Lisa?"

"I just don't think we're compatible. For one thing, I'm much older than you. I don't normally date younger men."

"I'm thirty-five. You can't be much older than that yourself. And to tell you the truth, I don't care about age."

"Well, I do. Look, I enjoy your company, and I love the group sessions, but I'm not ready for anymore than that. Thanks again for taking me out tonight," she stated,

A Man of My Own   189

stepping around him to open the front door. She held it open as he walked past her into the crisp night air.

Antwan didn't try reasoning with Lisa anymore that evening. Apparently, she had made up her mind that he wasn't the man for her, and she didn't want to be bothered with him. He wished it was that easy for him to let go of the growing feelings he had for her. Antwan didn't have any idea how he could care for someone who was so insensitive to another human being. From now on, he would have to keep his emotions in check whenever he was around Miss Lisa Bradford.

Lisa stood there watching Antwan drive away in his stylish sports car. She'd been more than surprised when he escorted her outside toward the glistening new blue vehicle looking like a rare jewel from the Nile. Peering through the window like she was in a jewelry store, Lisa had checked out the slick Bulgari-designed interior. "Is this your car?" she had asked, giving him a bewildered look. She was impressed with the keyless entry, the push button start, and the retractable hard-top after entering the foreign-made vehicle.

"Yes, it's my car," he replied. "I don't drive it that much because I like the feel of the motorcycle on the road. I've had it for almost a year. I just like to keep it locked up in the garage unless I'm going somewhere special with someone special," he stated, holding the door open for Lisa.

"Oh, I see. I certainly feel special tonight riding in this fabulous car. It's awesome," she responded, admiring the coordinating blue bucket leather seats and the aluminum trim on the door panel. Lisa's backside melted like butter into the soft supple seat cushions.

Entering the car from the driver's side, Antwan said, "I'd prefer to be on my Harley, but since you made it clear that you didn't want to ride on it, I thought you'd be much more comfortable in this."

"And you were absolutely right." They both laughed as he popped in the Helen Baylor CD.

"I have the automatic climate control on, but if you're uncomfortable, I can manually adjust it."

"No, it feels good in here. This is my kind of ride," Lisa said, inhaling the new car scent. "I like the display on your windshield. What is all of that?" she asked, pointing a finger upward.

"It's called a Head's Up Display. It projects the speed, audio information, and other pertinent data on the windshield, allowing me to keep my eyes on the road. It also has a special AudioPilot feature which automatically adjusts the volume to the surrounding noise."

"Um huh, that makes sense. I love all of the unique features you have in this car." Closing her eyes, Lisa leaned back against the firm headrest, concentrating on the inspirational music selection.

"Well, I'm happy that the lady is pleased," he replied, smiling at Lisa as they headed out for the evening.

Now, she was easing the front door open as his rear car lights disappeared from view. *Yes, he's a decent-looking man. Yes, he's an intelligent man. Yes, he's a very mannerable man, but does he have any money?* That was the question Lisa wanted answered. Although he was driving a $75,000 car, she knew that even the poorest black man would buy a flashy ride to impress the women. *And since he's only thirty-five, and never been married, and doesn't have any kids, every single woman in the church must be after him. Why is he interested in me? I certainly haven't done anything to deliberately entice him. Doesn't he know that if I wanted him, I'd have him by now? Oh, well, who cares?*

CHAPTER THIRTY
(I WANT REVENGE)

"Hey, Lisa, give me another Cosmopolitan and a Manhattan Dry for table three, please." Janine, the young waitress rested her elbows on the bar while she waited for Lisa to fix the drinks. She bopped her head to the rhythm of the fast beat coming through the mega sized speakers surrounding the dance floor.

"It's coming right up."

"Girl, it is really jumping in here tonight. What's going on? Is it a full moon or something out there?"

"I don't know, but I hate that the regular bartender didn't show up tonight. I'm going to shoot him if he doesn't show up tomorrow evening. He knows how busy we are on Saturday nights."

"Yeah, that's probably why he didn't show up. The lazy joker is probably somewhere else partying his ugly self away."

"If he's not here tomorrow, he might as well start looking for another job. You know, Uncle Johnny don't play that."

"I know that's right. I mean what good is a bartender if he's not dependable, anyway?"

"Here are your drinks, girlfriend. We'll talk later," Lisa stated, placing two drinks on the black tray. She rolled up the sleeves on her white, long-sleeved, blouse because it was getting hot in there. Wishing she'd worn a short skirt instead of long, black pants, Lisa couldn't remember what she'd been thinking when she got dressed for work tonight. Maybe it was that Antwan guy because she hadn't been able to get his gleaming smile out of her memory bank. And seeing him at the group meetings the last two weeks hadn't helped either. He was still asking her out after each session, though. Of course, she had politely declined. There was no need to deliberately break the poor man's heart since she couldn't use him for sex. Mr. Religion hadn't even tried to kiss her on the one date they did have.

"Sure, I'll be back in a few seconds no doubt," Janine replied, grabbing the tray with both hands. Lisa watched her as she eased her way through the crowd holding the tray above her head. When her eyes returned to the bar, a middle-aged woman wearing a silver, draped-neck dress with a dangling pair of diamond earrings had taken a seat in front of her. Lisa immediately felt a sense of uneasiness as she made direct eye contact with the stranger. Obviously, the lady was alone and full of confidence as she relaxed on her barstool. "Hi, how are you this evening?"

"I'm fine, and how are you?" the stranger replied.

"I'm stretched out, but I'll be all right. What can I get you to drink?" Lisa asked, leaning over the counter. She noticed the huge rock on the lady's left hand ring finger and surmised that she was married to a very wealthy man. Lisa wondered what she was doing on this side of town in a nightclub alone.

"I'll have a screwdriver with an extra shot of vodka," she stated, giving Lisa a sharp stare.

"All right, I'll be right back." Lisa turned her back to the stranger, wondering what her game was as she prepared the drink. She was back in a few minutes and gently sat the glass in front of the mystery woman.

"This is a nice place you have here," she stated, glancing at the dance floor. "Are you the owner?" she asked, returning her attention to Lisa.

"No, I'm the night manager. I'm just helping out at the bar tonight. My Uncle Johnny is the owner. Is this your first time coming here?"

"Oh, I've been here before, but it's been a while."

"I see. Is there anything else I can do for you?"

The lady took a sip of her drink, and then carefully placed it on the counter. "No, I just need a few more of these," she said, pointing to her glass. "I have something heavy on my mind, and I need some alcohol to numb my senses. Do you know what I mean?"

"Yes, I know exactly what you're talking about. I'll be back in a minute when you're done with that one."

Lisa kept watching the wealthy woman from the corner of her eye as she downed drink after drink after drink. Almost an hour later, she had a glazed look in her eyes and was slumping over the bar counter. "Miss, I believe you've had enough to drink this evening. Would you like for me to call you a cab?"

"No, I'm not ready to go yet. I just need someone to talk to for a little bit if you don't mind."

"Hey, that's what bartenders are supposed to do, listen to their customers. I have a few minutes since things seem to be calm for a while. What's on your mind tonight?"

The lady leaned in closer to Lisa as she spoke. "As you can probably tell from this rock on my hand, I'm a married woman. My husband and I have two teenage children, and we've been together for over eighteen years. He's had numerous affairs on me during the entire time we've been together. There's been one hoochie after another trying to take my man. You know, he's a doctor, and every sister in the world wants a doctor for a husband."

"Yeah, you got that right," Lisa chuckled as the woman spoke without slurring a single word. She could tell that the stranger was an old pro at drinking. Anyone else would be falling off that high barstool right now after downing that many double screwdrivers.

"Anyway, I've been able to get every woman who came after him out of the way somehow or another. A few of them left on their own after they found out he was married. But the rest of them had to be helped out of the way," she stated, keeping both eyes peeled on Lisa.

That uneasy feeling in the pit of Lisa's stomach started to deepen. *Why is she suddenly telling me all of this? She doesn't know me from Adam or Eve.*

"What do you mean by that last statement?" Lisa asked, eyeing her suspiciously.

"I haven't killed anyone if that's what you're asking, but I've been responsible for hurting a few, like this one particular heifer for instance. Now she thought that she was about to fix Thanksgiving dinner for my man while I was supposedly out of town with the children. But, I followed her in my car that whole day, and when I got my chance late that evening on a deserted street, I rammed into the back of her car as hard as I could. So I didn't kill her, but both of her legs were broken. The heifer wasn't able to walk for months. Then on top of that, I bribed her physical therapist to turn her stupid self into a drug addict. She ended up being admitted to a mental hospital. How do you like that for revenge?"

Lisa felt the blood boiling in her temples. Her head was aching so badly it felt as though it was about to explode. In fact, it felt like her entire body was being consumed with fire, as if she suddenly died and was entering the gates of hell. She could not believe the woman sitting there grinning in her face was Desmond's wife, and she was solely responsible for making her life a living nightmare for the last eight months. Suddenly, Lisa lost all control of her senses. She released a deep guttural grunt as she lunged for the woman's throat with both hands.

Belinda had already predicted Lisa's heated reaction. Sliding off the barstool, she was in a standing position long before Lisa could reach her. Perched like a lioness in the jungle, Belinda prepared for battle.

Throwing her left leg over the counter, Lisa started trying to climb over the top consumed in anger. She couldn't get to Belinda's narrow behind fast enough. Just as she placed one leg on the counter, Belinda grabbed her long wavy hair and snatched her thin body on over to the other side. Lisa hit the floor with a sharp thump, but she immediately started scrambling to get back up. Belinda stepped over and gave her swift kick in the side with one of her pointed toed shoes. Lisa doubled over in pain, clutched her side, and screamed obscenities.

By this time, everyone in the club was looking in their direction or either clamoring to get out of the front entrance. One of the bouncers had made it to the scene and was helping Lisa up. "Don't touch me! Don't touch me!" Lisa shouted, breaking free from his arms. "I'm going to kill this witch! I'm going to kill her!"

"Bring it on! Bring it on! Let me teach you a lesson about messing with married men! I could have killed your dumb ass a long time ago!" Belinda barked.

Charging at Belinda head first, Lisa's arms were flailing in the air like a windmill in the midst of a windstorm.

"All right, all right, that's enough. Let's break it up over here!" Uncle Johnny shouted, making his way to the center of the brawl. Grabbing Lisa by the waist, he forced his thick body between the two of them, "What the hell is going on up in here? What is this all about?" he asked, looking from a heavily breathing Lisa back to a disheveled patron. "Never mind, never mind, I don't even want to know. Take Lisa back to my office so she can calm down," he shouted to the bouncer.

"I'm not going anywhere!" Lisa tried to break out past her bodyguard, but he grabbed her arms and pulled her to the back of the building where Uncle Johnny's office was located. She was kicking and screaming the whole time and cussing out the onlookers as she was marched past them.

Uncle Johnny had a short conversation with Belinda, and then he escorted her outside to her Land Cruiser. He didn't bother trying to ask her any more questions because he'd heard enough to know this had something to do with his niece messing around with this woman's husband. He knew Lisa was a wild child. He just didn't have any idea she was foolish enough to touch a married man. Apparently, she had made a mortal enemy in this woman, because judging from the insane look in her eyes, she was here to kick butt first and then take names for later. So he tried to get her out of his night club as quietly as he possibly could after a ruckus like that. The last thing he needed tonight was trouble with the police.

***

Almost an hour later, it was after midnight, and the loud music was pumping throughout the club again. Lisa was still in the back office talking with Uncle Johnny as he tried to calm her down with a sensible speech. The only problem was that Lisa wasn't trying to hear anything close to being sane. Although the fire which consumed her earlier had died down, she was still extremely upset with her adversary, Belinda. Just knowing that Belinda had the gall to walk in there with a straight face and tell Lisa how she had deliberately harmed her filled Lisa with a rage like she'd never known before. Then on top of that, the woman had yanked her hair and kicked her in the side. *How could this woman possibly be that bold?*

"Uncle Johnny, thanks for everything. I have to get out of here right now. I can't stay here another minute, or I'm going to suffocate to death. I'm going home. I'll see you in the morning." Lisa winced from the pain in her side, but she had to get out of there right now.

"Make sure you go straight on home. I don't want you getting into anymore trouble tonight. Do you hear me? Don't you go looking for trouble, okay? You better leave that crazy woman alone."

"I'm not going after her. I just need to get out of here and get some fresh air. I'll see you later," she stated firmly, walking briskly toward the door.

As soon as Lisa burst through the exit door of the club filled with increasing rage again, she ran head-on into Antwan. He grabbed Lisa by the forearms and stared her dead in the face. "Are you all right? You don't look too well."

"What — what are you doing here?" she asked, showing her surprise.

"I was coming to see you. Why else would I be here? This is my friend, Randy. We were driving around talking, and I asked him to swing by here so I could see where you worked. Is everything all right?"

"Yeah, I was just leaving for the night. I'm really upset about something and I need to get away from here right now," she stated in a trembling voice.

"Give me your car keys," he demanded, reaching out his hand. "You're too upset to drive. Give me your car keys, and I will take you wherever you want to go."

Lisa didn't argue with him. She reached in her bag, pulled out the key chain, and handed it to Antwan. "Randy, thanks for bringing me over here, man. I'll give you a call tomorrow." Antwan glanced at his friend.

"Okay, I hope everything turns out all right. Don't forget to call me tomorrow," Randy replied, walking toward his car.

It was almost two o'clock in the morning when they made it to Antwan's casually decorated two-story condominium. Lisa felt the spirit of serenity as she entered his humble abode which was tastefully painted in light neutral colors. The strategically hung art pieces throughout the living room area immediately captured her attention. Each painting showcased a particular musical instrument.

Lisa's anger had finally subsided to the point where she could hold an intelligent conversation with the caring man who had rescued her earlier in the evening. Antwan led her to the tobacco-colored, leather sofa, held her hand while she sat down, and offered her a drink. "Would you like a cup of green herbal tea with fresh lemon and local honey?"

"That sounds great. Are you sure it's not too much trouble? I know it's really late," she stated, removing her black shoulder bag. Lisa rested her back against a soft pillow.

"It's no trouble at all. I'll be right back. You just sit here and try to relax. Do you mind if I turn on some soft music?"

"Not at all. It's your place. You can do whatever you want."

"Well, you're my special guest. I wouldn't want to do anything that would disturb you."

"You're so thoughtful. I've never met anyone as kind as you are."

"Thank you. That's the best compliment I've ever received," he replied, picking up the remote control and pointing it toward the stereo on the shelf in front of them. Seconds later, the jazzy saxophone sounds of Kirk Whalum filtered through the speakers. Lisa slid down in her seat and leaned her head back against the cushiony sofa pillow as Antwan fixed two cups of steaming hot green tea with chopped lemons.

"Here's your tea, Lisa. You haven't fallen asleep on me have you?" he was whispering, hoping she was still awake. He wasn't quite ready to say good night yet.

"No, I'm awake. I can finally feel myself calming down."

"Well, this tea should soothe your soul a little bit. Maybe you can tell me why you're so upset when you're finished."

"It's a long story. I don't think you want to hear about my sordid past. I've done things you probably couldn't even imagine that I would do."

"We've all sinned and come short of the glory of God, but we keep trying to be more like Him everyday."

"That's easier said than done. You're just the perfect man."

"Oh, no, let's not go there. I simply mean that I'm trying to be more like Jesus. I'm a long ways from being perfect by any standards."

"You do all the right things like going to church, and praying, and treating people right. You're the first man who has ever treated me decent."

"You deserve to be treated like a princess," he said, lowering his voice, staring into Lisa's eyes.

"My father used to tell me that all the time. He told me I was a princess and someday my prince would come along. It was a beautiful fairytale."

"Why does it have to be a fairytale? Why can't it be reality?"

"Because I always fall for the wrong man. I always fall for the man who doesn't want me or the one who already has someone."

"Really, and why is that?"

"I think it has something to do with my father leaving his family for another woman when I was a little girl. I'm working on it with my psychiatrist. You're beginning to sound just like her with all these questions."

"I'm just trying to understand the woman behind the enchanting face. I want to know everything about you, Lisa. I want to know about all of your secrets. You can tell me anything and everything. I don't care about any deed you've done in the past because I can feel your heart. I sense that you could be a better person if you just believe it's possible."

Lisa hesitated, giving careful consideration to Antwan's statement. Thoughts of Desmond flooded her mind, and then the image of his wife standing over her at the club tonight flashed in her head. Lisa could feel the anger rising from the pit of her stomach again. No woman had ever intentionally hurt her so badly and she wanted revenge. She needed revenge.

"Oh, I could just kill her! I want to kill that woman!" Lisa clutched her fist together in front of her chest as she ranted and raved about harming Belinda.

"Who are you so upset with? Please tell me what happened at the club before I got there."

"This crazy woman came in there and told me that she was responsible for my car accident because I was sleeping with her husband, Dr. Desmond Taylor." Lisa relayed the details of what Belinda had admitted regarding her accident in November, the day before Thanksgiving.

"Now do you see why I want to seriously hurt her for all the pain she's caused me? I can't let her get away with this. I'm not going to let her walk away from this scot-free, Antwan. I can't do it." Lisa was pacing the floor as she spoke, glancing back and forth at Antwan's startled expression. "Now you know why I didn't want to tell you about all of this. I knew you'd react this way. Listen, I've slept with a lot of married men, but I've never had any of their wives come after me like this." Lisa took a deep breath, contemplating whether or not to share more drama about her life with Antwan. Then, she figured, why not? *I'll just go ahead and purge my soul with him. I need to get it all out of my system. I'm not interested in having a physical relationship with him anyway, so I might as well tell him everything and be done with. Maybe then he'll leave me alone and let me go on about my merry business once he sees me for who I really am. I'm a cold, conniving witch who'll eat him for breakfast.*

Lisa spent the next several minutes telling Antwan about the life she'd lived in D. C. and Jacksonville. She even told him about most of the married men whom she'd dated over the years and how she'd tried to pry them away from their families. Finally, she shared why she fled from Jacksonville with criminal charges pending against her.

"I met Desmond shortly after moving here. He wined me and dined me for a short period of time. He moved me into a nice townhouse and made sure I was well taken care of. But after my car accident, I had a stroke while I was in the hospital and suddenly, he stopped coming to see me. He was there the morning when I woke up with my face all twisted. I'll never forget the horror in his eyes and the way he backed out of that room like I was a monster. Anyway, his wife said she followed me all day. Then, she rammed her car into the back end of mine which resulted in me going to the hospital with two broken legs. Now I have to do something to get revenge on both of them. It's bad enough I let him get away all these months with treating me like a dime-store whore. Now, his wife wants to do even more damage. No, no, I won't let this go. You can understand that can't you?" she asked, waiting for Antwan's approval.

"No, I can't," he stated, almost whispering. "I can't understand you wanting to get revenge on this woman or her husband. Don't you know that God is the only one who can truly get revenge on a person? If someone has wronged you, then turn it over to God and let Him take care of them. Believe me, there's nothing you can do to an evil person compared to what He can do."

"I'm tired of hearing about your God. Your God allowed that crazy woman to almost kill me!"

"That's right, Lisa, you were almost killed! But where are you today? Who do you think has brought you this far?"

"I don't know. I just know I want her to pay for what she's done to me."

"Then tell the police and let them investigate the case. She had to get her car repaired somewhere. They'll be able to trace that and build a case against her."

"Oh, please! I don't trust the crooked police to do anything. She is filthy rich. They'll believe anything she says."

"The law doesn't work that way."

"Just stop! You don't need to tell me how the law works! I'm the one with felony charges pending if I ever return to Jacksonville or D.C. What if that comes out during their investigation? What type of case will I have then?"

Antwan couldn't respond because he didn't know how to respond. Regardless of everything she'd just shared with him, he felt like she needed him even more now and he wouldn't let her down. He wouldn't walk out on her like all the other men had done in her life. *All she needs is a man of her own.*

"Look, I'm out of here!" Lisa grabbed her purse, rolled her eyes, and stomped toward the front door. "I don't know what made me think that you'd understand with all your Christian ways!"

Just as she reached out for the doorknob, Antwan came up behind her and wrapped both his arms around her body. Burying his face into the back of her head, he cried, "I'm not letting you leave like this. I'm not letting you leave here with this much anger. You have to trust me, Lisa, and listen to me, please. Just sit down and listen to me for a minute, then I'll take you wherever you want to go. I promise."

Exhaling, Lisa turned around to face Antwan. She'd never seen so much compassion in a man's eyes before as she held his penetrating stare. Several seconds passed. Lisa lowered her eyes as she walked back toward the sofa. Sliding into the soft cushion, she looked up at Antwan and waited for him to say something. "Stay right here, and I'll be right back. Don't move, okay?" Lisa just nodded her head, indicating she would do as he asked.

Antwan returned less than a minute later with a black Bible in his hands. Lisa gave him an exhausted look and asked, "What are you going to do with that? I don't need you preaching to me tonight."

"I don't have any intentions of preaching to you. I simply want to read you a few comforting Scriptures from the Bible. You see, the Bible teaches us that times like these will come and we have to pray our way through a situation before we can come out of a situation. Just sit back and try to concentrate on the passages I'm about to read to you. I promise you that nothing in God's Word will ever hurt you, Lisa. Do you trust me?" He stared into her brown eyes, waiting for her to respond.

"Yeah, I trust you," she whispered, barely audible.

"Then, please, relax and listen," he stated, sitting down beside her on the left edge of the sofa. Lisa relaxed her shoulder muscles and leaned her head over on his right shoulder. Antwan thumbed through the Bible searching for the appropriate text, hoping and praying that it would provide Lisa with the guidance she desperately needed. "The only emotion that can overcome evil is love, and this is what the good book tells us about loving others from Matthew 5:44-46: But I say to you, love your enemies, bless those who curse you, do good to those who hate you, and pray for those who spitefully use you and persecute you, that you may be sons of your Father in heaven; for He makes His sun rise on the evil and on the good, and sends rain on the just and on the unjust. For if you love those who love you, what reward have you?"

"Here's another passage from Deuteronomy 6:5-7: You shall love the Lord your God with all your heart, with all your soul, and with all your strength. And these words which I command you today shall be in your heart. You shall teach them diligently to your children, and shall talk of them when you sit in your house, when you walk by the way, when you lie down, and when you rise up." He looked at Lisa to see if she was still awake and she was, even though her eyes were closed. She was meditating on the soothing sound of his melodic voice as he carefully enunciated each word he spoke.

"Let me read you one more, and I'll let you get some sleep, okay?"

"Umh, don't worry about me. I could listen to you read all night."

"This passage here is my favorite one in the Bible from 1 Corinthians 13:4-8: Love suffers long and is kind; love does not envy; love does not parade itself, is not puffed up; does not behave rudely, does not seek its own, is not provoked, thinks no evil; does not rejoice in iniquity, but rejoices in the truth; bears all things, believes all things, hopes all things, endures all things. Love never fails."

"Those are the most incredible words I have ever heard. Do you read the Bible all the time?"

"Yes, I read this book almost everyday. It helps keep me calm. It helps keep me centered whenever I get caught up in the ways of the world." Lisa stared at Antwan in disbelief. She'd never had anyone to take the time to read Bible verses to her; not her mother, not her father, nor any of her other relatives, and she'd never seen any of the married brothers she'd dated over the years so much as pick up a book let alone read the Bible.

"You know, everyone comes into our lives for a reason. Some people are only meant to last for a season while others are meant to stay forever," he stated tenderly. "I hope you'll keep me around forever." Lisa didn't reply, she just stared into those deep eyes staring back at her as one single tear trickled down her cheek. Antwan cupped her face in his hands, and wiped the tear away with his thumb. "Lisa, I'm begging you. Don't try seeking revenge. Just turn it over to Jesus and let Him work it out for you."

As those words crossed his smooth lips, Lisa instantly released her pain, opening up the floodgate to a sea of tears. Antwan held her tightly in his loving arms until her body ceased shaking and her cries could no longer be heard. When he looked up a few minutes later, Lisa was snoring lightly on his chest, and the sun was rising over her shoulder. He silently thanked God for keeping them both safe through the night. *Thank you Father for your love and mercy. Please show us Thy ways and keep us safe from the evil one. In Jesus' name, I pray. Amen.*

Antwan continued holding on to Lisa, admiring her beauty as she slept, and smoothing her frizzy hair away from his face. She wasn't exactly the woman he thought he'd end up with. She wasn't the Christian-hearted individual he'd asked God to send him. But she had to be in his life for a reason, and he was willing to wait patiently on the Lord to find out exactly what that reason was. After all, the way his heart was beating against hers at this second, he didn't have a choice.

CHAPTER THIRTY ONE
(BAD NEWS)

Lisa woke up the next morning and glanced at the clock on the wall. She blinked her eyes, and then looked up at it again. She couldn't believe it was already past twelve o'clock. It took her several seconds to gain her bearings and realize where she was. Lisa's face was so close to Antwan's she could hear him breathing softly in her left ear. Feeling the moistness on his shirt where she had drooled on him during the night, she gently raised her head, and cautiously eased her body into an upright position. Moving her head from side to side, suddenly all of the events from the previous night came flowing back to Lisa's mind in living color. She frowned as scenes from the club last night invaded her consciousness.

Eventually, the frown was easily replaced with a slight smile when she recalled coming home with Antwan, and how he'd read those amazing Bible verses to her. Wishing she could recall some of the words, her eyes wandered to the black book resting on the coffee table in front of her. Judging from the tattered looking Bible, he'd had it with him for sometime.

Stretching out her hand, Lisa reached for the book she'd never opened even once before in her life. *How can I be over forty-years-old and never read a Bible in my life?*

Where do I start? I don't even know what the first chapter is in this book.

"Good morning." Lisa turned around sharply at the sound of Antwan's deep voice. He stretched both hands above his head, releasing a yawn.

"Ah, I believe the morning has passed already," Lisa replied chuckling. She pointed to the clock hanging above their heads. "I was just about to have another look at your Bible this morning, if you don't mind."

"No, why would I mind you reading my Bible? God's word is for everyone."

"Even a poor sinner like me?"

"Yes, my dear, especially for a poor sinner like you," Antwan stated, smiling into Lisa's eyes. She admired the way he had chosen not to preach to her last night because that was the last thing she needed to hear. Lisa heard enough of that everyday at home from her Aunt Oretha. Her aunt walked around the house day after day preaching to her about the demons walking the earth and she was tired of hearing that sermon. Anyway, Antwan had done the most romantic thing any man had ever done for her—he shared the precious words of God with her even after she told him about most of her evil past. *He has to be really special to do something like that for me. But is he special enough?*

"I'm going to go wash up," Antwan stated, rising to his feet. "Then, I'll fix us a little something to eat. How would you like a submarine sandwich? I should be able to pull that together in a heartbeat."

"Anything sounds good to me right now," Lisa replied, rubbing her stomach. She couldn't remember the last time she'd actually eaten anything substantial.

Lisa was about to sit down at the table with Antwan to eat half of the huge sandwich he'd prepared when she heard her cellular phone ringing in her handbag across the room. Making a dash for the sofa, she darted pass

Antwan to retrieve the instrument. "Hello, Uncle Johnny. How are you... Yes, I'm fine. What's going on?... When did that happen?... Are you sure? I'm on my way. I'll be home in twenty minutes." Lisa closed her flip styled phone, turned to face Antwan and said, "I've got to get home. My mother just died."

Antwan drove Lisa directly to Uncle Johnny's house. They were both quiet for most of the car ride over there. Antwan wanted to leave Lisa alone with her thoughts and memories because he knew how it felt to lose a blood relative. Regardless of how emotionally distant they'd become, the deceased woman was still Lisa's mother and that had to cause her some pain. Even though Lisa was still having her weekly sessions with Dr. Hopson, she wasn't ready to face the reality of suddenly losing her mother to a massive heart attack this morning.

As soon as the blue sports car pulled up to the curb and stopped, Lisa turned to face Antwan. "Thank you for last night. I appreciate you helping me like you did. I know you're a good man, and you'll make someone an excellent husband someday, but you're not the man for me. I'll have Uncle Johnny to bring me by later to pick up my car, but we don't need to see each other again."

"Wait a minute, Lisa. Let me say something, please."

"No, just let me finish," she stated, cutting him off, raising one hand in the air. "I wouldn't be any good for you. I don't know how to love you the way you deserve to be loved. I would only end up hurting you in the end because we have different values. Please, please leave me alone from now on. I don't want to see you anymore, all right. I need a man who can provide for me the way I want, not someone who's barely getting by working at a bookstore. Now, just go on about your life and forget about me because not even Jesus can help me." With that said Lisa bolted out of the car, slammed the door, and ran up the walkway toward the front door to her residence without glancing back even once.

Antwan sat there in total shock. Just when he thought they were making some progress toward having a meaningful relationship, she cut him off completely without any warning signs. *Maybe she's only trying to deal with the death of her mother the best way she can by striking out at me. I'll just have to be patient and give her the space and time she needs to grieve in her own way.*

CHAPTER THIRTY TWO
(REVELATIONS)

Lisa's dark Chanel shades shielded her eyes from the afternoon sun as she walked out of the small country church in Lake City where her mother's funeral was held. Only a few people in the community of less than ten thousand residents showed up for the short service and Lisa was thankful for that. She didn't feel up to smiling and shaking a lot of strange hands after the ceremony. She'd left the small town right after graduating from community college and didn't remember half of the people who were there offering their condolences, anyway.

Stepping out into the bright afternoon sunshine, Lisa held on to her older sister's hand. Jenna had put on a few pounds since Lisa left Florida, and chopped off most of her long wavy brown hair, but her sobering personality remained intact. They both wore short sleeved black Donna Karan dresses because of the scorching summer heat. Jenna was still clutching a wet white handkerchief with her other hand as they slid into the back seat of Uncle Johnny's Lincoln Town Car with Aunt Oretha already strapped into the front seat.

Lisa and Jenna sat there staring out the back window as Uncle Johnny shook hands with their father, James Bradford, a man neither one of them had seen in over twenty years. Lisa was even surprised he'd shown up at the funeral at all, dressed in a double breasted black pinstriped suit. He was still an attractive looking man for his age. His face barely held any wrinkles. If it wasn't for his graying hair, he'd pass for a much younger man. At first, Lisa was elated to see her biological father, but those feelings subsided with the lukewarm greeting she received from him. So Lisa said forget him and clung to her Uncle Johnny's arm during most of the ceremony.

Lisa noticed her stepmother, Della, didn't seem to be quite as happy as she was the last time they'd been together. She was dressed in a dark purple suit with sequins down the front of each side with a pair of high heeled pumps and a clutch purse to match. Della smiled and hugged Lisa tightly, but she didn't seem to have the spark of happiness in her eyes Lisa had remembered envying as a child. Although she was still about a size eight, Della had dark circles under her eyes that she'd tried to cover up with the wrong shade of concealer. In fact, Lisa detected a hint of sadness in her stepmother's face as they stared at each other for several seconds.

"I'm really sorry about your mother. I've always regretted hurting her and losing her as a friend, but I was young and foolish then. Anyway, it's just so good to see you and your sister, again," she stated, embracing Lisa with both arms.

"Thank you, Miss Della. I appreciate that," Lisa replied, returning her hug. They both stepped back to get a better look at each other while they remained holding hands. Lisa replayed that scene in her head several times as she continued thinking about the funeral.

While Jenna was shedding crocodile tears over Sadie's stiff body, Lisa couldn't even will herself to fake a cry. She just stared off into nothingness as the preacher said a few words over the woman who gave birth to her. The only time Lisa was really moved was when the choir sang, "Walk with Me, Lord." She remembered hearing the song as a child during one of the few times she'd ever attended service with her mother. Lisa thought it was odd that she recalled hearing the tune.

"I'm just glad it's over with. I hate funerals," Jenna stated between sniffles. "You know mama loved us, right?" she asked, staring into Lisa's clear brown eyes.

"I know she tried to love us the best she could. But sometimes our best is not good enough," Lisa stated stiffly with a straight face.

"She never got over Daddy leaving us for another woman. She tried to make us tough so we'd never experience that kind of pain. I know that she loved us."

Lisa dropped her head for a second before replying. "You're right. It's so difficult when I think about how bitter and sad she was all the time. Even when the men were around while she was laughing and having a good time, she never seemed to be really happy."

"No, she didn't. She lived the last thirty-eight years of her life in bitterness over a man she'd once loved and couldn't have. Mama met several good men after daddy left who wanted to marry her, but she wouldn't allow her heart to love again. So she died alone with pure sadness in her eyes and a whiskey sour in her hand."

Lisa shook her head at the thought of her mother sitting alone in a hot room with the curtains pulled, drinking her poor self to death. Then, it suddenly hit Lisa like a sharp clap of thunder lighting up the night sky that she'd been doing the same thing all of her adult life. She'd been searching for the love she could never have because she'd lost the love of the one man she really wanted, her father. While her father had moved on with his life and supposedly found joy with another woman, she and her mother had both subconsciously resolved to live the rest of their lives in misery and bitterness.

Thinking back to her college years, Lisa couldn't remember dating an unmarried man since then. After leaving Michael Wayne in Jacksonville, she'd hungered for wealthy, married men who were willing to have a kept mistress. She was hoping that one of her affluent suitors would leave his wife for her and prove that she was deserving of love. This was confirmation that she had been a foolish woman, just like Sadie.

Lisa decided right then and there that she didn't want to die alone and unloved like her mother had. She still had time to find a man of her own who would love her and cherish her for the woman she finally wanted to become. Lisa wanted to be a whole woman with an honest to goodness man who wasn't afraid to love her wholeheartedly. *Antwan could be the man for me. Is it too late? Have I ruined my last chance at love with a man who cares for me? Oh, God, don't let it be too late. I need a man of my own.*

CHAPTER THIRTY THREE
(AN ULTIMATUM)

Belinda drove herself home after confronting Lisa at the club that Saturday night. After checking Desmond's private cell phone line and realizing that the witch was still trying to reach her husband, Belinda had decided to put an end to the drama. She'd already had a couple more shots before leaving the house, so Belinda definitely had the courage for confronting Lisa at the nightclub.

When she entered the dark house and realized Desmond wasn't there, she made it to the bar and poured herself a couple of more screwdrivers minus the orange juice. Pacing the floor while waiting for Desmond to arrive, she felt like a hopeless fool in love. Belinda felt like she had sunk to an all time low by confronting her husband's mistress at some low-class bar and lounge. She was too doggone old to be fighting in bars over a man who had already moved on to the next whore. *It's time for this crap to end and it's going to end tonight. Either he straightens up and flies right or I'm taking all of his filthy money and leaving him. I can't take this anymore.*

Belinda lifted her head after she heard the front door slam shut. She'd fallen asleep on the sofa with an empty vodka bottle in her hand. She sat up in her seat and tried to fix her silver dress before Desmond made it into the living room. "Belinda, what are you doing up? It's almost three o'clock in the morning? My God, are you drunk?" he asked, furrowing his eyebrows.

"No, I'm not drunk. I'm just slightly intoxicated," she laughed, noticing his dark brown Armani shirt and slacks were both wrinkled.

"Slightly intoxicated my butt! You're sloppy drunk, woman. I will not have my wife conducting herself in this manner. Where on earth have you been? Don't tell me that you were out in this condition?"

"Yeah, I've been out. I've been out trying to kick your girlfriend's face in."

"Woman, you have lost your mind. Take your drunk self on to bed, please."

"I saw your old girlfriend, Lisa Bradford, tonight," she blurted out.

Desmond turned to face Belinda with rage in his green eyes as they became darker. "What in the world do you know about my relationship with Lisa Bradford?"

"I know you screwed her in my house. I found her nasty drawers in the dirty clothes to prove it. How about that for starters?"

"I don't know what you're talking about. Lisa has never been to this house."

"Whatever, Dez. I just know I'm sick and tired of chasing away your other women. I can't live like this anymore. Either you stop running around and cheating on me or I'm divorcing you, and it won't be a pleasant experience," she boasted, standing up.

"You can leave if you want to. But believe me, your money hungry butt won't get one red cent of my money."

"Oh, you want to bet? Why don't you have a look in the safe behind that expensive picture you have hanging on the wall."

"I don't have time for playing games with you, B. Now why don't we just go to bed and talk about this in the morning when you're sober."

"No, no, why don't we get this over with tonight," she insisted, pointing to the picture on the wall. "Just check my safe box that I left open for you, and tell me whether or not you really want a divorce."

Desmond casually walked over and removed the $20,000 antique painting he purchased at an auction last year, and removed Belinda's deposit box, which was sitting right beside his. Pulling out one large envelope after another with a former mistress's name labeled on each one, his mouth dropped opened once he reviewed the contents of each one. This was astonishing to him, Belinda had undeniable proof that he'd been with at least nine other women during the entire eighteen years of their marriage.

"What is this supposed to mean?" he asked, trying to sound calm while the blood raced to his head.

"It means that if you don't stop chasing cats, I'm going to sue your rich dog ass for every penny you've got for putting me through this craziness. I mean it, Dez, your whole family is going to know what type of life you've led."

"Woman, please. Do you think my family gives a hoot about who I sleep with? My own father would probably pat me on the back," he bragged, looking over at her.

"Well, that may be true, but I doubt if the judge will be standing in line to shake your hand," she stated firmly with hands folded across her chest. "Now, you need to end this affair with your new girlfriend tomorrow. And if I find out you're fooling with anyone else after this, it's over. Let me show you how serious I am," she huffed, heading to the safe. Belinda pulled out another large unmarked envelope and pulled out a long document. "You see here, my attorney has the original files from each folder, and she's already drawn up the divorce papers. Here, take a look for yourself," she stated, throwing the papers at him.

Desmond thought Belinda had lost her natural mind to be speaking to him this way. *She's got to be on something stronger than liquor. Doesn't she know I could choke her to death with one hand?*

After silently reading the divorce decree, Desmond let the papers slip through his fingers. Belinda wasn't the blind fool he thought she'd been for the last eighteen years. She had crossed all the t's and dotted all the i's on this one. There was nothing for him to do except release the deeply held breath he'd been holding longer than he needed to. She had him over a barrel of fire if he wanted to keep a dollar of his money along with a shred of dignity. He knew his wife was smart, but he'd never figured her to be this business savvy.

"All right, B. I'll play it your way," he relented, walking toward the master bedroom. He knew there wasn't any point in arguing with her any further until he could get a copy of those papers to his attorney.

Even though Desmond was livid with his spouse at first, he secretly admired the strong woman he was walking away from. She'd finally found enough backbone to stand up to the grizzly bear he'd become. With a sinister smile creeping across his thin lips, he thought, *Maybe we do have a chance if she keeps up this determined attitude and shows me some decent loving.*

"So are you saying you're going to change, Desmond?" Belinda asked, stepping into the bedroom behind him.

He turned to face Belinda's gaze. He saw a shadow of the young beautiful woman he'd halfway loved in college and then decided to marry over all the others who were vying for his attention. *What was it that had made me choose her?*

"I'm saying that I'm willing to try and make this marriage work if you are, B," he stated, staring deeply into her soul. "If you'll give me another chance, I'll be good to you."

"Oh, Dez, that's all that I've ever wanted to hear," she whispered, drawing closer to him.

Desmond's mouth consumed hers in a devastating kiss. Belinda melted into his arms as she returned the urgency of his fiery tongue. Naturally their bodies blended together against each other's familiar curves as they began tearing at each other's clothes. Within minutes, they were making passionate love like they hadn't been together in months. Peering into Belinda's pleasure filled-face, he was wondering if he would actually be able to keep his promise to her. She smiled up at him, hoping her husband had finally come to his senses.

CHAPTER THIRTY FOUR
(RETURNING HOME)

It was a long twelve hour ride back from Florida to Texas in the back seat of Uncle Johnny's car on a Friday evening. They had left Florida before day that morning just so they could make it home before the setting sun. While her uncle and aunt took turns driving on the interstate, Lisa spent most of her time sleeping in the back seat and dreaming about how she was going to claim Antwan as her own man. After the way she'd treated him before leaving, it wouldn't surprise Lisa if he didn't ever want to see her freckled face again. She had a man ready to love her in spite of her sordid past, and she'd done everything in her power to push him in the opposite direction. Now she would have to beg his forgiveness to get back into his good graces, if it wasn't too late already.

The second the car stopped in the driveway, Lisa bolted through the back door, and jumped into her shiny PT Cruiser wearing a pair of white shorts with a pink tank top, and a pair of white flat heeled sandals. Her loose, wavy hair was all over her head, but at this point, Lisa really didn't care about her tired looking appearance; she just wanted to see if Antwan still cared about her.

Taking out her cell phone, Lisa punched in the numbers to Antwan's bookstore as she headed toward downtown. A female voice picked up on the third ring.

"Good afternoon, this is the Black Experience Bookstore. How may I help you?"

"Hi, I'm looking for Antwan Saunders. Is he available, please?"

"No, ma'am, I'm sorry, but he had to go out of town for a few days for a book fair in Houston this weekend. He won't be back until Monday morning."

"Well, do you have a number where I can contact him there? I really need to speak with him, please."

"I can give you his cell phone number if you don't have it," she replied.

"That would be great!" Lisa exclaimed, memorizing the digits as the sales lady called them out to her. Dialing his cell number, Lisa anxiously waited for him to answer. After the sixth ring, Antwan's voice mail came on instructing her to leave a detailed message, which she did.

Turning the car around, Lisa headed back home, sadly disappointed she wouldn't see Antwan until Monday. Hopefully, he would return her call in a few minutes, and she'd be able to explain her feelings to him.

She was so hyped up about speaking with Antwan that she decided to go shopping instead of heading back home to wait by the telephone. Making sure her cellular phone was set to a high ring tone, she eased it back inside her handbag. Lisa was in search of a special gift for him, one that would show Antwan how much she had been thinking about him and sincerely appreciated how kind he'd been to her. Based on what she'd learned about him over the last couple of months, she knew Antwan was a sensible, level-headed guy who wouldn't care for anything expensive or overbearing.

Leisurely walking through the mall, Lisa came upon a "Things Remembered" store, and decided to stroll around inside for a personalized gift. A warm smile crossed her lips when she caught sight of a miniature metal sculpture of a gallant knight painted in flashing silver with golden highlights. Lisa thought it would be the perfect present to show Antwan that he was indeed her "knight in shining armor." The miniature figure was the picture of medieval nobility garbed in a full suit of armor, which vividly reminded Lisa of Antwan's many outstanding assets.

"You must have a special man in your life," the sales lady commented while ringing up Lisa's gift for Antwan. She glanced up into Lisa's smiling face for only a second.

"Let's just say that I'm hoping things will turn out that way."

***

It was after midnight and Antwan still hadn't returned even one of Lisa's three messages. She needed something to occupy her time because sleep would be a mystery for her tonight since she was worried about Antwan. Feeling like she'd lost her last chance at love, Lisa slumped down in her bed and imagined Antwan sleeping soundly in some hotel room in Houston. That's when Lisa began to see visions of him in that same hotel room with a young sexy woman on top of him winking an eye at her.

I've got to get up from here and stop this nonsense. I need someone to talk to. Lisa pulled on a pink housecoat, opened her bedroom door, and walked to the living room where she could barely hear the television program Aunt O was watching. Just as she entered the doorway, Aunt Oretha looked up at her. "Hey, baby, are you all right?"

"Yes, Auntie, I'm fine. What are you doing still up? You can't sleep either?"

"No, I couldn't rest for nothing. I decided to come out here and prop my feet up for a spell. Are you sure that you're okay?" she asked, keeping her eyes on Lisa's face.

"Ah, yes. I'm just really tired, but I still can't fall asleep."

A few seconds later, Aunt O looked up to see that Lisa hadn't moved from the spot she was standing in before, fiddling with her hands.

"Auntie, I need to ask you something. Do you have a Bible?"

"Of course, I do. Every good Christian woman has a Bible, baby."

"Well, may I borrow it just for tonight? I'd like to read a few passages if you don't mind."

It took Aunt O a second or two to catch her breath after hearing that unexpected statement. All these months she'd been preaching the word around here and urging Lisa to go to church, she'd never once seen her read the Bible, but that didn't matter now. She was thankful for whatever had gotten into her niece. "Sure, baby, look under that table in the hallway. It should be a big, white, hardback Bible under there."

"Thank you. I'll take it to my room and read awhile."

Aunt O stared at Lisa as she went to the hallway to retrieve the Bible, then passed back through the living room on the way back to her bedroom. She didn't know what to make of this sudden change. She just thanked the Lord for making it possible.

Lisa racked her brain trying to remember the Bible passages Antwan had read to her last week. She couldn't recall any of the words or anything. The only thing she could remember was how appealing his voice had sounded as he read each Scripture to her. He spoke as if he could feel the power of God behind every word that escaped across his lips, and Lisa had felt comfortable in his presence. He'd made her feel completely safe from the outside world. That was something Lisa hadn't ever felt around any other man in her life.

She flipped through the pages reading random passages in the big book. Finally, Lisa stumbled across a verse, Romans 10:13, that she repeated to herself several times: For "whoever calls on the name of the LORD shall be saved."

Lisa slid out of bed, got down on her knees, placed her hands together, and did something she'd never done in her life. She prayed, and asked God to save her. Instantly, peacefulness came over her entire body as she climbed back into bed. Moments later, she was sound asleep with the Good Book spread across her light breathing chest.

CHAPTER THIRTY FIVE
(FEELINGS)

Antwan entered his small hotel room after dark in the humid city of Houston. He was sweaty, tired, and weary from a long day at the International Book Expo. Since his maroon shirt and khaki pants were both wet from perspiration, he adjusted the temperature on the thermostat to a slightly cooler setting. Then, he walked across the room and eased into the plush burgundy wing chair beside his bed and slipped off his black loafers. Pulling out the cell phone from his front pants pocket, he noticed he had missed several telephone calls over the course of the day. The hip-hop music pumped so loudly throughout the convention center today until it was impossible to hear his cell phone ringing, and he'd forgotten to place it on vibrate.

Realizing Lisa had called several times, he was anxious to listen to her messages as he pressed the button to do so. "Hi Antwan, this is Lisa. I just got back into town this evening, and I'd like to speak with you. Please call me back at this number. I'll be waiting for your call." Then, he went on to play the next two very similar messages.

After listening to Lisa's last message, Antwan couldn't help thinking what was really behind that sweet voice of hers. With each succeeding call, he detected urgency in her voice and wondered what that could be about.

Although she didn't leave many details, he got the impression she desperately wanted to speak with him about something. Thinking back to their last verbal exchange, he couldn't fathom what she possibly wanted with him after hurting his feelings the way she had with her brutal words.

Lisa Bradford had made it clear he wasn't the man for her, for whatever reason she could think of, and he'd decided not to waste anymore time on trying to change her ways of thinking. *If she wants a rich, shallow man for a husband then let her move on. I'm through wasting my time and energy.*

He pressed another button, automatically erasing all of her messages, and placed the phone on the nightstand. Antwan started unbuttoning his shirt as he walked toward the bathroom. He just wanted to take a cold shower, washing all thoughts of the selfish Lisa Bradford out of his consciousness, and down the drain with the dirty water.

At first, he'd resigned to being patient and waiting her out, but his better judgment was constantly telling him differently. Antwan had seen enough women like Lisa to know that she was into breaking men's hearts without reservations, and she only wanted men who were unavailable to her for whatever crazy reason. He figured some women were just like that; they didn't really want a good man. They only wanted the so-called bad boys who knew how to use and abuse every woman they met. Well, Antwan wasn't like that. He'd never be that type of man because it wasn't in his spirit to mistreat people, especially women. But since he was one of the wise men, he knew when it was time to let go of an unfruitful relationship. He would have to let his feelings for Lisa go before she caused him even more pain.

Turning the showerhead on at full blast, he let the cold water engulf his body by placing his head directly in the line of spray. Shivering at the iciness of the water, Antwan looked down to realize the coldness was having the opposite effect on his body than he'd hoped it would. Instead of releasing his tension toward Lisa, his tense body was telling him that their relationship was a long ways from being over.

***

It was almost eight o'clock Monday morning when Lisa woke up, rolled over, and checked the time. She sat straight up after realizing Antwan hadn't returned her telephone calls all weekend. Hoping he'd made it home safely last night, she dialed the number to his condominium. Six rings later, his voice mail answered the telephone asking Lisa to please leave a message after the beep, but that's not what she wanted to do. Lisa wanted to speak with him in person.

Thinking he was probably at work by now, Lisa dialed the number to the Black Experience Bookshop in hopes of reaching Antwan. Seconds later, he was answering the telephone in his famous Caribbean accent, "Good morning, thank you for calling the Black Experience Bookshop, this is Antwan."

"Good morning. How are you?" Lisa asked, with a smile in her voice.

"I'm fine, Lisa. How are you?"

"Well, I could be better. I've been worried about you all weekend since you didn't return any of my messages. Is everything okay with you?"

"Ah, yeah, I'm great. I was tied up at the book fair all weekend, and I was under the impression we didn't have anything else to talk about. Isn't that right?"

"I — I really need to speak with you again if you don't mind." Lisa fumbled for the right words to say. She hadn't expected him to question her like this.

A Man of My Own   227

"I'm sorry, but the store is very busy today. I have to restock all of the books I took with me to Houston. I'll see you at the group meeting on Thursday evening."

"I was hoping I could see you sometime before then, Antwan. This is really important," she pleaded.

"Like I said, I have a business to run. I don't have time to play games with spoiled, grown women. So you have a nice day."

Lisa could not believe Antwan had cut her off so abruptly without even saying good-bye. That certainly didn't sound like the caring man she had come to know over the last few months.

Not being one to easily accept the word "no," Lisa pulled on a yellow Diane von Furstenberg sundress, slid into a matching pair of Moschino kitten heel thongs, grabbed her present for Antwan, and headed downtown. Twenty minutes later, she was parking her silver convertible PT Cruiser beside Antwan's black Harley-Davidson motorbike.

Entering the doors of the bookshop, Lisa scanned the perimeter of the room filled with shelves of books looking for Antwan Saunders. The sound of island music playing in the background and the strong smell of incense filled the air. Making her way to the check-out counter, a young lady wearing a huge afro asked, "Hello. May I help you?"

"Good morning. I'm looking for the owner. Is Mr. Saunders available?"

"Yes, ma'am, he's in the back doing inventory. I'll let him know that you're here. My name is Dana. What's your name?"

"Hi, Dana. My name is Ms. Lisa Bradford. I'm a friend of his," Lisa replied, trying to keep from cringing over the fact that the young woman had called her ma'am. She'd always hated that southern phrase with a passion and now that young people were referring to her by that name, she hated it even more.

It only took a few minutes for Antwan to emerge in the doorway leading to the back of the store. Lisa took in his casual appearance, admiring the purple polo shirt and Lee jeans that were molded to his fine body.

"Hi, Lisa. I thought I told you on the telephone I was busy today," he stated, sounding annoyed with her presence.

"I was hoping you could spare some time for me. I only need a few seconds to speak with you."

"Well, I'm sorry. I have a lot of work to do, and I need to get back to it. Now, if you don't mind, please, see yourself out of my store and out of my life," he stated firmly, turning away from her.

Lisa stood there watching his retreating back with her mouth opened. She started to say something, anything that would get his attention, but she decided to snap her jaws shut and not embarrass herself any further. Lisa turned her red face around and hurriedly walked past the young lady behind the counter. When she made it to the front door, she remembered the white, gift wrapped present she had for Antwan inside her yellow Prada purse. Turning around, she walked back to the counter, pulled out the small box, and handed it to the sales lady. "Dana, would you give this to Mr. Saunders for me, please?"

"Yes, ma'am, I'll make sure he gets it."

"Thank you," Lisa replied, forcing her lips to slightly curve upward. Then, she hurried to her car, fighting back the tears that were beginning to well in her eyes.

Antwan absolutely hated himself for speaking to Lisa so harshly. He'd never been that rude to anyone before in his life. But Lisa Bradford was a different type of person. She was the kind of woman he had to be stern with because he'd made a decision not to be a part of her life anymore except for the group sessions on Thursdays.

Maybe by their next meeting time he'd have her almost out of his system.

"Excuse me, Mr. Saunders," Dana interrupted Antwan's thoughts of Lisa. "Ah, the lady that was here to see you left this for you up front," she stated, handing him the small wrapped gift.

"Thank you, Dana," he replied, taking the gift from her hand. As soon as she disappeared through the doorway, Antwan tore into the wrapping paper. Once his eyes rested on the miniature knight-in-shining armor, he let out a quick laugh. He didn't know what to make of this present, but his gut instincts were telling him to be careful.

CHAPTER THIRTY SIX
(LISA'S NEW BIRTH)

Lisa arrived at the New Hope Baptist Church almost an hour early Thursday evening expecting to see Antwan setting up for the N.O.E.L. meeting. She hadn't tried to reach him since their exchange on Monday morning. Secretly, she had hoped he would have tried to contact her by now. Since she didn't want to appear desperate, she refused to call him again. However, she wanted to make sure she looked her best for their encounter at the group session tonight, which meant that she made a trip to the best hairdresser in town. The young ladies at Prestige Hair and Nails had washed and styled Lisa's hair to perfection in a tight updo with curly tendrils framing her face. She'd gotten a French tip manicure and pedicure to round out her day. For the meeting, she selected a conservative but romantic looking white Ellen Tracy chiffon dress. After applying her Clinique make-up, and spraying her neck with Romance perfume, she drove over to the church.

Walking inside the rear entrance, she checked every room looking for Antwan. By the time she returned to the kitchen area, Daphne was there arranging the chairs into a circle. "Hi, Lisa, I see you're here early tonight. How are you?"

"Hello, Daphne, I'm doing fine. Has Antwan made it here yet?"

"No, he called me earlier to say he would be running a little late tonight. Why, was he supposed to meet you here or something?"

"No, no, I was just hoping he'd be here early so we could talk."

"Well, I'm sorry, but I don't know how late he's going to be since he's normally the first one in the building. He asked me if I'd come down early and set up everything for the meeting tonight and he'd be here as soon as he could."

"Oh, thanks for letting me know. Is there anything I can do to help?"

"I'm almost done in here. I just need to get a few more things out of the car if you don't mind helping me with that." Lisa nodded and followed Daphne outside to her white Toyota 4Runner sports utility vehicle.

About an hour later, Daphne was closing the session out for the evening. Antwan hadn't even bothered to make an appearance or call to say he wouldn't be able to make it after all. Considering the fact that this was out of character for him, Daphne was definitely concerned. As soon as she said good night to all of the group members except for Lisa, who was waiting to speak with her, she dialed Antwan's cell phone number. He picked up on the fourth ring sounding drowsy. "Hey, stranger, what happened to you tonight?"

"Ah, man, I wasn't feeling well so I took some medicine and fell asleep. I just woke up a few minutes ago and realized I'd missed the meeting tonight. Did you have a good turnout?"

"Yes, we did. Everyone was present except for you. Someone standing here with me would like to speak with you," Daphne stated and handed the phone to Lisa before he could ask who.

"Hi, Antwan, this is Lisa. How are you?"

"Ah, I'm okay. I just took some sinus pills and sort of passed out for a while. I'm sorry I didn't make it out tonight."

"Me, too. I was looking forward to seeing you. Listen, if you have a minute, I'd like to come over and talk with you about something."

"I — I, ah, I'm still sort of drowsy and out of it from the medicine. So this wouldn't be a good time for me to have an intelligent conversation with you. Let's talk tomorrow or something."

"Sure. No problem. I understand. We'll talk later," Lisa replied, handing the phone back to Daphne. She walked out of the church as fast as her legs would move, thinking she'd lost the love of her life. If she'd learned anything in therapy, it was that it was time to let go and move on without a man in her life for the first time in years. *My worth is not determined by a man anymore.*

***

"Dr. Hopson, do you believe in God?" Lisa was stretched out on the green cloth sofa in her psychiatrist's office wearing a sheer teal caftan over a pair of white stretch capri pants. She'd slipped out of her teal strapped low heeled sandals, and had her ankles crossed as she relaxed on the cushiony sofa.

"What I believe is not important. What do you believe, Lisa?" Dr. Hopson replied, leaning back in her armchair. She was wearing a tailored summer dress instead of her usual suit with her hair pulled back into a bun today. Peering through her black frame glasses, she waited patiently for Lisa to respond.

"I don't know. I've never had much reason to before, but I've been reading the Bible more lately. Ever since Antwan read those passages to me the night that I was upset, I've found some comfort in reading Scriptures almost every night."

"And what have you learned from your readings?"

"I've learned that it's possible for people to change their lives if they want to because God doesn't care about our past or how much we've sinned. You know, I've done a lot of evil things, and I've hurt a lot of people over the years. I didn't think it was possible for God to love me. But according to what I've read in the Bible, He does."

"I see. How does this make you feel?" Dr. Hopson asked, leaning in closer to her client.

"It makes me feel like I can become a better person if I try harder. I promised Antwan and my Uncle Johnny I wouldn't try to get revenge on Desmond or his wife for trying to kill me, but it's been the hardest thing I've ever done. Sometimes, I become so consumed with rage against them, I just want to go burn their whole house down with both of them in it."

"And what do you do when you have thoughts like that?"

"I've been following Antwan's advice and praying my way through it or by reading the Bible until I calm down. I'm not obsessed with getting revenge like I was at first."

"I'd say that it's working then, and I'm very proud of you, Lisa. You're starting to show some control where your anger is concerned. That's a very good sign," the doctor stated, writing something in her journal regarding Lisa's progress.

"Well, I know Desmond is a Casanova, and Belinda Taylor is crazy. I thought I had some issues, but that sister is one insane woman. I have never tried to physically hurt anyone the way she did with me. But now I realize that pain is pain. It doesn't matter if it's mental or physical. I was just like Belinda at one point in my life as far as causing people pain. Now I don't want to be that way anymore. They can have each other if that's what they want. I'm so thankful to have my life and health right now that I intend to stay away from her and Desmond."

"And who do you think is responsible for saving your life?"

Lisa unfolded her hands, and sat up in the center of the sofa. She stared Dr. Hopson straight in the eyes and replied, "I know now that God saved my life."

***

Antwan was sitting in the third pew at New Hope Baptist Church wearing a Stafford three-button olive colored suit praising God. Although he didn't like wearing dressy attire since leaving his corporate job, he always wore one of his best outfits to church. And this was a fine September Labor Day weekend Sunday to be well dressed in the house of God.

It was toward the end of service when the pastor finished with his powerful sermon on "Living a Righteous Life," and the choir started singing a course of the gospel song titled, "None but the Righteous Shall See God." Reverend Palmer, a tall, muscular man with a mustache, had done an outstanding job as usual. He diligently informed the congregation of the virtues they needed to possess to enter into God's kingdom. Being one of the youngest ministers in the city at the age of twenty-eight, he was very well liked and admired. "The doors of the church are open. Whosoever will give their life to the Lord today, let him come," he stated, stretching out his hands over the podium. Two female ushers wearing black skirts with white blouses and white gloves, placed several chairs in a row at the front of the church as everyone in attendance stood to their feet.

One homeless looking male made his way to the front of the church and took a seat in front of the crowd. He lowered his head in tears as the congregation clapped and sent encouraging words his way. Moments later, Antwan's mouth dropped open in shock as he recognized the petite woman with reddish wavy hair wearing a royal blue chemise dress walking down the center aisle toward the front of the church. One of the male ushers ran to meet her halfway since Lisa looked like she was about to drop to the floor. Her face was covered in tears, and she was bent over holding her side as if she was in pain. The gentleman held her by the arm and escorted her into a seat. Lisa looked up at the crowd standing around her as several other young people came forward to give their lives to Jesus, too.

"Thank you, Jesus! Thank you for these souls today," Reverend Palmer said, clapping his hands and jumping for joy. "Ushers, please escort these candidates for baptism to the conference room so I may speak with each of them individually about the decision they have made today."

The ushers followed the pastor's instruction and assisted each of the newcomers to the conference room. Lisa's spirit was so filled with joy she'd forgotten all about looking for Antwan in the congregation. Once she started praying for salvation, the Holy Ghost came in and took over her body. She was walking toward the front of the church requesting baptism a few seconds later, crying with joy.

Antwan didn't know what to make of Lisa as he watched her small frame being led out of the church. He didn't even know she had been sitting in the back of the building all of this time. *Is she for real or is this just a ploy to get my attention? I know she has better sense than to play with God. She's an intelligent woman, maybe she has finally come to her senses.*

CHAPTER THIRTY SEVEN
(REUNITED)

Immediately after church was dismissed, Antwan went looking for Lisa. He waited for her outside the conference room door where she was meeting with the pastor and the other candidates for baptism. When Lisa stepped out into the corridor, Antwan looked into her beaming brown eyes and felt in the center of his heart she was a changed woman. Yes, she was still beautiful, but she had a glow covering her whole face and a smile that was almost blinding to Antwan.

Lisa was so stunned by his immaculate presence that she floated into his waiting arms. Just the expression of pure concern on his face brought tears to her eyes. Their bodies melted together as one with both of them crying like a set of newborn twins. Neither one of them spoke a word for several seconds. Lisa was the first one to lift her head to speak. "I'm sorry," she whispered through her tears. "I should have given you a chance," she stated, swallowing hard.

"It's okay. I'm sorry for the way I spoke to you the other day. I'm willing to start all over again if you are," he replied, inhaling deeply.

"Yes, yes, that's what I want more than anything in the world. I want a chance to show you that I'm really a changed person, and a lot of it is because of you."

"You did it all yourself. I'm just happy to stand back and watch you continue to grow because God is not through with you yet."

Lisa looked into Antwan's midnight eyes thinking he was the last man she ever wanted to be with. She no longer needed the riches she once felt were so important to her existence. She'd learned that loving someone, truly loving someone the way God loved her, was the only wealth she needed.

"I love you, Antwan," she whispered, sniffling through her tears while holding his face in her hands. "You're all I need from this day forward."

***

Lisa was in the midst of planning her wedding to Antwan. He'd proposed to her over the Christmas holiday in the midst of opening their presents. Admiring the two-carat princess cut diamond ring set in platinum, she couldn't help but to think about all of the married women she'd hurt in the past. Although Belinda was the most recent one she'd scarred, there was no way she would ever try to make amends with someone who was that crazy. The woman would probably think she was after her husband again and really lose it. But in her heart, Lisa had forgiven Belinda for causing her so much hurt

As she moved down the list of wives she'd mentally harmed, Lisa could see the emotional face of Alese Wayne, Michael's wife, on the day Alese confronted her about sleeping with her husband. *Now, she was the epitome of a righteous woman. Alese modeled perfect Christian behavior when I admitted to her face that I'd slept with her husband. I don't know many women who would do that.*

Lisa picked up her cellular phone and dialed the number to Alese's house. She silently prayed that Michael didn't answer the telephone because she'd never have a chance of speaking to Alese if he did. Although she needed to apologize to him, too, she wanted to speak with his wife first. Then, after the fourth ring, she heard a familiar voice say, "Hello, this is Alese."

"Hi, Alese," Lisa said. She took in a deep breath and exhaled before speaking rapidly, "This is Lisa Bradford. Please don't hang up on me. I just need to say something to you," she stated, then paused, listening to the silence. "Are you still there?"

"Yes, I'm here, Lisa. Why are you calling me after all this time?"

"I'm calling to apologize to you for trying to ruin your family. I was wrong, but I'm a changed person now, and I owe you an apology. Can you ever forgive me for intruding in your marriage, Alese?"

"Yes, I can forgive you. I'd just like to know what happened to you. What changed you?"

"It's a long story. Let's just say that I had a divine intervention in my life, and now I'm headed to the altar. I couldn't take my marriage vows without making at least one apology to a married woman I've hurt in the past."

"I see. I'm happy for you. I'm always delighted to see someone turn their life around. I know God is able to do what we want Him to do. And even though your actions really hurt me, Lisa, I still prayed for your soul to be saved. Thank you for letting me know my prayers have been answered."

Lisa could barely speak as the tears began to form in the corners of her eyes, and she could feel a lump swelling in her dry throat. She felt tremendous knowing that this woman whose marriage she'd tried to destroy, had actually prayed for her. "No, thank you, Alese," she managed to say. "Please tell Michael I'm sorry, too. He has an amazing family. I see now why he didn't leave you.

Everything I ever thought about you was wrong, and I'm so sorry for that."

"It's over now, Lisa. We're a much stronger family because of what we went through. I wouldn't want to do it again, but at least it's in the past. You take care of yourself and keep walking with God. You'll be all right."

"Thank you, again, Alese," Lisa whispered, hanging up the telephone. Her heart felt a little bit lighter now. She'd repented for all of her past sins, and she was building a new life with Jesus.

CHAPTER THIRTY EIGHT
(WEDDING DAY)

Lisa and Antwan stood on the edge of the pristine white sandy shore on the island of Trinidad reciting their marriage vows to each other for a beautiful Valentine's Day ceremony. The hem of Lisa's ankle length, white sleeveless wrap dress by Carilyn Vaile was blowing in the wind as she faced her soon to be husband. She flexed her toes while the heels of her white beaded T-strap sandals were sinking down into the warm sand. Antwan felt the cool breeze flowing through his Dolce and Gabbana white linen suit while he held both of Lisa's hands, gazing into her beaming brown eyes. He was happy from the top of his head all the way down to the tip of his matching Ferragamo loafers.

Everything was perfectly prepared exactly the way they had requested. The wedding coordinator, Tameka Jakes, offered them an all inclusive package deal for the wedding on the beach and a honeymoon in an exotic villa complete with a private swimming pool and household staff. The color of the pool with its infinity edges created the illusion of swimming in an enormous blue sea. They could look up at the sky from their outdoor shower or share a quiet meal on the shaded veranda.

Looking out over the bubbling ocean, Lisa thought it was the bluest water she'd ever seen against a magnificent golden setting sun with gorgeous palm trees in the distance. The four-piece calypso band playing lightly in the background added to the festive occasion, especially with the additional beat of the steel drum.

"I now pronounce you man and wife," the Justice of the Peace proclaimed. He was a tall lanky butter pecan skinned man with a heavy Caribbean accent. "You may kiss the bride," he said, smiling at the happy couple.

Lisa savored the taste of her husband's soft lips against hers. She'd waited all day long for his sweet kiss, and now she was able to revel in the joy of tasting him for the first time as his wife. Lisa felt like a famous movie star standing on the beach wrapped up with her true love. They feasted on the taste of each other for several seconds as their twenty or so guests began to chatter and laugh at the engaging pair. Antwan lifted his head up enough to smile at his new bride.

Most of the wedding guests were Antwan's family members who were happy to welcome him and his new wife to the lovely island paradise. Lisa's older sister, Jenna, was her only family member who had decided to make the airplane trip. She tried to talk Uncle Johnny and Aunt Oretha into coming, too, but neither of them could take the time off from work. And since Aunt O didn't like to fly anyway, it would have been useless to try pressuring them into coming.

Jenna was the first one to congratulate Lisa since she was the maid of honor and bridesmaid all in one wearing a red gown with a white chiffon draped front and a pair of red silk sandals. She'd gone on a low carbohydrate diet for two months in preparation for this event and had happily lost almost twenty pounds. Jenna was ready to slide into her brand new two-piece yellow polka dotted bikini and hit the miraculously looking beaches she'd heard so much about. She was also excited about the handsome island men who were paying close attention to her recently redesigned figure and the possibility of exploring the breathtaking island with one of them later.

There were several tables of food set up for the wedding reception right there on the beach. The tables were covered with glowing red and white tablecloths in a pretty net fabric which gave the setting a dreamy look. Each table was lined with the freshest flowers on the island including orchids, sunflowers, Gerber daisies, and red roses mixed with white ones. There were tables roomy enough to accommodate the buffet spread, cake, and beverage station. They were loaded with authentic native dishes including delicious curry chicken, jerk Maui with plantains, peas and rice, caviar and smoked salmon hearts, quiche kisses, lemon bars with raspberries, a tropical fruit bowl, and a three tiered wedding cake with white icing and red flower decorations.

Dr. Hopson walked up to Lisa carrying a lemon bar in her right hand. "Welcome to the family. You know I can't be your doctor anymore, right?" she questioned, hugging her niece with one arm.

"Thanks for all of your help, Auntie. I don't think any of this would have been possible if I hadn't met you when I did. I'm proud to be your family member even though I was shocked when you first told me about your relation to Antwan."

"I couldn't tell you I was related to him when I first recommended the N.O.E.L. program as one of the places for you to join a support group. I just hoped you'd find your way there."

"Well, I'm glad you helped me get better mentally and find a good man. I couldn't ask for any more than that."

"You make Antwan very happy, and that's all that matters to me."

"And me, too," his mother, Bertha, chimed in. She was almost the spitting image of Dr. Hopson, but appeared to be a little bit younger with longer hair. They both looked frilly wearing their off white lace dresses with matching hats. Wrapping her arms around both of them, Lisa squeezed the sisters to her as tightly as she could. This was her new family, and she loved them almost as much as she loved her husband.

EPILOGUE

Antwan carried Lisa across the threshold of their private villa, placing her sweet smelling body on the edge of the king sized white oak canopy bed. Lisa was so ready to consummate their marriage she didn't take time to change into the sexy lingerie she'd bought for their honeymoon. Nor was she concerned about the elegance surrounding the grandly decorated room fit for a king and queen to enjoy with fresh cut flowers and chocolate candy on the satin pillowcases. The luxurious Lorraine paneled gold drapes blocked out the glow from the lowering sun. They were stunning with matching braided trim and fringed tassels hanging down to the floor on each side.

Antwan stripped down to his Calvin Klein knit briefs, and then began helping Lisa out of her one-piece wedding dress. He kissed and gently caressed every part of her vanilla fudge body as it was revealed to him for the first time. Relaxing against his warm handed touches, Lisa had never imagined she could feel this good from being with a man. She was excited just from the strong masculine scent that he exuded as he made his way down her heated body. They'd both made the commitment to be celibate until their wedding night, now Lisa felt like a born-again virgin. She couldn't believe that the man she'd first thought was so unattractive, was now her husband

and looked hot enough to grace the cover of a bestselling romance novel.

"I want to love you like no man has ever loved you before," he whispered in her ear.

"You've already done that," she replied, placing soft kisses all over his smooth midnight face.

Antwan closed his eyes, relishing in the affection his new bride was bestowing upon him. Her sweet kisses felt like tiny butterflies landing all over his sensitive face. He hadn't touched a woman in over two years, and he hadn't realized how much he'd missed intimacy until tonight. This was a part of his life that he thought had seen better days. Now, he could feel a heat rising at the core of his body telling him this would undoubtedly be a fantasy fulfilled.

When Lisa slid her small hand over his wide chest, Antwan let out a gasp of hot air directly into her face. Breathing in the breath from her man, Lisa eased up, pushing her chest against his until he was lying flat on his back on top of the gold satin bedspread.

They kissed and kissed until Antwan couldn't take the torture any longer. He loved the feel of their skin softly touching each other. He caressed Lisa's freckled face, tenderly kissing each closed eyelid. Every part of her felt like cotton candy evaporating in his hands as he became acquainted with her body.

Lisa cried out, "Take me! Oh, please, take me!"

Antwan responded to her cries by shifting his body so he was on top of his new bride. Lifting both arms above her head, taking her small hands into his larger ones, he skillfully glided himself toward her womanhood. They moved together sensuously, synchronizing their rhythms. Just as Lisa was about to reach the peak of her happiness, Antwan stopped.

"What are you doing? Why are you stopping?" she asked, fluttering for breath underneath him.

"I'm not ready yet, I need to enjoy this feeling a little bit longer. You feel so good," he moaned in her ear.

"Well, you can wait if you want to, but I'm ready." With that said, she tightened her legs around his torso even more. Increasing the pace of their lovemaking, it didn't take long for both of them to appreciate the joys of holy matrimony.

Moments later, still gasping for breath, Lisa actually thought she was going to pass out from sheer happiness. Fighting to remain conscious, she collapsed in her husband's solid arms. Listening to his rapid heart beat, Lisa knew she'd found the man her soul could love, her one and only soul mate.

Antwan held on to his ladylove as if he was afraid she was going to slip through his fingers at any second. They remained in that position for several minutes, holding onto each other, inhaling the unique fragrance their bodies had created together in a short amount of time.

Lisa drifted off into a happy sleep lying in Antwan's arms in the center of their king sized bed. Quietly, he eased his body out of the bed, and placed both feet on the floor. Lifting himself up, he walked over to the table by the window, reached inside his black leather briefcase, and pulled out a large manila envelope filled with pictures. He tipped back over to the bed, dumped out all the photographs on the bed, and then spread them out with both his hands. Now, his surprise was ready to be delivered to his new bride.

"Lisa! Lisa! Baby, wake up, I have a present for you. Happy Valentine's Day, sweetheart," he said, watching her turn over in the bed to face the sound of his voice. "Look at these pictures!"

Lifting herself up on both elbows, Lisa rapidly blinked her eyes several times, trying to focus on Antwan's standing figure. She realized he was pointing to the bed so she looked down to see what he was pointing at. That's when she saw all the pictures that were spread out over the bed covers.

"Baby, what's going on? Why do you have all these pictures of someone's house all over our bed? Whose house is this anyway?"

Antwan threw his head back, letting out a hearty laugh. "Why don't you make a guess, and I'll tell you if you're right or wrong?"

"Listen, I'm too drained to play games with you. Just tell me what's going on, please."

"Okay, okay, this is our new house! It's your Valentine's Day and wedding day present!"

"What! You're kidding me. There's no way we can afford a big house like this," Lisa stated, staring at her husband in disbelief. The 3,500 square foot, four bedroom wood framed house painted in bright yellow with white trim looked absolutely beautiful. There were two white oversized rocking chairs placed on the extra wide front porch. Judging from the size of the yard, it had to cover at least three acres of land.

"Well, the house and land is already paid for in full. I bought it last week," he stated, pulling out the deeds to the property from his attaché case. With renewed energy, Lisa jumped out of the bed and into Antwan's arms, wrapping her lean legs around his torso.

"Why didn't you tell me about this before we got married?" she asked as he lowered her body onto the ruffled bed sheets.

"I wanted it to be a surprise. I also wanted to be sure you were marrying me for the right reasons," he replied, sitting down beside her. "You see, I worked in the corporate world for almost five years before suffering from a nervous breakdown. The last two years that I was employed with Smithdine, I made over $250,000 a year, including all of the bonuses I earned at the end of each quarter. I was working sixteen hours a day for six days a week. I bought the condo, five suits, a nice car, and a Harley-Davidson motorcycle. The rest of the money was invested into low-risk stocks, bonds, and mutual funds. Today, my net worth is close to a million."

Lisa was too stunned to speak. Feeling as if she had been holding her breath after being tossed into deep blue sea water, she started gulping for air. Antwan held her hand and patted her lightly on the back as she regained her composure. Lisa thought life was truly a paradox, just when she fell out of love with money; she fell in love with a man who had money.

"So, you see, we can afford this house as long as we don't get carried away and start trying to live above our means. You can come to work with me in the bookshop, and we can build our business together until we're both ready to retire. Then, we can leave it to our children, if we're so blessed to have any. Otherwise, we can sell out and have enough to live on for the rest of our lives. How does that sound?" he asked, looking into her teary eyes.

"It sounds like I have a man of my own."

The End

Other Titles from Barbara Joe Williams

A Writer's Guide to Publishing & Marketing (2010)

Moving the Furniture: 52 Ways to Keep Your Marriage Fresh (2008)

Courtney's Collage (2007)

How I Met My Sweetheart: Anthology (2007)

Falling for Lies (2006)

Dancing with Temptation (2005)

Forgive Us This Day (2004)

Email her at: amanipublishing@aol.com

Visit her website at: www.barbarajoewilliams.com